Also by David Craig in the Brade and Jenkins series:

Forget It
The Tattooed Detective
Torch

Other novels by David Craig:

The Alias Man
Message Ends
Contact Lost
Young Men May Die
A Walk at Night
Up from the Grave
Double Take
Bolthole
Whose Little Girl Are You?
(filmed as *The Squeeze*)
A Dead Liberty
The Albion Case
Faith, Hope and Death

By the same author writing as Bill James:

The Last Enemy

The Harpur and Iles series:

You'd Better Believe It
The Lolita Man
Halo Parade
Protection (TV tie-in version, *Harpur and Iles*)
Come Clean
Take
Club
Astride a Grave
Gospel
Roses, Roses
In Good Hands
The Detective is Dead
Top Banana
Panicking Ralph
Eton Crop

Writing as James Tucker:

Equal Partners
The Right Hand Man
Burster
Blaze of Riot
The King's Friends (reissued as by Bill James)

Non-fiction:

Honourable Estates
The Novels of Anthony Powell

BAY CITY

David Craig

Constable · London

First published in Great Britain 2000
by Constable & Company Ltd
3 The Lanchesters, 162 Fulham Palace Road
London W6 9ER

ISBN 0 094 80070 7

Typeset in Palatino by Photoprint, Torquay, Devon
Printed and bound in Great Britain by MPG Books Ltd,
Bodmin, Cornwall

A CIP catalogue record for this book is available from the British Library

Author's note

The geography in this book is broadly right. There is a Cardiff Bay scheme to redevelop the docks, though further ahead than in this novel. Some details have been changed. Bethel Baptist Chapel, which I attended as a child, became a night-club and the building was eventually demolished. There is no police station in Bute Street and Crichton Street is no longer a beat for prostitutes. All characters and incidents are fiction. This is a story.

1

A little before midnight, when they knew Semprina would be working the usual stretch of Crichton Street, Brade and Jenkins broke into her flat. Jenkins had a flair for burglary and locks. He had a flair for information as well. He had all sorts of flairs. He had an Oxford degree.

Inside Semprina's place they stood for a while not moving and getting used to the dark. Although Brade always felt at his safest and most comfortable in darkness, he thought they might be able to try a shaded flashlight a bit later on, for very brief spells only. Semprina lived in a tower-block and there were a lot of people about the building still. Among the girls, Semprina had plenty of friends, and some might come to investigate if they saw a torch beam prowling behind her curtains. In fact, it would be more sensible to switch on the flat's lights. Sometimes Brade wondered whether furtiveness had become such a habit that he dropped into it without thinking. Detectives detected and grew obsessive about not being detected detecting. From outside, the flat's lights frankly on might suggest only she had brought a regular client or clients back for an all-nighter. Her colleagues would have too much trade delicacy to interrupt.

This was not an official police visit, of course. In a proper raid there would have been no long drawn out, conspicuous fiddling on the landing with the front door Yale. Brade or Jenkins or Brade *and* Jenkins would simply have done a bit of shoulder work on the nothing door. Brade estimated they had about an hour and a half. Semprina did not usually finish until 1.30 a.m., when possible business from the clubs began to dwindle. They would not stay that long. He and Jenkins were here for a quick look around only, and Brade did not expect to find much. Besides, there was more than Semprina to worry about, or they would not have been in the flat at all. Jenkins' information said she had someone living in. Jenkins' information said this guest or lodger had been here for above a week, days as well as nights, like true domesticity. Yes, Jenkins had a flair for information. He had even known the flat would be empty now. But he did *not* know who this guest or lodger was, nor what kind of hours he kept. He might come back a long time before Semprina. The flat had no rear exit. They mustn't get cornered. He and Jenkins should be able to stay unhurt even then, two against one, though, naturally, neither of them was armed, and the guest or lodger might be. Who would issue arms for an illegal bit of entering? In any case, Brade would prefer their visit to stay secret. Jenkins claimed to have left the Yale unmarked on entry, and he might be right. They would also go carefully in their tour of the rooms, no tell-tale disturbance.

'God, it smells clean,' Jenkins muttered.

Brade had been to Semprina's flat a few times before. Once he had watched her feather-dusting bookshelves nude. That was only months ago, but in a totally different era of his life, his grubby life of tarts and porn mags before Kate and the coming child. He thought he remembered the layout here and began to move towards her living-room, a cautious shuffle rather than a walk, with an occasional pause. Jenkins followed. There would be nothing on the floor for them to stumble over. Brade opened the door to the living-room and went in. The curtains were closed but patches of light came through from the landing. To Brade the room looked as it always had. He spotted nothing to suggest more than one person lived here now, and it was this other person who interested them. Jenkins' information said he might be important and Jenkins had a flair for weighing importance. You could not get a good Oxford degree without that and Jenkins' Oxford degree was good. Or he said it was. Jenkins lacked a flair for understatement. Brade sympathised. A black in a white man's police force, Jenkins had to let people know his qualities. He believed in positive discrimination, for himself.

Brade stood just inside the living-room doorway and Jenkins went past him and did a slow, sharp-eyed tour, moving a couple of cushions on the red, real leather settee and examining ornaments and crockery through the glass of a china cabinet, like a valuer. He opened no drawers or cupboards. They took a quick look at the kitchen and then entered the one bedroom. Here Brade did open the built-in wardrobe but saw only women's clothes. For someone like Semprina the sleeping quarters were astonishingly plain, Brade had always thought that. In his view a tart's bedroom ought to *look* like a tart's bedroom. Wasn't it part of what you paid for? Frippery could be a turn-on, and the more vulgar, the bigger the turn-on. You felt you were going to the bad in a gaudy rush. He had never mentioned his disappointment to Semprina because that would have been hurtful. Here, the floorboards had been sanded and varnished and there were two small rugs near the bed. The room could illustrate an article in a gracious living magazine about the holy glories of wood. There was a mirror but only one, and that small and in the dressing-table. She had a couple of pictures near the wardrobe, not easy to make out now. Brade recalled them as pale, dull watercolours of old countryside scenes – gates and smocks, the kind of stuff someone's wife might call art.

He did not remember the luggage stand, nor the couple of cases on it. To Brade they seemed high quality, *not* real leather, because leather is heavy, but smartly fashioned thick canvas in sort of green and black tartan, clan Anon. Jenkins lifted them in turn and signalled that the smaller, boxier case was empty. He tried to open both but they were locked. Immediately, he began to work on the empty one. This was intelligent. Jenkins had a luggage flair. If these cases belonged to the visitor, it was best to assume he would leave nothing valuable or significant here, even locked up, because a bit of tartan canvas could be slashed. Vital to know what he had taken with him from the empty case, and there might be traces inside. Traces? Smells. Oil specks. Brade wondered whether the case had contained implements of a profession, a gunman's profession, and Jenkins would wonder the same. If it had, this was the kind of visitor to his patch that Brade liked to know about.

And that accounted for his own and Jenkins' visit to Semprina's flat. The point was, Cordial Maximilian ran Semprina. Jenkins' information – from sources he did not disclose, of course – said there had been a power shift among some prominent local careerists lately, Cordial and two others. Traditionally these three warred brutally for shares of the markets – the drugs market, the girls market, the protection market. Now, Jenkins had been told they were moving into an alliance, moving very fast, very urgently. This could not be bigger or more depressing news. It suggested a considerable joint enemy for the three of them to fight. Had the visitor with smart luggage been hired to help somehow? Well, Brade could have made a guess at the somehow, even without help from Jenkins. If this visitor had moved into the flat it would only be with Cordial's knowledge and on Cordial's orders. Probably, Cordial had provided him with accommodation and a girl while he lined up the job they wanted him for, whatever it was. There could only be one or two skills Cordial needed to hire, with gunnery the most likely. Jenkins' information said gunnery, no question.

Brade felt troubled. He went back to the sitting-room and took a look around the edge of the curtain to the landing. He could see only a tiny distance. It was a tic, not security. When he returned to the bedroom Jenkins had just opened the small case. He began to sniff its interior very thoroughly, checking the corners like a dentist's suck-pipe. At the end, he looked up at Brade, gave a nod and did something between a pout and a wince. Even in the half dark these signals said to Brade, Yes, cordite. Several wide lengths of tape, plain not tartan, had been sewn to the lining. The work looked amateur but practical and strong. These tapes would be enough to hold two pistols and a box of bullets in place, preventing awkward clanking when the case was moved.

'I'd say a pair of Sokolovsky .45 automatics,' Jenkins whispered. 'Meaty very pricey pieces. Velocity to pierce body armour.' He did not explain whether he knew this from the costly smell, the placement of the tapes, his tipster, a voice from the Beyond or sheer gifted instinct. 'Do you want me to do the other case, Dave? Identification?'

'There won't be any, just socks and vests.' Identification did not matter very much. Role did, and they probably knew this now. 'Can you relock that one?'

'Of course.'

'And then we get out,' Brade replied.

'I could do the other very fast – same mechanism.'

'No time. Safety worries.'

'You mustn't fret about me.'

'Mine.'

'Oh, Dave, you put on nerves because you equate them with sensitivity,' Jenkins said as he refixed the lock. 'But I know you're all fearlessness.'

'We get out,' Brade replied.

They had been summoned to a meeting with Raging Bullfinch at headquarters in Cathays Park next morning. 'I hear rumours of an alliance forming between Simeon de Courville, Cordial Maximilian and A.W. Moss-Cober,' he said.

'Oh,' Jenkins replied. 'This is astonishing. Might we ask where such reports come from, sir?'

'I hear,' Bullfinch said. 'It's part of my job to hear, you know.' He was a plump-faced, slit-eyed very high flyer with a future to look after and for ever driven to enlarge his powers and, therfore, his earnings. Some setbacks recently seemed to have disturbed Bullfinch's zest and balance, and these days he could go into a bad anxiety state if he saw any threat or possible threat to his prospects. At such times, Bullfinch grew loud and agitated and raging. His bright mind would flutter about madly, like a bird trapped in a room, still high-flying but panicked and high-flying. So, the nickname. 'Those three combined would be formidable,' he said.

'Indeed,' Jenkins replied. 'A very remarkable change.'

'Are you saying one has things wrong?' Bullfinch yelled.

Jenkins held up his hand in a peace gesture, but did not speak. You could read the move as an apology or insolence. Jenkins had a flair for ambiguity.

Bullfinch asked: 'Have you two come across any signs of this alliance – any new, unusual developments down there?'

'What kind of developments, sir?' Brade asked.

'I don't know,' Bullfinch replied. 'Anything.'

'Not to date, sir,' Brade replied.

'I wish to be notified,' Bullfinch said. 'Instantly. Do you hear, Dave – instantly?'

'Absolutely, sir,' Brade replied.

In the car on the way back to Brade's office in Bute Street, Jenkins said: 'I wonder about him sometimes.'

'Oh, yes?' Brade replied.

'Don't you wonder, Dave?'

'He likes a peaceful scene, no crooked superpower cartels. What policing's about.'

'As if –'

'I hate as ifs.'

'As if he's getting . . . as if he has . . . well, as if he has an interest.'

'He *has* a fucking interest. It's his job. He knows how hard it is to nail people as big as those boys, especially if they're into a confederation. No Rico statutes here. Do you know about the Rico statutes, Glyndwr?' Christ, why ask? This sod knew everything.

'Standing for Racketeered Influenced and Corrupt Organisations, in the United States,' Jenkins replied.

'Extending the conspiracy laws. The FBI are able to charge big villains who sit in their mansions a long way from the actual dirty action. Our leaders are pressing to get some of that here, Glyn. No luck yet.'

'When I look at Bullfinch and listen to him I feel all the time as if . . . But you hate as ifs.'

2

In bed with Kate the following night, and thinking very constructive thoughts about fatherhood, Brade caught the sound of someone light-footed moving about his living-room. A while ago now he had given several of the docks girls keys to his flat after things became especially rough down there. At that time, he was living alone, and they might have needed a quick refuge, possibly when he was out. Obviously, such easy entry he restricted to those girls he half trusted, or only a little less. He had never reclaimed the keys. Partly that was forgetfulness. But also he felt that to demand them back would be insulting, mean. Of course, one of the girls could not have returned hers, anyway. Petronella, that friendly, bandanna'd kid who so prized his tattoos, had died in the Gloria Complex blaze, probably arsonised.

He left the bed without waking Kate and went to see who had come in.

'Dave,' Semprina said, 'I'm full of fear.' As if ashamed to sound so heavy she tried a smile, but it got nowhere.

'Sit down. You're all right here.'

'God, I'm sorry to turn up like this so late. Your wife –'

'Asleep. She'd understand, anyway, if there's a crisis. It's happened before.'

'Thanks, Dave.'

He put an arm around Semprina's shoulders and held her head to his chest for a few moments. Her hair smelled fresh and mild, though she probably had not been home and shampooed it after work. Brade went to the sort of sideboard and found almost a quarter of a bottle of Tia Maria and a dozen cans of Bass. He mixed them a drink each in two half-pint glasses. 'I never think of you getting scared,' he said. 'Other girls, perhaps. Semprina, never.'

'It's not about me,' she said. 'This is a guy I met.'

Brade drank. He had not tried Tia Maria and Bass before. They seemed completed by each other. 'A client?' he asked.

She stayed silent. He drank again and waited. Brade was used to this kind of stop-start conversation, and by now he knew the pace and procedure. Occasionally, when a girl felt worried about something, *truly* worried, she would come out to his flat for a talk. He did not expect any preliminary phone call. Like Semprina tonight, the girl would just arrive by taxi or in her car and hope he'd be there. Often – also like tonight – it would be very late, after her last trick. He wanted the girls to regard him as available. Some things they would not discuss with their pimps, and so they thought of Brade. In any case, several girls operated entirely freelance and unpimped. To Brade it seemed an increasing trend, legacy from the Thatcherite encouragement to go-it-alone small businesses. But, as for Semprina, she was run by Cordial Maximilian, of course, and would in fact rate as star of all his girls since the rough death of Petronella. Max himself had probably come up with the trade names Semprina and Petronella. Marketing was one of Cordial's chief skills.

'This guy's missing,' Semprina said.

'They come, they go.'

'No, not like that.'

'A client?' he asked.

'A sort of client.'

'They come, they go,' he said. All the girls would occasionally fall for a special tom, or special as they saw it, and for someone to have moved in with her would rate as special, even if he'd been put there by Cordial.

Semprina glanced around the room. 'This place is looking a lot nicer – tidier, cleaner. Since you got married. And to be a dad, I hear. That's lovely.'

'I needed to grow up.'

'Yes, I think so,' Semprina replied. 'We all worried about you.'

'Kind.' Although Brade might not be senior detective at the docks, he *was* the police officer most locals knew, and quite a few half trusted him, or only a little less. But despite this closeness to the folk there he did not actually live at the docks these days. He had a flat in a smart private block on the northern edge of the city, near Llandaff cathedral. It seemed to him that only a girl genuinely troubled would lay out time to make the journey. 'Something really bad, Semp?'

'I can talk to you like confidential?'

'As ever,' Brade said. 'So this lad has vamoosed?'

'I believe he could have bad bother, Dave.'

'Why?'

'I do.'

'What kind?'

'Bad.'

'What kind?' Brade asked.

'I don't know why he was here.'

'Where?'

'I don't know why he was in town at all. He had great luggage, a great suit.'

'So, you've lost a top-wallet customer. Sad, but it's not a police job, Semp.'

'He left the luggage.'

'He'd moved in with you?' he asked, giving it surprise.

'This was like a relationship, Dave, like a true relationship.'

'How like?'

'This was for more than a week,' she replied.

'And then he goes, without the luggage?'

'He expected to come back.'

'Have you been through it?' he asked.

'What?'

'The luggage.'

'It's his, for God's sake, private.'

'Oh, absolutely. Have you been through it?' Brade asked.

'It's locked. I think one case is empty.'

'Have you been through the luggage?'

'Cordial took it away.'

'Cordial knows him?'

'It was Cordial who told me to look after him. You know, *look after him*. I wouldn't do it, would I – get someone living in – unless Cordial said?'

'Well, ask Cordial where he is.'

'I don't want to. I don't want to, and I don't think he knows, anyway. Cordial is angry about it, and frightened.'

Brade shook the bottle and squeezed a bit more Tia Maria into each glass, then topped it with Bass. He had on his old Cardiff High School black and white striped rugby shirt which he slept in most nights. It pleased him that the shirt would still go around his frame after more than twenty years. It reached to a respectable length half-way down his thighs. 'Is there a name?'

'Of course there's a name,' she said. 'Didn't I tell you we kept house together for eight and a half days, cookery, morning paper, the lot?'

'His real name?'

'I don't know, do I?'

'A friend of Cordial?' Brade replied.

'Business mate.'

'So the name will be false,' Brade said.

'Can you look for him? Yourself, Dave Brade in person. Not something official – posters and dogs. I start something official, Maximilian would go mad.'

'So, does he know you're asking me to do it? In person.'

'No. Of course he doesn't. And don't tell him, Dave.'

Brade heard Kate stir in the bedroom. Then she called his name. He stood and went to her. 'A friend here,' he said. 'Some difficulties.'

Kate was on her back, still mostly asleep but her eyes about an eighth open, enough to show a bit of grey-green even in the poor light. 'Oh, bad difficulties?' she muttered. 'Business difficulties?'

'Probably.'

'Who? One of the girls again?'

'Semprina.'

'Will she be OK?'

Would she? 'You sleep now,' he replied.

She closed her eyes and turned on to her side. Brade returned to Semprina.

'I'm a pest, Dave,' she said.

'What name – the visitor?'

'Vincent.'

'Vincent what?'

'Peter Vincent.'

'It sounds made up,' Brade replied.

'Of course it does. Too . . . clean.'

'What about his pockets?'

'Dave, for God's sake, I *liked* this guy.'

'What about his pockets?'

'No, I didn't do his pockets.'

'Christ, not his luggage, not his pockets,' Brade said. 'No look at the credit cards or licence? How do we get an identity? You did do his pockets, didn't you, Semp? That would be only comradely.'

'It might be Peter Vincent,' she replied. 'But no.'

'I could ask the computer – if he's got form,' Brade said. 'Has he got form?'

'How would I –?'

'He knows Cordial, so he'll have form,' Brade said. 'What made you like him, besides the luggage?'

'He's kind. He's . . . well, like nervy?'

'How nervy?'

'You know, edginess. A thinker.'

'In town for some sort of job? A Cordial-style job.'

'Look, I'm not here to grass, Dave.' It was a snarl. She sounded suddenly violent. 'That's what I meant – confidential. I want you to find him, that's all.'

'Along what lines?'

'What?'

'The thinking,' Brade replied. 'He's deep?'

'In his face sometimes, and the way he stood.'

'*How* did he stand? *What* was in his face?'

Semprina left the moquette armchair where she had been

sitting and with the glass in her left hand went and took up a position on Brade's bit of thin orange hearth rug. She became very still, staring towards a photograph of ice-floes at the South Pole on Brade's wall. 'You see, Dave? A thinker.' She did not turn to speak to him but kept the pose, so Brade would understand better about the thinking that went on in Peter Vincent, alleged. Semprina wore a short black leather skirt and black cotton jacket over a cerise shirt with big pointed collar. She was about twenty, tall, her dark hair cropped short to show off the fine smooth profile and sombre eyes. This was a face that might do fifteen blow-jobs a night yet still kept its refinement. Her shoes were purple and white, the kind of shoes a tart had to wear to show a cruising car quickly she *was* a tart, in case the skirt and arse didn't. 'Like that,' she replied, not moving. 'He would stand like that, except not the glass.'

'Killed conversation, did it? Non-drinker?'

'He didn't talk all that much.'

'But you still liked him. He must have had something else.'

'Poise? Is it called poise, Dave?' She went and sat down again. 'How would you know about poise, though?'

'Accent?'

'It could be London. That way of just standing, and the thinking – they got to me. You seen anything like that?'

'How did you know he was thinking?' Brade asked. 'Did he say, "This is the thinking position"? He might have just been standing. But, anyway, you liked him?'

'Like him,' she replied. '*Like* him, Dave. It's not over. You'll find him, bring him back, won't you?'

'So, now, a description. Did he meet anyone else that you know of, besides Cordial?'

'He went out a few times, alone. I don't know where or who he saw.'

'Day? Night?'

'Both. He's around six feet, maybe a bit less, a lot of fair hair. Thin build, with –'

There was a knock at the flat's front door.

'Jesus,' Semprina said. She crouched forward urgently now, knees hard together, gazing at Brade. 'It's nearly 3 a.m. Who's calling? Dave, don't open. Shout you're busy. Have you got a spy hole in the door?'

Brade moved towards it and opened up. The Reverend Clifford Hale-Garning stood there holding a possibly full bottle of tonic wine, a finger through the handles of four earthenware mugs. He wore an old vermilion track-suit, the trousers tucked into calf-high brown fashion boots, an ochre silk knotted cravat and a sweatband around his grey scrubby head. Cliff would be in his mid-sixties.

'Ah, I thought I heard talk, Dave, and wondered if you were all right for drink and, as it were, society.' He looked past Brade into the living-room and gave Semprina a small, approving wave. Hale-Garning occupied the flat above Brade's and constantly listened through the floor and ceiling for sounds of a party he might join. That was fine and usual when Brade lived alone. Cliff had not really adapted yet to the changes, except that these nights he knocked the door, did not use the key Brade had given him too, in that previous era, and never reclaimed. Perhaps Cliff *couldn't* adapt – a survival matter. Hale-Garning did some dogsbody role at the cathedral and never gave up his fine, late-life struggle against boredom and decline. Now, stepping eagerly forward, he set down his mugs and tonic wine bottle on the table. He poured three drinks then went to the record player but stopped. 'Kate's sleeping?' he asked. 'Sleep's important – for a future mother.'

'Thanks, Cliff. Could you drive Semprina home? She's upset. And it would save her a taxi fare.'

'Of course,' Hale-Garning replied. 'What's the matter?'

'Confidential,' Brade said.

'I'm a priest, for heaven's sake. I'm used to secrets.'

'Perhaps she'll tell you then.'

3

From the jib of what was these days not much more than an ornamental crane alongside what was these days not much more than an ornamental dock hung a figure that could never be called ornamental. It *could* be called a display death, Brade decided.

The man was about forty feet above the water and would be sure to catch the eye of many in the docks marina housing, marina apartment blocks and the marina hotel opposite. He would also be visible to motorists using the roads on both sides of the former Bute Dock East, which had become a pond, with ducks and swans. In fact it was a breakfast chef arriving early at the hotel who made the first call. There would have been more since. But it was that first call, of course, which the Control Room had passed on to Brade, asleep by then and a bit blurred and weary. He had slipped back into slumber for a little while until Kate rewoke him. 'The call, Dave. Whatever it was, you said you'd go at once. Was it something?'

'Yes, something.' He had made himself get on to his feet. 'Not much of a life for you, these disturbances.'

'I'm not the one who has to get out of bed, love.'

It angered Brade that people in the marina housing should be confronted by this dangling figure on the crane. They had paid a lot for their bright properties and deserved a better view to wake up to. He knew why he thought display. On television news not long ago he had watched the execution of an alleged multiple killer in a Middle Eastern state. Before an attentive crowd, the supposed culprit was winched up by the neck on a construction crane much higher than this one, the aim obviously to let plenty of people see him kicking there so they would know law and order were on the ball, and could feel comforted and, if necessary, deterred.

Today's display – the man rotating sluggishly above Brade now – would comfort nobody. And he could not have kicked because his wrists and ankles were bound. He would certainly be meant to deter. But the message was not for the general populace. This deterrent had someone's name on it. Identify the corpse and Brade might manage a guess at who was being warned.

From where he stood staring up he did not recognise the face or physique or gear. Perhaps he should have allowed Jenkins to open the other case in Semprina's place after all. These clothes might have been in it. The face was only intermittently in sight as the figure slowly spun, and was probably fifty feet away from Brade on a grey, misty morning. Besides, hanging did things to the features. He was white, thin, near forty, his hair long, fair and thick. To Brade the clothes looked classy, and not just classy for someone strung up over a mock dock. The man wore a double-breasted grey suit, perhaps three-piece, of established cut, no vents. The jacket was still buttoned and Brade could not be certain of a waistcoat underneath, but it did seem that kind of suit, a waistcoat kind. The hanging figure had on a very white shirt and muted tie, possibly blue or grey, with what could be silver motifs across it. Someone considerable in the Diplomatic Corps might wear a tie like that, or a top Buck House flunkey – people careful to be turned out right but also well-placed enough and confident enough to let their locks run on a bit. The man's shoes looked expensive, too, and pretty new or recently repaired. They were narrow black lace-ups with not much wear to the soles. The soles in fact gleamed yellowy-brown up there, despite the poor light, close together and forming one image, like a misshapen tossed pancake.

Brade deliberately forced himself to consider options. This man's style suggested a media executive or charity administrator or metropolitan hit man or Social Services director somewhere or metropolitan hit man or Royal Press secretary or whiz-kid QC or metropolitan hit man or snooker club proprietor or fast-track ambassador. Brade tried to imagine him in that thinking pose Semprina had acted out. He hoped he would not have to ask her to look at this face when they brought him down. What good would an identification as Peter Vincent do, anyway? Of course, Cordial might be able to offer better help. And Cordial had the wonderful luggage.

It would take aptitude and strength to get him on to the end of the jib like that. The crane was only a piece of historical décor, with no electric power now. It stood there to remind people that this demure lake had once been a dock with a dozen busy cranes emptying and filling ships. Somebody must have climbed out on to the crane's arm in the dark with a rope and passed the end over its pulley wheel. Then from the dockside they would have tugged him up. Had he been dead already? The down length of rope he saw was fastened to a bollard which had been left in the redevelopment as another piece of period. That bollard would have held freighters when the dock earned its keep. Now it kept fine tailoring aloft and dry. They had put a constable on the bollard to make sure nobody undid the turn and two half hitches and dropped the figure into the water. The turn and half hitches suggested someone good on knots and ropes. Perhaps a member of the team had been in the Scouts or Girl Guides.

Jenkins was already at the crane when Brade arrived. 'I've sent people to knock doors in the marina for witnesses.'

'Any witnesses would have called us, wouldn't they? If someone looks out and spots a hanging, he/she dials 999.'

'Many avoid spontaneous contact with the police these days, Dave, even in a good cause, and even middle-class marina dwellers. It's a sad, deplorable fact.'

The crane stood on a red-brick walkway at the eastern side of the lake, with a bank of bushes and trees between it and the road. To keep back spectators, a tape barrier had been fixed from rails around the lake to one of the trees. About twenty men and women watched from a decent distance, nothing like the turnout for the Middle East seminar. It was too early for many people to be around. Nobody seemed to have told the media yet. A plaque on the crane said it had been made in 1933 for the Great Western Railway and operated first in the Commercial Dry Dock. It was last used in 1987 and then donated to the council by Associated British Ports. Even in a Depression year like 1933, business had been good enough here to require a new electric crane. 'We should bring him down,' Brade said. 'He might be alive.'

'He what?' Jenkins said.

'Bring him down,' Brade replied.

'Raging Bullfinch is coming. He wants things left as they are until he's eyed the scene. You know he's into hands-on leadership, Dave.'

'Fuck Bullfinch. Bring him down,' Brade said. 'Spectacle.' He turned and yelled at the watchers. 'Get moving, will you? You're an obstruction.' A few of them walked off. The rest took no notice.

'I've called for the diving squad,' Jenkins said. 'We can lower him into their dinghy. Otherwise, Splash! He's hanging about eight feet out.'

'So, where are they?' Brade asked.

'It takes the squad a while to get all their gear together, Dave.'

Brade walked over to the barrier. More spectators dispersed

when they saw him approach. A reel of spare tape lay by the railings and he unwound a length and cut it free with his penknife. Making a coil, he put it over his head and across his shoulder and chest like a bandoleer. A couple of strands of barbed wire were stretched around the four metal legs of the crane at about ten feet above ground to keep kids from risking themselves, but Brade saw where some of it had been cleared and he climbed up at that spot to the cabin. A metal ladder started here.

The jib had been left at a low angle when they installed the crane or the man would not be out so far over the water. This made things a bit easier for Brade and he began to work his way slowly up. Footholds were easy using the internal struts and he had on a pair of his supple Charles Laity ankle boots. But, although the jib might be nowhere near its steepest, progess tired him and he could hear something like a wheeze or intense fermentation high in his chest. He had the notion he might spout a sudden bile-phlegm-tonic-wine mix arcing from high into the dock, and possibly catching the fair hair and grey suit on its way. Now and then his eyes clouded for a moment and he fought nausea. He would feel ashamed to mess up gear Semprina thought so much of. Plainly, Brade should have sent someone else, someone younger and fitter, or waited for the dinghy. But it had been important to show Jenkins that a night of full-pace activity left Brade entirely unimpaired. Jesus, impaired, impaired, impaired was what he fucking was, though, right through.

Spreadeagled on the struts, he paused and looked down at the hanging figure. Brade was closer to him now, but above. The clearest views took in the top of his head and the polished leather of his grand black lace-ups. Once, when the face did come round towards him, Brade thought for a second he saw a fair moustache, a Diplomatic Corps or Buckingham-Palace-aide type of neat, small moustache under a longish Diplomatic Corps or Buckingham-Palace-aide type of nose. Did Semprina speak of a moustache? Then Brade amended. Although he was correct about the nose, the moustache might not be a moustache but a gag of some sort stuck across his lips. The idea upset Brade. It meant the man had not been dead when they brought him here and were getting him ready to hoist, nor when they actually hoisted.

Jenkins struck the leg of the crane a couple of times, perhaps with a fallen branch, like a code signal on the central heating pipes in an old-style jail. When Brade looked down towards him he saw Raging Bullfinch in shirt-sleeves coming over the earth bank from the road. He had left his Rover 400 there among other police vehicles. 'Fuck him,' Brade muttered and climbed on. At the top of the jib he lifted the coil of barrier tape from his body and fixed a loose loop around the hanged man's rope. The loop slid down and rested on top of his fair hair. Brade decided he had his chest-guts more or less cowed and was relaxed as he began to descend, paying out the tape as he went.

On the ground he said to Jenkins: 'Two men to lower him, Glyn. When he's at our level, use the tape to pull him into the dockside and welcome him with an embrace.'

'Was this necessary, Dave?' Bullfinch asked.

'Yes, sir, it was. Ends a fucking peepshow. And he might be alive.'

'He what? There's a boat coming.'

'Where?' The hanged man had begun to descend very slowly. 'If they let him fall in I'll kill them.' Brade had given Jenkins the tape and Glyn took up a position at the dock's edge with a couple of uniformed officers standing on the lower railings and leaning out, ready to pull the man ashore.

'Here's the dinghy now,' Bullfinch said.

A couple of divers launched it at the end of the lake near another piece of ornamentation – a big gantry and chute which used to load ships with coal when coal was still a Cardiff export. The divers roared up on their outboard. Jenkins ignored them. Once the hanging man was a couple of feet above the water Glyn pulled on the tape and drew him towards the dockside. The WPC stretched out and took a hold on the great suit. The other officer gripped the bound ankles with both hands. Jenkins went to help. Between them they brought the man over the railings and laid him on the walkway face up. The face was lean and unscarred, eyes open and blue-black. Brade did not know him but felt that affinity men can register who have been turn-and-turn-about fucking with one woman.

Bullfinch went and stood over the body for a moment, like an angler with a catch. Then he bent down and searched the clothes. He found nothing.

Brade joined him and felt for a pulse. *He* found nothing.

'Showy, Dave,' Bullfinch said. 'Bloody Tarzan up a crane and now Florence Nightingale. Compensating for getting here late, as I hear from a spectator? The marriage bed proves too consoling after all those deprived years?'

'Dave was here first, sir,' Jenkins replied. 'Here before anyone. I don't know how he does it. Well, it's a kind of sublime intuneness with this patch, his patch. He can sense what's coming up. Somehow.'

Nothing had come up, thank God.

4

For Glyndwr Jenkins, lying to Bullfinch like that came as part of the job, and he was more or less sure Brade would have protected him the same way. Yes, more or less. Dave could be variable. Besides, even without the need to shelter Brade now, it had become policy for Jenkins and him to fuck up Bullfinch whenever he grew pushy. In Bullfinch's special dictionary pushiness would be defined as leadership qualities. Perhaps that was fair enough, and Jenkins knew he could be accused of golden boy pushiness himself. All the same, he and Brade still tried to fuck Bullfinch up.

Jenkins, first at the crane by a good ten minutes, had observed something on the far side of the lake that he did not mention to Bullfinch, or consider mentioning to Bullfinch – standard obstructiveness. But he did not mention it to Dave Brade, either. Although Jenkins was familiar with all that *Hill Street Blues* crap about loyalty to a partner, he also knew there must be limits to what you shared. Hadn't Dave himself frequently told him that a good detective never revealed all he discovered to colleagues, and above all not to ... above all not to those above? A wise detective kept a store cupboard. A happy detective hoarded.

Besides, what he had seen at the crane might not signify much. Standing under the jib while dawn edged its dirty grey way in, he had looked up first at that excellently clad and shod body and then done a swift eye tour of the surroundings. Gazing across the ex-dock, Jenkins had thought he spotted several small, quick, oh-hide-me-do movements. They happened around the edges of a mountain of uncleared debris, where a dozen Victorian workshops and warehouses had recently been crashballed in the righteous cause of marinadom. Although he kept binoculars in the car he stayed where he was for now, afraid that by the time he came back with them the movements would have finished. He did not believe what he saw was a man, or woman. It had been less bulky than a human shape. He thought of it as angular and slight – not much beyond two-dimensional. Three or four momentary weak gleams might have come from its surface, street light reflections, perhaps. Possibly metallic then.

As he stared, waiting for a repeat, he had felt his memory nudge him about something, but not something he could get clear. Something he had read recently? Part-recalled pages from several volumes jostled in his memory, the type merging and blurred. Jenkins read a lot of books. Brade considered it a disease. Jenkins struggled to nail this slippery recollection, just as he struggled to sort out what it was he had glimpsed by the rubble. Perhaps the two were linked. Memory could operate like that. Memory lacked system and might have been kicked into strange, undefined action by those movements.

He had detected nothing more near the debris. Then, he did risk going for the binoculars. He sprinted both ways, still anxious about deserting his spot. And perhaps this break in concentration and the physical effort helped unscramble his communication lines. At any rate, as he unlocked the car boot and reached in for his glasses, he suddenly realised what his mind wanted to hand back. A few days ago he had reread a couple of chapters of James Thurber's portrait of Harold Ross, first editor of the *New Yorker* magazine. To illustrate Ross's famous fussiness, Thurber recalled how when vetting a John Hersey article on the Hiroshima atom bomb Ross blue-pencilled a description of bicycles damaged in the blast. Hersey had said the blast made them 'lop-sided'. Ross declared bicycles were not structures capable of lop-sidedness and changed the word to 'crumpled'.

Why had this passage bullied its way into Jenkins' brain now?

Might it be because Ross meant the angular, virtually two-dimensional character of bicycles? So, was it part of a bicycle Jenkins had glimpsed on the west side of the lake, a chunk of the frame, perhaps being tugged out of sight behind the debris?

He had returned to his place beneath the crane and examined the rubble heap through his glasses. Wrong priorities? The man hanging above him was conceivably still alive. Shouldn't he try to cut him down immediately? He lowered the glasses and glanced up at the body again. It rotated, half-rotated, slowly but otherwise seemed totally still. Jenkins could persuade himself the man was unquestionably dead, and *did* persuade himself. This figure might have been on the end of the rope for hours when he was spotted, and could even have been killed before they hoisted him. Jenkins resumed his survey with the binoculars but saw nothing more. Not long afterwards, the scenes of crime people began to arrive, then a lot of uniforms and then, eventually, Brade, still three-quarters sunk in the wholesome, clinging aftermaths of marital bed sleep – some change for him, an overdue change.

Of course, Dave would have been fascinated by the notion of the bicycle for the same reasons as Jenkins was fascinated. Therefore Jenkins had not told him. Brade often warned that once you let information go it was gone and could become someone else's – *would* become someone else's. How high rankers got high rank. Your jewels ended up in that someone else's fucking diadem. No way to run a career. 'And I'm the force's top expert on how not to run a career, Glyn,' Brade would say. Possibly he had never expected his advice on secrecy to be used against him personally by Jenkins. Just the same, Brade *was* those two things, a colleague and of higher rank. So Jenkins did not feel all that bad about censoring. Not really bad at all.

This evening he drove back to the docks, parked outside the Bay's new, vast, neoned leisure hangar and, carrying a flashlight, began to search the few derelict warehouses, workshops and small factories still standing in Collingdon Road, where down-and-outs sometimes set up short-term living quarters, snort-term if they had the cash.

He was looking for a lad named Basil Carl Endicott, but not a lad. Endicott must be in his fifties, at least, a tramp – a tramp who tramped eternally by bicycle around Bute Street, the Pier

Head, Atlantic Wharf, Schooner Way, his gear in bags and baskets hanging from the frame. He was as much a feature of the Bay as the glow on foreshore mud and the doctored dock. In his little travels Endicott saw plenty. Glyndwr knew he should have thought of the bike and him sooner. Although his machine was old and weathered, it would still be capable of giving off glints under street lights in the run-up to dawn.

Apparently, Endicott had once been something biggish in a docks chandling firm, but the business collapsed and he himself never properly recovered. The bicycle might be one of the few items he had hung on to. Not many people now recalled Endicott's real names, and he was known around the Bay as Pedal Power. Occasionally he grassed minor tip-offs to Dave for very minor cash. He talked *only* to Brade because he trusted him and *only* him to use material in a way that never fingered the source. Endicott, wobbling about on his wheels at all hours and sleeping in decayed buildings, was targetable. In one of these places he could be painfully and easily and privately killed for opening his mouth if rumbled.

And it was because of this fine and mystical understanding between Brade and Endicott that Jenkins did not open *his* mouth about what he might have seen. Brade was brilliant, though only half educated, but did he deserve exclusive hold on Pedal? After all, the guidance manual insisted that a grass never belonged to any individual officer but to the whole police force. Although Jenkins would certainly not go that far, this morning he had decided Pedal Power could be a voice to him as well as to Dave. If he found him, Jenkins would convince Endicott there was more than one detective who knew what care meant. Also, Jenkins might bump up the kind of sweetener Brade would pay. Jenkins had been to the cash point on the way down here tonight. It would have to be his own money, at least as a start. Perhaps he would be able to reclaim it later from the informant fund, if Endicott did talk and if Endicott out on a night spin had witnessed anything worthwhile at the ornamental crane. Jenkins revelled in cash points. It was a type of transaction some whites seemed to consider off limits for a black, and in the street they would stare at him as if he had not keyed the cash but mugged the dispenser. As he walleted the notes he felt triumphantly wicked.

He stood back from the wrecked Collingdon Road buildings and tried to work out which of them still had a roof, or a bit of roof. Dossers looked for at least that much comfort. Two of the ruins were open to the sky and he ignored these. Two of the others had pretty well all their slates and one showed about a third or half. He went to one with a full roof and saw he would have to climb in over a load of tyres and soaked and reeking old furniture and mattresses dumped across the entrance as easier than a journey to the tip. Perhaps the place was once a motor repairer's, its doorway big enough to take a car or truck. Although the Bay people boarded up these buildings months ago, most of the planks had been torn away. Good. That meant settlers keen to establish domicile. Pedal Power would have trouble taking his bike across the tyres and furniture, but in many homes bicycle storage was a problem and he would persist. Jenkins felt glad about the bike. It ought to make Endicott easier to find. Upright or flat, bicycles needed space, had geometrical prominence, unless, of course, they were nuclear lopsided. Crumpled.

Inside, the beam of his torch found a woman between forty and fifty sitting on the floor, legs stretched out, her back against a concrete pillar. Perhaps she had been sleeping when the light or Jenkins' footsteps crunching bits of brick and glass disturbed her. She had on two raincoats, astonishingly new-looking blue and white trainers, tweed trousers and a khaki balaclava helmet. 'This is only temporary as far as I'm concerned,' she said.

'I'm glad.'

'The torch –'

'I'm sorry,' Jenkins replied and took the light off her face. There was a brown paper carrier bag at her side with what appeared to be clothes in it. He saw no food or drink traces nearby. Her eyes seemed dark and were very large, perhaps sleepless large. Under the balaclava her face might be round, plumpish, motherly. Jenkins wondered if she had pinched the trainers from a son before quitting the family for adventure.

'I'd say that torch is like a police torch, very strong, for investigating,' she said. 'I don't think that's a torch of someone after a billet.'

'Yes, I'm the police. But don't worry. You're doing nothing wrong.'

'Giving myself piles, I expect, sitting on this cold floor.'

'There's the Salvation Army up the road.'

'As I say, only temporary. I wouldn't want to bother anyone. There have been one or two little reverses, but they'll sort themselves out. I can see you better now. Plain clothes. You're looking for someone particular?'

'No, no,' Jenkins replied. 'Just dawdling. Routine.'

'I should think you're looking for someone particular but can't say because of confidentiality. A grass?'

'No, no, indeed. Only checking out the buildings.'

'For? You're black? Or is it shadows? It's good they're getting blacks into the plain clothes side, also. Like Virgil Tibbs in *In The Heat of the Night?*'

'Yes. Sidney Poitier did help.'

'Have you got a white colleague who's by comparison crude and uneducated, like Rod Steiger as the Chief, chewing all that gum? And his gut?'

'Look, could you use a ten?' Jenkins replied. Before he'd finishing speaking he knew it was an insult, as if he had no interest in a conversation with her about colour and films, just felt he had better fork out to a derelict.

'Don't ask me to believe the police send people around now giving tens to vagrants.' Her accent was Cardiff but refined Cardiff, the *a* in *ask* widened and softened to *awsk,* just as uptown folk pronounced Cardiff as Cawdiff. Jenkins leaned forward and put one of the new ten pound notes on top of a greenish cardigan in the carrier bag. 'Get a good breakfast. And a cushion from Oxfam. You've got me worried about your arse.'

'Oxfam? Yes, I'd like to help the unfortunate.'

'I was wondering about your name, madam – in case someone comes to us looking for you. If you've walked out from somewhere, I mean.'

'But you wouldn't ask me whether I did?'

'I might.'

'Am I on the Missing Persons list, is that what you're wondering?'

'Like that.'

'Who'd put me on it?' she replied.

'There's a lot of loneliness these days.' He left her, climbed back over the furniture and made for the next building with a roof, about twenty yards up the road. It was smaller, trimmer, even now – might have been a store once, perhaps a chandler's store. Here, too, boarding-up wood had been torn away. He went in through a side door and immediately saw the bicycle standing against a wall of the one big central room, two or three bags still tied to the frame. There was something ordinary and comforting about it, like the laden bicycles of onion sellers around the streets from Brittany when Jenkins was a boy, the 'Johnny Onions' men. He moved the torch beam slowly along the wall and reached Pedal Power who was standing a couple of feet from the handlebars. As always, he looked full of dignity and presence and had a dark, decently square-cut beard. Could he still manage trips to the barber? Would a barber's shop let him in, even if he had money? Would customers fancy the same comb? This time Jenkins remembered to keep the light's glare down. Pedal Power's brown brogues looked expensive, perhaps also brought from the happier days. 'Mr Endicott,' Jenkins said, 'we all value you as an observer.'

'I was just leaving,' Pedal Power replied. He wore a beige belted raincoat that had seen hard living and a plum-coloured corduroy cap. Jenkins could understand now why Dave Brade regarded Endicott as symbolic – three-speed downfall. That would upset Dave. He was going to be a father and longed to believe the city and what remained of its docks would soar to eminence again pretty soon, and definitely in time to offer his family a sound future. He disliked signs of the opposite – Endicott, for instance. Dave tried to think positive. He would lovingly cite all the plump development money about now, and the swank and status that came via the new Welsh Assembly and all its bits and pieces. Of course, perhaps the scale of crime would grow in harmony. Never mind, Dave could deal with it. And Jenkins would help, more or less full out. Yes, more or less. There would always be career details to think about.

'Leave Pedal alone.' The voice, male, high, sharp, determined, nervous, came suddenly from behind Jenkins. As he half turned to see who was there something struck his arm, maybe a blow meant to knock the torch from his hand but too high. Jenkins held on to it and, swinging around with the light at face level again now, saw a youthful, fair-bearded, thin, pale, bony face bent forward at him full of terror and rage. Jenkins saw, too, the piece of old cast iron drain-pipe which had hit him raised again for another try, but aimed at his head this time. The instant crazy thought came that the man looked posed for a picture captioned 'Poet with cosh'. Glyndwr moved fast to the side and the metal took him on the edge of the shoulder only and slid away. Painful for a moment, but no real damage. He could still punch with that arm, did punch with it and caught the man full on the left cheekbone. He dropped the piping and then folded down in a rush to the concrete floor himself. In the torch beam Jenkins saw he was still more or less conscious. He helped the man to his feet and propped him against the wall, holding him steady with one hand. 'What's bothering you?' he asked.

'Have you come for Pedal, you bastard?'

'To talk to him.'

'I don't believe it.'

'What's he to you? Who are you?' Jenkins replied.

'Who are *you*?' the man said.

'He's the police.' Now, it was the tones of the lady from along the road. She must have followed Jenkins and come in behind him. Quickly, she went and stood alongside the young man, her body helping to keep him upright. They both stared towards Pedal Power.

'Police?' the young man asked. He had on the kind of heavy, sleeveless leather jerkin you could get in army surplus stores if you wanted to. He wore it over a navy blazer with silver buttons, most of them present. The blazer was out at one elbow and looked much too big for him, its material bunched on his chest under the jerkin, so that the buttons clustered like Christmas tree trinkets.

'I'm going now,' Pedal Power said. Jenkins heard him shift the bicycle and when he put the light beam over there again saw that Endicott was nosing his machine towards the doorway.

'No,' the other man cried out passionately. He turned to Jenkins. 'If you're police, don't let him. We can look after him here, guard him. There are others in these buildings. We have a grand strength, united.'

'Going where?' Jenkins asked.

'He's afraid. And afraid for us,' the woman said. 'Yes, *for* us.' She seemed to decide the young man did not need her to lean on any longer and walked forward and put a hand on the front wheel of the bicycle, as if to detain Endicott. 'Pedal's doing a Captain Oates. You know Captain Oates – on Scott's expedition and sacrificing himself because he had frost-bitten feet and was endangering the others? "I am just going outside, and may be some time." Cold feet but not cold feet. Brave. Now Pedal is going outside.'

'I'll be fine, Beryl,' Endicott said.

'Endangering you how?' Jenkins asked.

'Don't you know?' the woman replied. 'Isn't that why you're here?'

'Just a little move,' Pedal Power said.

'We do try to look after one another in these properties,' Beryl stated. 'Oh, non-stop mutual thieving, too, naturally, but we're a community.'

'Did he see something at the old crane this morning?' Jenkins asked.

'Well, I'll be away,' Pedal Power said. He pushed the bike gently towards the door. The woman let her hand fall from the wheel.

'Pedal, have you thought, if this one's police, black or not, he might be able to look after you,' the young man said. 'It's their role.'

'Goodbye, Terry, goodbye Beryl,' Endicott replied.

'Stop him,' Terry said.

'You saw who hanged the hanging man?' Jenkins asked.

'And perhaps the one who hanged the hanging man knows he was seen,' Terry said. 'And so, bad hazard. I thought he'd sent you for Pedal Power. He didn't send you, did he?'

'I told you, he's the police,' the woman said.

'He didn't send you, did he?' Terry asked. 'Someone like that – someone who could hang the hanging man – he'd have power everywhere. He might run all sorts, police included. But whatever he tried we could look after Pedal Power here. We can fortify our homes.'

'But Pedal Power won't have it,' the woman said.

'Get him back – if you're police,' the man said.

When Jenkins went outside, neither Pedal Power nor the bike was in sight. The other two joined him. 'You know about it now,' Terry said. 'Your responsibility.'

'I need the name,' Jenkins replied. 'If I'm to help.'

'He told us nothing,' Terry said. 'To protect us he told us nothing.'

'Someone who might run a police officer?' Jenkins asked. 'That what you said, Terry?'

'Leave it now, will you?'

'But someone local big enough and rich enough to run a police officer and hard enough to take on eliminating the crane man, or helping?' Jenkins said. 'I can think of two names.'

'Perhaps we all can,' Terry replied. 'Anyone who knows the Bay can.'

'This would be Jule Corbett or Adrian Garrant, those prime middlemen of the Bay,' Jenkins said.

'Perhaps it's best no names,' Beryl said. 'Best for *us*.'

'Where will he go?' Jenkins asked.

Terry said: 'As a matter of fact, I've got a poem dealing with the homeless and the police.'

'I thought you might be bardic,' Jenkins replied. 'The thinness and class of beard.'

Terry produced a grimy exercise book from the jerkin pocket. 'Give me a bit of light.' Jenkins turned the beam on it and Terry tore out a page and handed it to him. 'There are other copies.'

'Where will he go?' Jenkins asked. 'I've got a colleague. Endicott might be willing to speak to him.'

'Brade?' Beryl said. 'About this Pedal Power won't talk to anyone. Too perilous. This is a death, for God's sake. A man with his mouth taped.'

'Brade's subtle,' Jenkins replied. It hurt appallingly to advertise Dave like this, but necessary, perhaps, as a last shot. 'I could do you for withholding evidence, you know.'

'No, we haven't got any,' Beryl said. 'Plus, you seem too decent.'

'No, I'm not decent,' Jenkins replied. He went for his car and drove up Collingdon Road and then back down Bute Street and on to the Pier Head. He did not see Pedal Power, though. Endicott would have other spots where he could go to ground. One or other of the girls might give him lodgings. He would know them all from his travels. Or he might have cycled out of the Bay altogether. Maybe Jenkins should have called in and asked patrol cars to look for him, but that would mean saying why he was wanted. It would mean opening the store cupboard.

At home, he sat on the side of the bed and read Terry's poem. It was gifted and dismal and touching, about someone sensitive who could not keep up and *would* not keep up with life's savage changes. Dave Brade might have bloody empathised.

'What's that filthy bit of paper, for heaven's sake?' Mair asked, lifting her head from the pillow and staring at the page.

'A statement.'

'Statement for a court?'

'Wider than that. About somebody's soul.'

Mair sat up properly, interested. 'That sounds lovely, inspiring.'

'Well, yes, it is, in many ways.'

'Female?'

'Men have souls as well.'

'He's speaking direct to you?' Mair asked.

'To me, to the world, if it will listen. But it's the kind of poem that assumes the world won't. Nine-tenths of the world's poetry wouldn't get written if poets thought the world wanted it.'

'So, where do you meet a poet?'

'A little ivory tower I discovered.'

'In my view, now you've told me all that, the dirt actually *improves* this document – gives it more genuineness. And is it useful, Glyn?'

'It shows me someone's thoughts and feelings – always a plus.'

'You expected something else?'

Jenkins said: 'Not to be ungrateful, but I imagined he was handing me a tip-off – something dangerous he had to disguise as a poem. He lives in an exposed spot. He says he and his friends can turn it into a castle. As a warrior he's a fair poet, and what he has given me is just a poem. A scream for help.'

'And can you supply it? If anyone can I'd say it was you.'

'You're biased, and thank God for it.' He put the poem on the chest of drawers and began to undress. 'What's going to happen to people living rough around the Bay, Mair, when their accommodation is flattened in the bright cause of redevelopment?'

She thought a while. 'They'll move on, or back to where they came from, won't they? People are strong. They can't be allowed to hinder a magnificent scheme. Don't get mawkish.'

Mair believed entirely in the new Cardiff Bay, or Bae Caerdydd as she preferred to call it. Although she had come south for her job with the Wales Tourist Board, Mair was raised in a heartland district of North Wales and still seemed more at ease speaking Welsh. God, what a fusion of far-flung ancestries when she and he decided to move in together a year after her divorce. It worked more or less all right, though. Mair turned towards him as he climbed into bed, her arms open and a great smile on, because she was biased. Yes, it worked more or less all right.

5

Dave Brade felt troubled about the type of people now turning up in the Bay. A couple of weeks after that little expedition along the crane jib to the hanging man, another stranger arrived on his turf, or a stranger to him, anyway.

Yes, a party-giving chappie sailed into the Bay. Although Brade did not know this newcomer either, Jenkins did, from their glittering education days. Just the same, Brade was invited to the party. 'His money?' he asked Jenkins. 'Where from, Glyn?'

'I've lost touch with Kim since Oxford,' Jenkins replied. 'We shared a tutor, you know.'

'Ah,' Brade replied.

'Oh, yes. My scholarship was history but I switched to moral philosophy – knowing I'd be coming into the police. I'd have expected Bullfinch to be here.'

These prestige get-togethers came up all the time for Brade. Venture capitalists venturing capital found it a comfort to put him on their guest list. This applied even to venture capitalists whose capital was honest. People courted Brade's friendship – or what Jenkins called Brade's 'good offices'. Looking at the mob of happy, noisy, pricily dressed folk today Brade wondered which of them longed to kick to death which of the other happy, noisy, pricily dressed folk, and which of them might actually do it any autumn night soon. Mostly, he thought of men doing it to men. But women could be on the end of it, too, either end.

'I love the way you say it,' Brade said across his amiable Campari.

'What?' Jenkins replied.

'Oxford.'

'How *do* I say it?'

'Like offhand. Not dwelt on.'

'It's just a place, Dave – just a place with a goodish university.'

'Like offhand yet stuffed with pity for those who never fucking got there.'

'*You* never fucking got there, did you, sir?'

'Like he's bound to have made his loot honestly because you two were students together,' Brade said.

'They say *undergraduates* at Oxford,' Jenkins replied. 'Students are art college.' He nodded a bit to emphasise the booming wisdom of this and smiled at Brade, like a kindly teacher. 'Plus possible family money. His father. Printing, I think, and give-away newspapers.'

At the top of the room a bell sounded slowly four times, perhaps imitating the half-hour chimes of a watch at sea. 'Ladies and gentlemen – may I, may I for a moment or two . . .? I'd like just to say that my associates and I are immensely grateful such a crowd has come today to hear about our project. Immensely.'

Kim Pillar, this one-time friend of Jenkins, when they were undergraduates not students, began to address the gathering. He stood eager, engaging, broad and full of vocabulary alongside a side table on which rested the handsome brass bell. Near it was a cardboard box. 'Thank you, thank you,' Pillar said. The waiters stopped moving about with trays and stood grouped against a wall. People grew quiet. Some would want to concentrate on their suspicions of Pillar, even fear, especially as the food and drink were so good and the big flat's antique furniture so unrepro. This boy had depth. It could be diabolical.

His voice was cheery and soothing. He had a tone which, regardless of the words spoken, would seem always to seek friendship, and friendship of a wholesome kind. That might be damn tricky here. 'It is a project we feel sure you will all recognise as richly in harmony with your wonderful Cardiff Bay scheme,' Pillar said. 'I hope my sounding of the bell in that fashion will give a fair clue to the type of idea we want to put before you – put before you with pride.'

Brade loved the message. He revelled in anything that highlighted the city's great history. The past was so manageable, so charted and, yes, wholesome – so easy to falsify, when convenient.

Pillar said: 'It's a sea project, a special one, a resoundingly right one, in our view, which brings the brilliant present and future of this dockland area into living contact with its famed, distinguished earlier times.'

The brilliant present. Yes, Brade could just about buy that, but did any of these people in the audience know about the hanging man? Well, of course, all of them. It had been in and on the media. But did any of them know about the hanging man before Brade had known, and even before Jenkins had known? By now, of course, the body was definitively identified: not Peter Vincent but Clive Everton Indiment and not of the Diplomatic Corps or Buck House either, but, as had always been more likely, a metropolitan hired artist specialising it was thought in quick hits at fifteen and upwards grand a time, though he had never been convicted and now never would be. Indiment must have needed that sort of money for his wardrobe and shoes. Semprina had considered him a thinker. But he had also been a damned good shot with a heavy handgun up to ten yards, a major skill. There had been no need to show him to Semprina or Cordial. Scotland Yard kept a file on Indiment despite his lack of form, and he was identified from pictures. Brade yearned to look at the luggage. But to ask Cordial would point to Semprina, and that could turn out rough for her.

Pillar took hold of the cardboard box, which Brade now saw was not a cardboard box but a cover with no base. Making a quick movement Pillar lifted it, like a magician reaching his rabbit. He grinned with delight and pride, then stood back to admire the sight and to give people in the room time to admire it. Excitedly he rubbed at his forehead. There came foot stamping from guests with drinks in their hands to signify applause, and cries of 'Bravo!'

A beautiful model of a ship lay displayed. It was about two

feet six inches long and made of wood, with metal, plastic and cloth extras. Brade recognised her immediately. His heart soared and tears of pleasure clouded his eyes. She was a Victorian three-masted vessel with some sails set, and a funnel astern for an auxiliary steam engine. Pillar said: 'I know I don't have to tell such an audience, familiar with Cardiff's great story, the name of the barque you see before you – and I am advised by experts she *is* a barque – this is not merely Pillar going poetical! – she is square rigged on her foremast and mainmast and fore-and-aft rigged on her after mast.' He turned with large modesty to someone behind and said in a deferential whisper which everyone could hear, 'I did get that right, did I, Mark? Good.' Brade could have told him he had it right. He could have given him the whole life story of the ship.

Pillar said: 'This is that famous little one-time whaling vessel, the *Terra Nova*, which sailed from Cardiff in 1910, stocked with good South Wales coal as a gift, and which went on to carry Captain Robert Falcon Scott, the mighty explorer, on his glorious but tragic mission to the South Pole.' Pillar paused to give people time to admire the model and sink into the oratory.

'Yes, glorious,' Brade muttered.

'I heard a wash-out,' Jenkins said. 'Weren't they beaten in the Pole race by some Norwegian? Then Scott dies and four others.'

'Glorious,' Brade replied. '"To strive, to seek, to find and not to yield."'

'Ah, old Tennyson,' Jenkins said.

'On the cross over their cairned grave.'

'Cairned? That ancient kind of glory – the disaster kind. The Light Brigade. You and Lord Alf, Dave – death-wish people.'

Pillar said: 'While you take time to admire the vessel may I say very, very shortly what my associates and I propose, ladies and gentlemen? It is a high-grade floating restaurant which would be another detailed model of the *Terra Nova*, but bigger, obviously – more than life-sized in fact – and moored at a dockside somewhere in the Bay.' He paused again, this time so the idea could be absorbed, weighed and wondered at.

Brade liked the word Bay. This Bay – Cardiff Bay – was not just a patch of sea semicircled by cliffs and beaches, as, say, the famous Bay of Plenty in New Zealand is, or the possibly more famous Bay of Pigs in Cuba. This Bay was a concept, an advertisement slogan, a downtown redevelopment scheme, mostly land-based, although the sea lay there at the edge. It was industrial, commercial, had infrastructure, a barrage, streets, the Welsh Assembly buildings, cinemas, road tunnels, crime, a brilliant, architecturally vivid opera house (in drawing-board, dream form only), Harry Ramsden's fish and chip palace, crime, the ornamental dock and ornamental crane, a visitors' centre, crime and politics. When Brade thought of the party-giving lad, Pillar, as *sailing* into the Bay, he did not mean the lad actually came over the Bristol Channel horizon by boat. He arrived down the M4 from London in an SL 600 Mercedes, just as Indiment had arrived down the M4 from London, though by Escort, not Mercedes. *Sailed* was to reflect Pillar's style: that confidence, jauntiness even, the glow, bounce and careless grace of a sleek coloniser. His car was parked in the apartment block yard now alongside vehicles of his partying friends, most of these vehicles as comfy as his and also with non-local registrations. The new Bay had a lot of interested parties as well as parties.

'Fuck family money,' Brade whispered to Glyndwr. 'Where does his real capital come from?' But Jenkins' fine face was turned away, looking for more drink or possible pussy or for an excuse not to answer. Apparently, he and Kim Pillar had not only been college men together about ten years ago, they had played for the same rugby team. THEY HAD PLAYED FOR THE SAME RUGBY TEAM. In South Wales this was big-time bonding and approached the sublime. Jenkins might not want such a chummy chum subjected to Brade's rude and endless curiosity.

The chum resumed his address once everyone had examined the model: 'What a draw this would be – people taking their dinner – something rather finer than the hard tack the expedition had to make do with now and then! – dining in a replica of that famed and noble wardroom, slightly extended! It's what I meant in my original remarks – the merging of Cardiff's prestige as a port in the past with the wonderful present and future prospects for Cardiff Bay. Now, be honest, folks, doesn't the idea wow you?' His enthusiasm billowed, played on the crowd like a sunlamp.

Bay. Many bays around the globe offered shelter and protection after the harshness of the open sea. A bay might be wide and beautiful. To Dave Brade the word suggested scope, even glamour, and these were grand for an enormous reconstruction project set to transform those dud dock acres. Already *was* transforming them. Cardiff Bay. Yes, he adored the title, adored being part of it. At the same time it worried Brade to hear people like Pillar use the name as a trading ploy. Brade stuck at it: 'His money, Glyn?' Find how someone got wealthy and you knew how he meant to get wealthier. This was basic police thinking, learned at Nellie's knee, but possibly true, just the same. Jenkins still did not answer.

Pillar said: 'When the *Terra Nova* lay moored in Bute Dock East it cost 2s. 6d. each for people to visit, as the money went then. And not much of a take-up! Just over £13 was raised and donated to Cardiff Royal Infirmary. But my associates and I *know* things would be different today. Our *Terra Nova* will be a magnificent draw.'

Most of the time, to watch this reshaping of dockland thrilled Brade. Now and then it terrified him. That episode at the superannuated Bay crane had terrified him, and still did, especially as he and Jenkins had caught nobody for it yet, or even hatched a shortlist. And this lad Pillar's well-stocked cocktail party could terrify him, as well. Brade smelled fat funds and he heard trouble. He was accustomed to the old dockland and had been more or less able to control the old dockland, those home-grown, familiar, small-time predators. But the finance behind the new Bay and all its glories might attract different quality wild life, might have already attracted that wild life. Pillar, beautifully garbed, exquisitely articulate, was wild life? Incomers like this could be big-time troublesome.

Brade murmured: 'Glyn, in my mind I see a high-grade floating restaurant which serves dainty food and wines to the affluent, plus whatever else they might need to make the evening go with zing. I see a pusher's goldmine.'

'Ah, you're thinking of how things used to be in Bay City.'

'Where's that? I remember Bay City Rollers.'

'Before them. In Chandler.'

'Pedal Power used to be a chandler, didn't he?'

'*Raymond* Chandler, for fuck's sake.'

'Who?' Brade asked.

'He wrote about Santa Monica in California, where he lived in the thirties or forties. It was very civic and respectable and very corrupt. He coded it as Bay City in his tales. Gambling hulks in the port. The police all taking. And so the need for Philip Marlowe. *Who?* you'll ask, acting thick.'

'I'm talking about now,' Brade replied. 'Does this operator big deal drugs?'

'Who?'

'The wordsmith. The sportsman.'

'I told you, I haven't seen him since –'

'Oxford,' Brade said.

'Oxford. What's with you, Dave?'

Pillar grew weightier still and said: 'That renowned moment of the *Terra Nova*'s visit in the city's grand story needs to be commemorated more vigorously than it has been to date. This is my own feeling, and the feeling of my associates. Oh, we recognise that there *are* memorials, like the lighthouse in one of your parks, a Scott tablet in the City Hall, and a *Terra Nova* bed in the Royal Hamadryad hospital.'

'Research,' Brade said. 'But some he's not mentioning: isn't there a famed floating restaurant in one of the English ports, a real drug-trading emporium – called the *Eton Boating Song*, or something hearty like that?'

'Yes, I think I've heard of it,' Jenkins muttered.

'Splendid. So has he,' Brade replied.

Pillar went on: 'But we wish to augment these local tributes to that fine vessel and its crew, believe it is right to augment them. And to do it here in the Bay, near the very spot where the *Terra Nova* docked at the start of her brave voyage nearly a century ago. What could be *more* right?' Again his delight shimmered in the air, like first-class washing out to dry.

'Yes, it *was* a brave voyage,' Brade said.

'Fucking suicidal and mad?' Jenkins replied.

'Brave,' Brade said. 'Obviously, your mate's picked up jolly reports about the *Eton Boating Song*, too. He's pinched the idea and will give it a nice local marketing touch here, he thinks?'

'You're rushing to judgement, Dave.'

'Pillar's proclaiming in his gorgeous voice, *No need to load us with steam coal, but we can load you with coke*. Was he already dealing at Oxford? That the basis of your friendship?'

'One thing I love, it's a pun,' Jenkins replied.

Brade shifted away from him for a better view of the ship. Pillar continued his presentation. No question he had style, had glamour and pitch. Quite often Brade wanted to think the best of people and found he wanted to think the best of Pillar, despite his filthy fucking scheme to turn a symbol of courage and endeavour and sheer magnificent *Britishness* – Brade did believe in that, in Britishness – at least historically, Pillar was going to turn this revered emblem into some snort-smoke-and-mainline trading station, if that was the plan. And it would be.

Perhaps this was how the times were moving. Maybe Pillar had spotted it. The elegant quick outsider might be more aware of the spirit of the new Bay than Brade was. Possibly Pillar would even survive against the equally elegant and quick enemies among this crew today, so prompt with hearty applause and the comradely cries of 'Bravo!' For instance, and what an instance, Brade saw Julian Corbett, one of the Bay's great middlemen, and in continual contact with all kinds of outside developers, applauding much too heartily. Perhaps Jule did not have a piece of this proposal. His bulky, strong-minded wife, Henrietta, wearing a heavy, long, brownish, friar-style dress, and her hair tied with a brownish ribbon, did not clap at all. Henrietta Corbett never wasted energy on *politesse*.

Real skill and knowledge had gone into the making of the miniature *Terra Nova*. Nothing cheap. Brade admired the care. Her decks were loaded with little replicas of all the expedition's equipment. Toy ponies looked over the half-doors of their stalls and toy huskies slumbered on the open deck. Brade knew it all so well that now and then he would fancy he could have commanded the expedition. At home he had a book about it, *The Great White South*, and often he would dwell on that marvellous account of the valiant sea trek. Brade loved heroic tales and yearned to achieve what used to be called gallantry, though he feared the word had probably slipped out of use now. Maybe climbing the jib like that to bring the corpse privacy had been gallant in a way – a very elementary way, but just about his limit, especially after a wearing night.

At the end of Pillar's speech came more happy applause and several people moved forward for another close look at the model. Brade found he could almost imagine a kind of nice-natured, wholesome fascination in them, as if they were admiring a wild-flower collector's newest. Brade frequently tried to believe in the goodness of people. Jenkins took him across the big room to meet Pillar. 'Dave hates everyone who moves into this area,' Jenkins told him. 'At least at first.'

Pillar's handsome, impish face stayed handsome and impish. 'Even an old pal and rugby team-mate of yours, Glyn?' he asked. 'Some of those times – so unforgettable.' Jenkins was copying Pillar's phone number from the handset into his notebook. 'And you should give me yours,' Pillar said.

'Sure.' Jenkins wrote it, tore the page from his book and passed it to Pillar. 'Dave would like to know how you came to be rich, when I'm stuck here as his understudy, so far. It's his way.'

'Rich? Perhaps you dislike our *Terra Nova* proposal, Mr Brade.' His voice now was mild, humble even. 'But Cardiff Bay used to be called *Tiger* Bay, didn't it? Notorious, dangerous, mixed nationality slum. Jungle perils. Surely it's good to transform that.'

Yes, it *was* good. 'But who transforms it?' Brade said.

'World-wide when people heard Cardiff they thought only coal and Tiger Bay. Not very attractive notions, surely. Oh, plus Shirley Bassey. The *Goldfinger* vocalist came from Tiger Bay, didn't she?'

'No,' Brade replied. 'The publicity said she did because Tiger Bay had charm and magic.'

'You regard the *Terra Nova* project as vulgar, disrespectful to great men?' Pillar asked.

'Probably something like that,' Jenkins replied when Brade didn't.

Pillar said: 'But we will have only the integrity of the area at heart, believe me. It is in our interests that the emergence of the new Bay should be painless and successful.'

Would it happen? Decades before Brade came to work in dockland and to love it, bloody and prolonged rioting took place there. Because the authorities always insisted this had had nothing to do with race, he assumed it did. The reputation was a drag when a city sought outside investment for spectacular millennium rebirth. So, get a new logo. Rechristen. Goodbye *Tiger* Bay. Hello, Hello *Cardiff* Bay. Naturally, there might be hazard in the scale of change. Would Cardiff Bay turn out more threatening than Tiger Bay had ever been, even at its fiercest? Well, all right. That's what policing was for, wasn't it – what Brade was for, plus Jenkins and a few others, of course?

'Such partners in the rugby scrum, you two,' Brade said. 'It would pain me to see a comrade of Glyn run into shit clouds. There are roughnesses here. Sadly, we had a visitor who could not keep his feet on the ground. I expect you read the papers. Have you thought about the enemy, enemies?'

'I've had other enemies, Mr Brade.'

'So young, yet already tried in the fire.'

'I came through all right.'

'You've run here from trouble? You might bring your own helping of unpleasantness with you, then,' Brade said. 'Yes, how *did* you get your money?'

'My associates and I want nothing more than to add an asset to the superb Bay development. We will strive for that, fight for that.' His face looked grave, still humble, not off-putting beyond what his kind of ideas-man face was bound to be.

'I'd heard from Glyn about the rugby,' Brade replied. 'Some next-to-fucking-nothing college side, wasn't it, playing against nunneries? Things here could be tougher than that sort of game.'

'I'm sure the law will look after any legitimate enterprise, Mr Brade.'

6

At home in the Bay Julian Corbett had three visitors. He was expecting them, though no appointment had been made. Jule tried to act serene. If you rated as one of dockland's most prominent entrepreneurs – middlemen or even fixers as they were slangily called here – if this was your profession, and a deal you handled went wrong, you knew there would be feedback. A lot of money might be put into some of these projects and people wanted returns. When Jule handled a transaction, the parties generally *did* get returns, healthy, long-lasting returns.

But, of course, a catastrophe like this fucking Indiment on the end of a rope could always happen and then a middleman might get hit with the blame. No might, he *would* get hit with the blame. On the surface, there was some justice in this, Jule did not dispute it. If you took a percentage you stood liable. He, personally, had recommended Indiment, and then, before he even started, the dim sod gets himself hoisted like that. When you bought someone with Indiment's CV you did not expect sloppiness.

Although Corbett had heard early about the body he did not go down there to view. He had shunned any association with such a disaster. Or any *public* association. It struck Corbett as especially bad that Indiment should have let himself get hanged when wearing a superb suit – what the local paper had described as 'hand-tailored, Savile Row'. It made Indiment seem a real idiot to have been jumped when glossied up like that. A showpiece, not an operator. Sometimes people in this sort of work grew vain and casual.

As soon as Corbett answered their knocking and opened the door, Simeon de Courville said: 'I got to tell you we're disappointed, Jule. I speak on behalf.'

'I know, I know,' Corbett said. He wondered if he could get this over fast with a bit of contrition, and keep them in the porch.

'It's cost us heavy money,' de Courville replied. 'But why do I tell you? You negotiated it.'

'In good faith,' Corbett said.

'I don't think any of us disputes that, Jule,' A.W. Moss-Cober replied. 'But try to see how we're left by it, will you?'

'I know, I know,' Corbett said.

'You see, Jule, when we're setting up that kind of operation we have to rely totally on you, on your contacts in London and your skills,' Cordial Maximilian said. The three of them stood in a small semicircle, like carol singers.

'I wouldn't want anything else,' Corbett replied. 'You engage me and I'm honoured and use everything I know to meet your specifications, believe me.'

'Fuck specifications,' Simeon de Courville said. 'We pay out to what we're told by you is an unstoppable artist in all types of weapons and less than two weeks later he's up there over the duck pond and for fucking ever unproductive.'

'We do need to be thinking of a replacement, Jule,' A.W. Moss-Cober said.

'Urgent,' de Courville said.

'You and Henrietta were at the *Terra Nova* presentation, I hear,' Cordial said, 'so you'll realise why our fears are still sharp. You'll realise Glyndwr Jenkins is an old-time pal of the *Terra Nova* boy, Pillar?'

'Indiment in the air like that makes us look like jerks, Jule – me, A.W. and Cordial,' de Courville said.

'Oh,' Corbett replied, 'I don't –'

'What it was meant to do,' de Courville said.

'There *is* contempt shown, Jule,' Cordial said, 'for you as well as for our new little firm.'

'Maybe we should come in for a short conversation,' de Courville said.

'Oh, of course, of course,' Corbett replied, and stood back so they could enter. 'Rude of me to keep you outside. We'll go in here.'

Corbett lived in the manse of Bethel Baptist church, where his father-in-law, Floyd Llewellyn, was minister. Corbett led the three men through a connecting door into the chapel itself and switched on the lights. Cordial looked about admiringly at the wall texts, pulpit and pews. 'I remember this so well from my Sunday school days,' he said. 'Wonderful. Many's the Bible story I still treasure.'

Floyd was away for a week at a religious conference in Ealing. But Corbett did not want to take de Courville and the others into the manse because Henrietta would almost certainly join them if they used Floyd's study. She believed in having views.

'*Without shedding of blood is no remission.*' Cordial read the text aloud. 'I always got a bit of a fright from that one. How about you, Jule?'

'Obviously we still got to find someone to take out this Pillar for us, Jule,' de Courville said. 'We feel you'll want to arrange this, so as to make up for the fucking fuck-up with Indiment. There was £10,000 of our cash in that noose.'

'I know, I know, boys,' Corbett said. De Courville was very bald, his face shiny and mobile. He made you think of a corrupt child, a child who knew about the innocence of the young but had chosen something else. This included unrestrained violence when he felt like it. He seemed close to feeling like it now.

'We want to make it clear we're grateful to some degree for the shrewd way you framed the agreement with him, Jule, half in advance, half on completion,' A.W. said.

'Oh, definitely,' de Courville said. 'If we was down twenty grand we might of been really fucking vindictive with you, you see, Jule. Plus, your own percentage which we did advance in total. That's another three grand.'

'We know you'd want to help us out now, in view of that fee,' Cordial said. 'A second try.'

Oh, Christ, Corbett would have loved to let them have half of it back, now, tonight, or even the full lot, just to be free of this job. A hanged man, plus rumours of an understanding between these *Terra Nova* people and the police – it was so damn dark, so unpredictable. But he knew they would not allow him to return the fifteen per cent, in whole or part. They would regard that as a betrayal, as if he wanted to ditch them. He did. It was not something to proclaim, though. 'I hope Julian Corbett knows when he has a responsibility,' Corbett replied, 'and I hope he will always try to fulfil it.'

Moss-Cober said: 'What we were sure of, the three of us, as a newly formed but solid syndicate, Jule, was that you – like us – could not tolerate the invasion of the Bay by an alien firm seeking to establish and maintain monopoly.'

'This *Terra Nova* restaurant would take all the up-market drugs trade and the more select whoring,' de Courville said. 'That's their business plan. If it ever worked, where are we then, Jule, you, me, A.W. and Cordial? True, we *are* thinking of our own special scheme to resist them, but if they got Jenkins and through Jenkins got Brade . . . Well, I ask again, where are we?'

He and Cordial were sitting in the front pew, half turned to face Corbett and Moss-Cober who had taken places in the one behind. Cordial stood and slowly climbed up into the pulpit. He walked with a stick after that street gang fight when he was run down by a Renault, run down twice. In the pulpit, he did not speak but gazed out as though over a congregation, his face tender and thoughtful. Part of an ear was missing, also because of the street battle. Perhaps as he stared into the middle of the almost empty chapel he searched for memories of himself as a Sunday school child, a wholesome and whole kid then, all his ear present and no injury to his legs. After a while he glanced up at another wall text, *Boast not thyself of tomorrow for thou knowest not what a day may bring forth*. He nodded a couple of times and shrugged.

'So you'll find us another chap, will you, Jule, to dispose of this Pillar and end all prospects for the *Terra Nova*?' Moss-Cober asked.

A.W. was in the kind of greenish-brown gamekeeper's tweeds he liked. 'Another *chap*.' Corbett found Moss-Cober's word strange, and yet it was what he might have expected from him. It gave the planning of a murder a happy ordinariness, allowed no melodrama.

Cordial came down from the pulpit and resumed his place in the front pew. 'The other thing that seemed very clear to Simeon, A.W. and myself, Jule, was you would want to get back at Adrian Garrant. We can't imagine that someone who has been handling business liaison for so long in the Bay as Jule Corbett – and handling it with real distinction, I have to say – well, Jule Corbett is not going to allow someone like Garrant to overtake him, through connection with this new, grasping, cliquey, jumped-up outfit.'

'Obviously, Garrant slaughtered Indiment for them,' de Courville said.

'I did hear a whisper,' Corbett replied.

'No question,' de Courville said. 'Them *Terra Nova* people bypassed you when picking a local rep, Jule, and went for Garrant. Bloody insulting.'

'I've got a girl, a prime girl called Semprina, who's full of genuine distress because of Indiment's death,' Cordial said. 'This was something quite close to love. I'd like to see that Garrant knocked over in due course as well as the immediate target, Pillar.'

Oh, Christ again. He was supposed to line up someone to do Pillar for them and, after that, Adrian Garrant. These expectations would get known, of course. Such things always did. Then, Jule Corbett would be a priority target himself. *Boast not thyself of tomorrow.*

They talked for a short while longer. When the three were leaving, Henrietta must have heard movement and came to the front door to see who had been visiting. She wore a navy smock thing above khaki trousers and looked big and glorious, Corbett thought. He knew he was lucky to have her. But Hen's mind could be brutal, deeply unfoolable. 'So are you people panicking about this ostentatious guy on the crane?' she said. 'You want Jule to help put things to rights while they still can be?'

The bluntness, the truth, obviously embarrassed Cordial, Simeon and A.W. Henrietta could do that to people, *liked* to do that to people. 'This really was a most terrible incident at the crane and very much the kind of taint the Bay can do without, I feel,' A.W. replied.

'What we hope above all is it don't lead to repercussions,' de Courville said. 'That would be truly deleterious.'

'And Floyd, your dad, how is he, Henrietta?' Cordial asked. 'Sometimes Floyd, sometimes Gareth. Many's the day I think of him gently, brilliantly instructing us. Perhaps you'll say it was instruction that did not bring much permanent improvement to yours truly. Perhaps not, perhaps not. But my memories of Floyd are all warm, grateful.' Although Floyd's real first names were Gareth Rhys, he admired Floyd Patterson, the first heavyweight boxer to win the world title twice, and liked to be called after him.

'Jule engaged that guy for you, did he, the guy who was hanged?' Henrietta replied. 'Did you mention that to me, Jule? I forget these things. Jule has a stack of enterprises – I lose count. I hope you boys are not blaming him, trying to pressure him.'

She had so much loyalty, so little tact, the wonderful, big-mouthed cow.

7

'Rendezvous? Nowish?'

'Where?' Jenkins replied.

'I'm at the for ever unvandalised phone box in Bute Street. By the Welcome to the Bay placard. Pushers call suppliers on it, untapped.'

'What's happened?' he asked. Almost as soon as he picked up

the receiver he had thought he knew the voice. Then when she did placard as refined-Cardiff placawd he was sure.

'Or will it embarrass you to be seen with me?' she said.

Yes, it might embarrass him, especially if she still had on the two coats, brilliant blue and white trainers and her Battle of the Atlantic balaclava. 'Embarrass?' he said. 'I don't understand. Why would it, Beryl?'

'But will *I* be embarrassed, spotted talking to the law?' she replied.

'No spiked helmet. Have you seen Pedal Power since?'

'I hear you're a whiz-kid,' she said. 'A white hope. Well, as it were. I'll wait by the box.'

He took a Rover from the police station yard, drove the half-mile to the phone booth and picked her up. She had a skateboard and held it between her legs in the passenger seat, one end touching the floor. As she settled into the car Jenkins found himself pushing his nose towards Beryl like a scenting hound, trying to find if she smelled and if so of what. Would she taint the vehicle for the next user? Immediately he realised what he was doing he felt ashamed. Temporary problems had hit her, as they might hit anyone. Dosserdom and its balaclava and derelict lodgings waited for most of us if we made a couple of slips or lost our taste for family and the household virtues. In fact, Beryl had no balaclava today but wore the rest of her gear. He had guessed right about her face. It was round, chubby more or less, kindly looking. Yes, she would make someone a good mother, perhaps *had* made someone a good mother, even if she stole his trainers. Possibly his skateboard, too. Her hair had been cut pretty short and curled in around her ears. It was brown-stroke-red, possibly well on its way to grey here and there. In her present accommodation, mirrors and light would be scarce and she might have decided not to attempt a dye-match. Jenkins thought her hair looked clean, though he failed to see how it could be.

Now, she seemed to have forgotten the dangers of getting noticed with him and did not try to sink down to below window level. Instead, she sat up full of jauntiness, beaming around like a royal procession, as though she enjoyed car travel and never mind who knew it. Perhaps this trip recalled a lifestyle she had ditched and suddenly found she missed. The skateboard would be more fun, though.

'This is urgent,' she said.

'I guessed.'

'We came across Pedal's bike.'

'Who?'

'Terry and myself.'

'Is it all right?' he asked.

'How do you mean?'

'An accident? It's not . . . well, crumpled?'

'Bikes aren't the shape to get crumpled, surely.'

'Lop-sided then,' Jenkins said.

'It was leaning against a building. Does that make it lop-sided? No damage.'

'But Pedal Power himself?'

'No,' she said. 'Terry's watching it.'

'Where am I going?'

'Behind the Norwegian church,' she replied.

The church was a showpiece on the Bay waterfront. They might meet Mair. In her job with the Tourist Board she often brought official parties from all over Britain and abroad to admire the transformed dockland. This morning she had mentioned over breakfast that she would be in Cardiff Bay today – the Bae – with a group of visitors.

'Bags and baskets, all there with the bike,' Beryl said. 'And his stuff. I don't think anything's been taken. But he wouldn't leave it like that. He understood security, from when he was in business. This is shirts, a tie, spare shoes in the bags, a suit, all his formal wear. He didn't know when these garments and shoes might be reneeded. Many boardrooms were angling for Pedal. He'd never leave such garb about unattended.'

'The brogues he had on the other night were very fine.'

'But the shoes in the bag, hand-made for him personally. For his personal feet, each separately measured. I said to Terry we should phone Brade. Terry said you – because you were bright enough, interested enough, to come looking for Pedal.'

'Found the bike how?'

'Were we looking for Pedal, you mean? Wouldn't you? He's seen too much. He's in danger. As co-dwellers, we have a responsibility.'

'Terry told me *I* had responsibility.'

'Yes, and it made no difference. Oh, I'm surprised he wanted me to phone *you*. Brade's name – it has solidness, honour, dignity.'

Jenkins thought he saw Mair and some guests on their way into the silver, telescope-shaped Visitors' Centre, created for the Bay by architect William Alsop. 'Dignity?' he replied. 'The married man.'

'Brade's got all sorts of famous, tidy skills.'

Jenkins parked at the Pier Head and he and Beryl walked around to the back of the Norwegian church. Terry was there with the bicycle. He stood very close to it, protectively, as if gangs would be here soon, wild for such lavish pickings. He pointed out towards what would be a lagoon once the Bay barrage was finished. 'Many feasible scenarios for what happened to Pedal,' he said. 'E.g., if he was attacked while the tide was up, they could have lowered him into a boat here and taken him out for deep dumping.'

Mair and her party would be looking with admiration through the glass end of the Alsop construction towards the almost completed barrage and promised lagoon, and then beyond to the Channel and to Flat and Steep Holm islands.

'If who attacked him?' Jenkins asked.

'I think there's blood on the crossbar,' Terry said.

Beryl was carrying her skateboard but put it down now so she could crouch for a close look at the bicycle. 'I hate to think of someone murdered so near a place of worship,' she said, 'or even an ex-place of worship.'

The church was built early in the century for seamen at a time when Cardiff did plenty of maritime trade with Norway. These days, the small, white-walled church with its stubby spire operated as a gallery and culture centre. It was sure to be on Mair's itinerary.

'Yes, perhaps blood,' Beryl said.

'I'll have the bike picked up,' Jenkins replied. 'We'll get a proper analysis.'

'No,' Terry said at once. 'Please.' The threat of losing the bicycle seemed to have changed his reading of things. 'He might come back.'

'Not if he's been dumped in the Channel,' Jenkins replied.

'That's only one possibility.'

'Of course. But Beryl says he would not leave the bike and his gear voluntarily.'

'He might have been head-hunted for a board of directors,' Terry replied. 'Living in the properties, he was only marking time until the call came. But, clearly, he would not need the bike in this new appointment. A company Jag.'

'Wouldn't he have taken the special suit, tie and shoes?' Jenkins asked. 'Beryl says everything's here.'

She lifted one of the bags from the handlebars and put it on the ground, then began to check the contents. 'Yes, his suit is still present, as beautiful as ever.'

'Just the same, I want to move the bike back to Collingdon Road,' Terry replied. 'I can look after it there. And it will be available should he return. Pedal would expect us to do that for him.'

Jenkins said: 'If we know whether it's blood on the crossbar we can make a better guess about –'

'I'm inclined to agree with Terry,' Beryl said. 'This bike – once it's disappeared into your forensic machine –'

'Unthinkable,' Terry said.

'Oh, where would we be then?' Beryl asked. 'This bicycle is in our trust, plus the fine possessions.'

'This bike is evidence,' Jenkins replied. 'Or might be.'

'It would be better with us,' Beryl said. 'And if you take it in you'll have to tell everything you know about Pedal Power to colleagues, won't you? I had the feeling you were acting individually on this, the way some snoops do. Off your own bat.'

They came out from behind the church, Terry pushing the bike, Beryl nursing the bag of clothes in both arms. Jenkins had picked up her skateboard. As they emerged, Mair and a group of about a dozen official sightseers were a hundred yards off, strolling towards the church. Mair took a gaze at Terry and the bike and Beryl's two coats and the trainers and Jenkins with the skateboard and gave him a bit of a smile, a North Walian bit, short on merriment, a smile which said, *Keep clear, please, you dead-fucking-loss*. Terry and Beryl were not the kind of Bae Caerdydd features she would want highlighted. Suddenly, though, a member of her party broke away and hurriedly approached Beryl, Terry and Jenkins. This man was in denim jacket and jeans, not a formal outfit like the others. He had a pigtail. Around his neck hung three cameras and with one of them he began to photograph Beryl, Terry and Jenkins, probably with the Norwegian church in the background atmospherically. He might be a professional. Others of Mair's guests saw what he was doing and paused, though Mair herself did not. Several produced cameras themselves and delightedly pointed them. Jenkins turned his back and held the skateboard against his chest so it would not be visible. Beryl and Terry gave salt-of-the-earth poses. Beryl said: 'We'll be in the *Geographical Magazine*. It's not all tribal tit pics.'

After a while the visitors continued to the church.

'Am I right?' Beryl asked.

'What?' Jenkins asked.

'That you're on a personal mission with this one?'

'Let me know immediately if Pedal turns up then,' Jenkins replied. 'You think he's been attacked because of what he saw? So, who was it strung up the crane man? If Pedal's dead you're no longer bound by any obligation to silence.'

'I feel even *more* bound in that case,' Terry replied. 'The obligation gets to be sacred. Besides, he might not be dead at all.' He mounted the machine and Beryl rehung the bag of clothes on the handlebars. Terry began to cycle towards Collingdon Road.

'Are you going to skateboard it, Beryl?' Jenkins asked.

She took it from him but said: 'I'd prefer another lift in an unmarked car.'

Over their meal in the evening Mair groaned: 'Christ, Glyndwr.'

'Who was he, the first one?'

'A freelance doing pictures for one of the municipal journals. But he also sells to the national Press.'

'*Geographical Magazine*?'

'He thought you three might be right for "something grainy" in the *Guardian* or the *Independent*. He considered you looked "so genuine and endemic" and "a sort of brilliantly natural counter to all the Bae publicity crap" – the kind of crap I make my career with. Thanks, Glyndwr. The pictures will be no help to me, the

Tourist Board or the Bae. He loved the two raincoats and trainers and your skateboard. Plus the racial variety, naturally – the "comparative smartness of the black – for a tramp". He especially liked the "dignified, even noble, shyness" when you turned your back, though he'd got a stack of you face-on before that. So what in the name of all that's pious was happening?'

'The phrase is "all that's holy".'

'Fuck off.'

'That one you always get right,' Jenkins replied.

8

'Our view was that you handled the *Terra Nova* presentation pretty well, Kim – really gave them the charm and commitment, yet a pleasant shyness, too. Well, the grand Kim Pillar trademarks. And the conversation at the end with your officer friend and his colleague – this was promising.'

'We're prepared to let you work at your own pace, Kim.'

'I think it's a strength this officer friend is black, Kim. His bosses have to be careful how they deal with someone like that – I mean, discipline of him, surveillance of him – they need to be moderate or they're into extensive fucking bother with the racial discrimination experts, and quite right. About an Oxford friendship of that sort – you with your St John's Wood background – it *was* St John's Wood? – you from such-and-such a milieu, him a back-street black – about that there's a kind of sanctity. Yes, that's what I'd call it. This Oxford comradeship was a fine break from social class, as well as from race considerations. This is something their superiors have to give its due.'

'But the Brade figure. Obviously we're watching him during your presentation, Kim, and afterwards when you're talking to them. Not a sympathetic face. He's got his unhelpful side, do you think? Naturally, we've taken the trouble to know a bit about him. He's not the planning authority, of course, and he's not the Bay management and he's not the Chief Constable, or anything like, but we will need him, I think. We might – only *might* as of now – *might* be able to arrange some influence at a few ranks above Brade. But problematical and, even if we do manage it, we always need a workaday officer or two, a street level officer or two, especially when they've somehow built up the sort of influence Brade seems to have in docks matters.'

'We're certainly willing to show him a lot of patience, Kim, at this stage. In any case, to take out a policeman, any policeman, anywhere, even a spot like this – it's risk. No certainty of long-term advantage. You've told us you can reach him via your chum, Jenkins, and we're ready to accept that. At this stage. And especially if we fail to bring it off with this figure above Brade – not Chief rank, but weighty. Yes, if we fail there this Jenkins becomes of real significance. *Glyndwr* Jenkins. That's magnificent. His parents gave him the name of a Welsh prince to help him integrate? And he's bilingual Welsh-English, I hear. Bloody superb.'

'We've got an investment in you, Kim. It embarrasses me to remind you that you owe us, but it *is* a factor. We can't let some middling detective like Brade foul up a project of this size, can we?'

'It's a project that could put you more or less right with us again in due course. We're giving you your fucking head. Yes, your head. At this stage. We regard renting the flat for you in the Bay and the furniture and entertainment costs as entirely worthwhile.'

'We know you recognise we've been reasonable to you, Kim.'

'Oh, certainly, and I'm grateful,' Pillar replied.

'How much would you estimate you skimmed in trading until October last, Kim, when we did our little audit? We know the figure, of course, because we've got the accounts. But we'd like to hear your own estimate.'

'And very nasty reading they make, those accounts.'

'You took us good, Kim. Do you know *how* good? Did you have a system, or was it just as it came?'

'I still don't see it as skimming,' Pillar replied. 'Some carelessness there might have been by me, and even some incompetence, yes. Not skimming, though.' He could hear a whine in his voice. It appalled him. He needed a joke. He was Kim Pillar, known for his wit and ease and lightness of touch. But he could not find a joke for now.

Dominic gave a fair chuckle. 'Not skimming? You varsity boys, you're remarkable with words.'

'Skimming, Kim. We put a figure of £1.6 million on it.'

'Many would find that a difficult amount to regard forgivingly, Kim. And all gone, you tell us. Car, country house in Wiltshire, fittings – you're a spender, Kim. I don't normally mind that. I think people *ought* to do things with their money. I can't stand fucking meanness. But you'll notice I said "their" money, signifying their own. Now, Kim . . . well, imagine you'd taken 1.6 million from, say, Leonard Bright. It's doubtful whether you'd be sitting there today in a suit and this marina-style flat.'

'Oh, Leonard the Lunge,' Pillar replied. 'Dominic, you mustn't ask me to compare you and Geoffrey with him. Lunge first, work things out afterwards.'

'You would not have been given the chance to repay,' Dominic said.

'I *am* grateful,' Pillar replied. It was best to stick to the simplicities with these two at this time.

'Oh, what use would you be to us dead, Kim?' Geoffrey said. 'We'd still be down the 1.6, plus whatever it cost to have you hit. Is this constructive? You're a true and rare creative force. It's in your body language. This *Terra Nova*! Brilliant. Are we going to smash someone who has flair like that – I mean without a lot of thought first? You were alive enough to see the potential here. Yes, alive.'

'We prize you, Kim. Hence, that little demonstration on the toy crane at the toy dock. Indiment had been hired to do you, of course. In a way it's flattery. The competition sees that with Kim Pillar out of the way the *Terra Nova* scheme can't function. Indiment was commissioned by someone who does not like your talents. We're not sure yet about his employer, but Indiment is high-fee, so it's someone weighty. Or a syndicate. All kinds could envy you and your abilities, couldn't they? We *were* certain, though, that he'd been told to take you out. We had to arrange that pre-empting, you see. Just consider – if we'd been short-sighted and evil, thinking only revenge because you milked us, we could have let him go ahead and made a saving. To get a hit man hit and given a bit of projection up a crane is damn costly, but to the point, I think. We think. Half-baked lad to move in with a whore like that, so obvious, so trackable.'

'Thanks, Dominic, Geoffrey.'

'Geoffrey's had some research done on Brade. Well, as you'd expect, Kim, knowing Geoffrey's thoroughness.'

'Just some basics,' Geoffrey said. 'This is a complicated type. I'm sure Kim can manage an appraisal of him without any help from me. Yes, Brade's complex but no mystery. Just take my findings as an extra, Kim – possibly of use, possibly worthless.'

Pillar said: 'An extra! That's funny, Geoffrey. I'm damn sure any work on him you've done or had done will be –'

'Brade packs a lot more power than might seem. He's admired. He's believed in. He could help us, certainly. We're going to need some first-class protection and I'm sure he could provide it, particularly if we fail a little higher.'

Pillar said: 'You're doing your own negotiations with someone?'

'What you'd expect, Kim,' Dominic replied. 'All possible influences. We're working to bring in this higher cop. And then we needed someone to handle Indiment's death and the deterrent display, and we'll probably keep a connection there. A local called Garrant, Adrian Garrant. You can leave all that aspect to us. You concentrate direct on Jenkins and Brade. Kim, we know you're the very boy to get to Brade for us. This is where talent and breeding and polish and education come in. You plus your black college brother, your rugby team brother. Things don't get closer than that, not without actually dicking each other, and we gather that wasn't happening, was it? Both girl men, weren't you?'

'There used to be a lot of weakness in Brade,' Geoffrey said. 'Personal weakness. Tarts, magazines. Perhaps not any longer. He's married, a kid coming, stability.'

'Yes, a pity,' Dominic said. 'We could have made hay with his frailties. However . . . Our middleman lad down there – Adrian Garrant – he supplies this information on Brade's new state. We'll probably retain Garrant. There's another possible, called Julian Corbett, but he's had some nasty and near escapes. Shop-soiled. Probably working for a local syndicate, anyway. Heard of A.W. Moss-Cober and confederates?'

'They've been around for centuries, apparently,' Pillar replied.

'You're going to have a triumph with this Brade, Kim,' Geoffrey said.

Dominic said: 'We're confident you won't try to make a run for it, Kim – abroad, somewhere like that, no matter how much of the 1.6 you've still got stuck away liquid, you filching bastard. We considered putting someone in with you and your family at that lovely Wiltshire place, just to keep an eye and so on. I even thought my father and mother. They could act as butler and housekeeper. That house, the size, it's a pile which could take staff. And they'd keep in touch with me about you and your wife and baby, Edward. They're adaptable and would enjoy living in such a big spread. But Geoffrey and I decided it's not necessary.'

'Not a bit,' Pillar replied, 'I would never think of –'

'Are you going to run for it and leave a fine place like that behind, possibly also your wife and the bairn, and the cars and this unique project of yours, the *Terra Nova*?'

'Hardly, Kim,' Geoffrey said, 'correct us if we're wrong.'

9

'They're comic, really,' Pillar said.

'No, not that.'

'Oh, don't worry, I'd never let them see anything. No giggling. I act eternal gratitude. You know how I can grovel, if grovelling's needed, Jane.' He went into a big triumphant laugh and waited for her to join him, but she managed half a smile, nothing more. *He* was the one with the jokes in this family. Well, he didn't mind that. 'They put on a power show but they know I've got them.' He punched the air a couple of times, one for each, Dominic and Geoffrey. 'Got them.' He believed it. He felt pretty sure he truly believed it. He felt pretty sure this was not just bullshit, to comfort Jane. It seemed they were using a local middleman named Garrant, but Pillar did not mind. Naturally they'd need someone who knew the Bay scene from inside, and who could handle a tough assignment like the death of Indiment. But he, Kim Pillar, remained as ever actually in charge of the project.

Dominic and Geoffrey still could not do without his thinking, his imagination and boldness. That, after all, was why they asked someone to see off Indiment before Indiment could see off him.

Jane said: 'I don't understand how you –'

'They spelled it out, love. I'm indispensable. You should see the Bay flat they've laid on. And the furniture.'

'They'll use you, yes. But they won't –'

'They depend, I tell you.' For a second he grew ratty. 'No, not *use*. I've got flair. They're self-interested enough and bright enough to recognise it. I can think a theme like the *Terra Nova*. They know they could never have done that, or follow it through from notion to working unit. Themes are all the thing in our business now – create a mood, give the punters a milieu. *And* I've got connections. Well, *a* connection. So far. But that can be developed, extended. Good old Glyndwr. We're going to need some heavy help down there, especially early on. We have to look around for protection. It's basic with this sort of initiative. Dominic and Geoff claim to be lining up someone else, a higher rank officer. Of course. Oh, of course. I don't swallow it. But I can probably deliver what's needed – via good old Glyndwr. *They're* grateful – Dominic and Geoffrey. Would they offer this kind of deal otherwise?'

'Deal?'

'A package. I provide what only I can provide, and they'll write off 1.6, for God's sake. That's what they add it up to, the "skimming". I didn't argue. Their figure might even be under. Did *you* ever count it, Jane? On totting-up I'd be more inclined to believe *you*.'

She whitened and became agitated: 'Darling, I still don't see that extra income as – what did you call it?'

'Not what I call it – what *they* call it. Skimming.'

'Such a miserable, damn slimy word, Kim. I definitely think it could be argued you were entitled.'

'I'd argue it, did try to argue it.'

'A kind of bonus for success. They can't deny the success, surely. You brought them mighty profits. Nine, ten million, didn't you say? Setting up the Leeds operation. *And* Huddersfield and Sunderland, for God's sake. It's like people in the City – the annual percentage payout.'

'How I see it,' Pillar replied. 'Not them.'

She frowned. 'And they're not really writing it off, are they?'

'I'll watch them, of course I'll watch them. And if – if it looks like they might turn truly shitty despite everything – say because they really do fix something with a bigger cop – if there's something like that, we just get ourselves quietly together and run, love. Europe, or further. Easy. I'm not into stupid stubbornness, or gallantry. I don't think of them as anything but damn dangerous. There's evidence, Lord knows.'

'What evidence?'

'But they don't believe I'd ever go, because of this spread and so on.' He threw a couple more punches, but gently now, lazy blows in which his fist just grazed the grey stone wall of the big hall. 'I do love this place, and I know you do, too, Jane. It's us – you, me, Edward. Our natural spot. We deserve Maidrew. We're right for it. But I could leave it, all the same. So could you. They misread us. We've had our escape route settled from the start, haven't we – the ejection seat? There's money to cover it. Incidentally, I have to say they're sharp about that.'

She frowned again. 'They know there's a bale-out fund?' she asked, her voice shaky.

'They know there's money. Liquidity, as they say. Naturally they know. They can see we spend, but not that much.' He did a couple of pirouettes on the flagstones in the middle of the hall and waved both hands in the air to signify the outlay on the house and refurbishing, and perhaps the cars outside and Jane's couple of horses in the stables. 'Dominic realises there'd be change from 1.6, even if we'd paid cash for the property, which he'd know we didn't.'

At once she said: '*How* would he know? He's digging into our lives? Christ, Kim – there's tabs on us?' The front door of Maidrew was open in the afternoon warmth and Jane Pillar walked out to the porch and gazed intently across parkland and woods in their grounds, as if looking for spies.

'He'd know because nobody puts down three-quarters of a big one in cash for a homestead. It would be flashy.'

'Even so, this place – doesn't it yell at them that you've been . . . that we've made a stack?' She gazed for a while longer. 'God, we're so open here. What was that film called? *The Killing Fields.*'

He went and stood behind Jane and put an arm around her shoulders. 'They trust me,' he said.

'They *what*?'

'Sort of trust me. Dominic spoke about putting his parents in.'

'In where?'

'Here. Maidrew. With us. The servants' quarters. While things sort themselves out.'

He felt her go rigid under his arm.

'But he decided against,' Pillar said.

'*Dominic* decided against? This is *our* house, isn't it?'

'Darling, he backed off.'

'Well, thanks, oh, thanks, dear Dominic.'

'I'd have refused, obviously.'

'And what would he have done?' she asked.

'Oh, he'd have accepted that. Is someone going to put his mother and father into an environment where they are clearly not wanted?'

'He'd know from the start they were not wanted, wouldn't he? This would be to dump a couple of custody officers on us.'

'Anyway, it's not going to happen. They know they can't mess me about.'

Jane did laugh now, but only for a second and the laugh dwindled to a wince. 'God, Kim, I wish I had half your cheek. Half your confidence.' She reached up and put a hand over his where it rested on her shoulder. 'It's always amazed me, thrilled me.'

'Pulled you.'

'Yes, that, too. Edward's got it.'

'Of course,' he said. 'That's what blood's about.'

Jane seemed to have relaxed but stiffened again now. 'Blood?' she muttered, then turned and walked quickly back into the house. 'I'll just pop upstairs and see he's still having his nap,' she said.

'I tell you we're all right, love,' he called.

'Yes. I know you can look after us, Kim.' She waited at the foot of the stairs and he joined her.

'In their way, Geoffrey and Dominic look after us all, too,' he said. 'Well, they look after *me* – and that means they look after us all, doesn't it?'

'Look after you *how*?'

'As I say, in their own way.'

'But how do you mean?' she asked.

'In their own way, love.'

'But it can't be spoken about.' She turned and continued up the stairs to see their son.

10

There was a summons to see Bullfinch at headquarters in Cathays Park. When Brade arrived he found Jenkins already there. Bullfinch waved a copy of the *Guardian*. 'Have you seen this, Dave?'

Brade didn't mind the *Guardian* and its mature passions but preferred the *Financial Times*, despite the cost. He examined a big atmospheric picture captioned, *At the heart of the Bay.* Brade thought Jenkins looked noble, even with the skateboard. He recognised the other two from around the properties, and the bicycle. The Norwegian church, a trifle out of focus behind, gave them a kind of international spooky grandeur.

'Glyndwr says this is to do with inquiries about Indiment,' Bullfinch stated.

'These Collingdon Road folk, they see things, hear things,' Brade replied.

'The *Guardian* loves to make us look fools, with its damned semicolons,' Bullfinch said.

'Glyndwr is not identified as police, is he, sir? I mean, supposing he looks a fool, anyway. He's here as a bit of true dockland, surely. His blackness probably counts – the whole multi-racial aspect of the Bay's good history. The *Guardian* would love that.'

'I'm damned uneasy,' Bullfinch replied. 'Where will it stop? Are these people significant? Or the bicycle or skateboard?'

'Potentially, sir,' Jenkins said.

'How?' Bullfinch asked.

'This could be a very useful picture, sir,' Brade replied. 'It suggests a community bond between police and locals. Although Glyndwr is not identified, many around the Bay will recognise him. Carrying Beryl's skateboard for her – it *is* Beryl's, I take it, Glyn? – this has a kind of, yes . . . *sweetness* to it, part of the admirable, traditional style of policing which people wrongly think has gone. It's the type of "image" shot our public relations people strive to set up. Glyn does it by sheer flair. *May I take your skateboard for you, Beryl?* One can see why Glyn's fast track. I don't know whether they actually mentioned skateboards on the accelerated promotion course at Bramshill, did they, Glyndwr?'

Jenkins said: 'I saw a chance to help a lady in difficulty.'

'The sort of publicity that will bring others forward when they have information,' Brade said.

'Either of these two have any?' Bullfinch replied.

'Potentially, sir,' Jenkins said.

'Yes, you said. What the fuck does it mean?' Bullfinch asked.

'They have to be worked on a bit,' Jenkins replied.

'But Glyn's carrying the skateboard and so getting a kind of equality – comradeship – with those two will make them more forthcoming,' Brade said. 'Terry's quite a poet, I believe.'

'I've read some of his work,' Jenkins said.

'Bravo!' Brade replied. He turned to Bullfinch: 'Jenkins is building community links in several directions, sir. I know community is one of your foregrounded issues.'

'Oh, certainly.'

'In fact I've heard people say playfully – yet not without some point – that Community is your middle name, sir.'

In the car on the way back to Bute Street Brade said: 'I christen thee, Raging Community Bullfinch. How does that sound, Glyn?'

'The bike – it's a worry, Dave,' Jenkins replied. 'Found abandoned.'

'I gathered. Were you going to tell me, if you hadn't been fucking forced into it by the darling picture?'

'Pedal's a grass of yours, isn't he?'

'So did he see something down there?' Brade replied.

'It has to be possible.'

'You know it, do you?' Brade asked. 'Well, we'd better find him, if he's findable. First rule in this game, look after your informants. No, that's the second rule. First rule is never tell your colleagues all you know. And you don't, do you, Glyn?'

Brade took off part of the afternoon to drive Kate to the antenatal clinic for a routine check and the hospital people decided something urinary was not quite right and she should stay in at least overnight and possibly for a couple of nights. She objected, wanted to be at home, but they and Brade insisted. He was anxious. When he visited her in the evening, she looked fed up but all right. He felt some relief but would have liked to feel more.

Later he had more visitors at the flat, a deputation this time. 'We got a project, Dave,' Simeon de Courville said.

'We feel this will delight you,' Cordial Maximilian added.

'This project got what's known as a theme,' Simeon said. 'This theme – superior to anything else around, Dave. This theme – what's known as authentic. Better than the damn *Terra Nova*. This theme will be Jim Driscoll, the world-famed boxer, born in Cardiff. Peerless Jim. Featherweight champion of Wales and fought for the world title. Black curly hair, bright blue eyes.' In his enthusiasm for the boxer Simeon's brilliantly bald head grew a bit more brilliant, took on a purplish redness like a rough sunset. 'This project is a Jim Driscoll theme restaurant in the Bay.' He did a businesslike fighting stance for a second. Simeon was compactly built with astonishingly narrow hips. 'The whole eatery part to be built around a kitchen that's raised up and will have the shape and size of a boxing ring, with ropes, a canopy, everything.'

'Not spit buckets,' A.W. Moss-Cober said.

'Originality, Dave,' Simeon said. 'Patrons will be able to see the cleanliness and so on of the kitchen and, at the same time, atmosphere. A tribute to a great local. This idea is private for the moment, please. And there'll be an MC, in full gear, of course, black bow and dinner jacket – he comes to the ropes every so often and announces to diners like a fight verdict the special dishes of the night, and vintages on special offer. "Ladies and gentlemen, at the weigh-in this morning the sea-bass was eleven pounds six ounces."'

Just as he encouraged the girls to come out and see him, Brade liked it when old-style crooked tigers like Cordial Max, Simeon and A.W. needed to consult him, and especially when they needed to consult him at home. It was urgency. It was pilgrimage. He felt central. He felt loved. He felt bound in to their tatty pasts and vital to their slithering allied futures. Simeon de Courville said: 'So, what the fuck, Dave? We got to ask straight out what you doing about the boy on the crane. I mean, if anything. This is standstill.'

'Oh, he was dear to you?' Brade replied. 'How dear?'

'All our channels of info say what's going on at police level is no fucking thing whatsoever,' Simeon replied. 'Someone got power to damp things down in that area? This boy on the crane, and you doing fuck all, or fuck all that works – this is worrying when we think about our project.'

'What we hear, Dave, is Jenkins was first to the scene,' Cordial remarked. 'Does that mean he's got the case?'

'I was delayed a little,' Brade replied.

'Marriage *is* lovely,' Cordial said. 'Bed comradeship, if you don't mind me saying, Dave.'

'Kate's in hospital,' Brade replied. 'The pregnancy.'

'Oh, but this is a worry for you,' Cordial said.

'Yes.'

'It will be fine, I'm sure,' Cordial replied. 'Blood pressure up? Urinary?'

'Urinary.'

'Ah, this is how it can be with them sometimes, that urinary. It's only routine, Dave. Don't fret. But Jenkins – he's in the forefront of this inquiry?'

'We're a partnership, Max,' Brade replied. 'We –'

'Exactly him is what disturbs us, Dave,' Simeon said. 'Not racial in any way, I hope you know Simeon de Courville better. White, black, Welsh, Scotch, Mex, Afro, Isle of Wight, Aussie, Chetnik, Simeon can wear it. But Jenkins. Oh, problematical.'

'We see this hanged man as symbolic, Dave,' Cordial Maximilian said.

'This was not some negligible,' Simeon said. 'This was quality, in its own way. In his trade – all right, yes, a *particular* trade – but in that trade this boy was a prince.' His voice went to an injured whisper. 'Sticking plaster across his mouth. I hate to hear of someone like that treated so contemptuous, Dave. And this gets in the media, the sticking plaster. Everyone knows it, colleagues, family. Hurtful.' Volume returned. 'You personally, once you *did* fucking roll out of bed and get there, you done well, hiding him from view, the tape and initiative. I've heard gratitude nationwide for that. This was to make up for being so bloody late? But where's the commitment since, Dave?'

'Had you three hired him to do a hit for you, then?' Brade replied. 'So naturally you're pissed off when he's annihilated. And I expect you'll be trying again. And if that also fails – well, the boxing restaurant. Christ, *another* theme eatery?'

A.W. Moss-Cober said: 'Probably you've heard rumours of our little merger, Dave, but you're still surprised to see us acting together for once, instead of the traditional battling. The *stupid* traditional battling, as we now regard it.' A.W. was seated very tidily on Brade's moquette settee in his field-sports suit. 'Suddenly we realise we have to get into alliance if we're going to . . . well, live. People who can kill Clive Everton Indiment and hoist him as a warning flag must be considerable, must be evil – and must be resisted.'

'Especially if – I got to say this, Dave,' Simeon told him, 'especially if the police seem like they don't have no interest in Indiment, except when you yourself showed delicacy, early. Unless you wanted the bastard out of sight because of something you needed hidden. You can be devious, Dave. You in with them? It got to be asked, Dave. Why we're visiting.'

A.W. Moss-Cober said: 'Simeon believes it's Jenkins' influence that stops police activity over Indiment. I'm afraid I suspect something higher. But we do hear Jenkins has been down there solo, at night, around the Collingdon Road properties. Was he making sure no witnesses?'

'Who would Indiment have taken out for you?' Brade replied.

Cordial said: 'Always you've liked to keep us in a nice state of mutual aggro, Dave, tearing the fight out of one another.'

Cordial put his arms wide, the polished stick hanging from a wrist. His profile was towards Brade so as to play up the scars to his temple and left cheek and his vermilion-blue ear fragment after the street damage. Brade saw a broken nobility in his pose, perhaps more like a wounded soldier home from the Front, and Max held it, held it. For a while Brade fell into a kind of grief. Max had a long, foul history in the docks, was as symbolic as the hanged man, and his ear gone was like an era gone. In some ways that had to be an advance, naturally. Yet Brade felt regrets. Sad to see Max decline so fast. A game leg and stick aged anyone, and a pusher-pimp above all. They could make the profession appear seedy, a last resort for the disabled. 'Look well upon me, Dave. This is what your clever evil strategy produced.'

In the sideboard Brade found some last cans of Bass. These folk deserved the grandest hospitality. He handed three around and opened one for himself.

Cordial went and sat down. Thoughtfully he drank for a while. He turned to Moss-Cober then de Courville: 'I wanted to assure Dave that our little confederation means no threat to him or the Bay. We know how to conduct ourselves, Dave. There's been the odd foolishness, yes, but, as A.W. mentioned, that's over now. A *creative* alliance, a *constructive* project.'

Simeon said: 'What we hear – or what *I* hear, anyway – A.W. got a different notion – what I hear is Jenkins and the new man, Pillar . . . what I hear is like they're blood brothers. In a manner of speaking, that is, Jenkins being black. Through no fault of his own, clearly. But this is to do with what's called Balliol, being an absolutely genuine college in Oxford, probably gowns.'

'I think you can see why we're uneasy, Dave,' Cordial remarked. 'There could be undue influence. Pillar-Jenkins, then, via Jenkins, you.'

'Ah, Indiment was commissioned to kill Pillar for you boys, that it?' Brade asked. 'He's the competition? But someone got in first and did Indiment instead? Always a hazard in your line. Of course you're angry. You haven't lost the whole commissioning fee though, surely. Half down, half on completion, which there won't be. We found no money in his pockets – not that I'd be able to let you have it back. An execution, for God's sake.'

'Are you certain – no money?' Cordial asked. 'Fifties?'

'Bullfinch searched him.'

'Are you certain – no money?' Cordial asked. 'Fifties?'

'I watched.'

'Oh, in that case, all right.'

'Jenkins, Jenkins, Jenkins,' Simeon said. 'He's the core of it.'

'Or Bullfinch,' Moss-Cober said.

'I wonder if you've done much to find who's behind Pillar, Dave,' Cordial asked.

'Terra Nova,' Simeon remarked. 'Their project. Do you know what *terra nova* means, Dave? This is Latin, I done inquiries. *Terra* is land and *nova* is new – great name for an explorer's boat long ago when there was bags of Latin. But *now,* like today, what is their *terra nova*? It's the fucking Bay, yes? Pillar and team think they can come in and snap it up, push lovely local firms off the map, open up their own dirty distribution. Marina trading new style. Drugs, Dave, high-calibre stuff, too. Girls, obviously. Flagrant. That's the outlook if you back them. But *our* project – the Jim Driscoll Memorial Restaurant – it would be clean, believe me. As you'd expect. Anything powdery and untoward kept totally out of sight. Customers caught mainlining in the toilets banned for life. A superb boxer. Would we tarnish that memory in any way? But this invading crew, they think they can come in and stick any difficulty on the end of a rope. Dave, this was a lynching, its message aimed at us. That plaster over his mouth – what Cordial was saying, symbolic. It shows their plan to block all decent protest. I for one would be upset to see you go along with them, Dave. And I'm sure I speak for A.W. and Max.'

Cordial glanced admiringly about and did a little bow to the photograph of the Antarctic ice-floes and their appearance of white purity. 'We would never intrude in this way, Dave, unless it was a matter of real gravity. I certainly appreciate your refined neighbours would not want to be in the lift with a throw-back figure like Simeon. This is the place that one-time girlfriend of yours made you buy, yes? And when she'd dragged you out here to live she ditches you and goes to someone else. Savage.' He frowned with sympathy, then gave a tremendous smile. 'But things turn out brilliant again, this fine marriage and a pregnancy. It will be great, believe me. Urinary is no sweat.'

'We feel in danger of being discarded by you, Dave, because of influence from above or below. I admit I'm not certain which,' Moss-Cober said.

'Dominic Ardnell and Geoffrey Fonnet,' Cordial said. 'These run Pillar. Perhaps they'll have a middleman like Adrian Garrant or Jule Corbett down here as well, but Pillar's their main lad.' He paused. 'Well, it's Adrian middling for them, isn't it?'

Simeon stood and went to the window. He looked out towards the cathedral spire, a searching stare, his head very still, almost uncrinkled, wise. They said he once thought of a career in the military police. He wore one of his fine, Italian silk suits, beigish-gold with quite a shimmer, and tan and white shoes, possibly Gucci. He did a lot of heavy wrist jewellery, chains, bracelets, that kind of decoration, and something clicked against the Bass can as he waved his hand in a generous way. 'I've always said there's a place for churches, regardless. They mean well.'

'So, are you tied in with them, Dave?' A.W. asked. 'We need to know, before we finalise the Driscoll, its scale and so on. For a worthwhile business plan we must have an idea of what the opposition is. You two will aid them, you and Glyndwr?' A.W. was tidy, slight, nimble and extreme. From several angles his longish face could look caring. He had done some jail and now and then you would still catch a kind of wide-open-spaces terror in his reactions when he first entered a room bigger than a cell. He liked gamekeeper's tweeds, woollen ties and heavy brown shoes. In the Bay they called him Thornproof. He planned fine careers for his children. One or two of them were what he called 'gifted'. A.W. had integrity and when he offered businesses protection he wholeheartedly tried to give it, even if this led to bad damage for some of his people. Always he generously subsidised their funerals, anything up to £6000 or £7000.

'We are being cut adrift, are we, Dave, are we?' Simeon asked. 'I told them no. I told them Dave Brade would not let himself get used by some fucking silver spoon college pair. But I look at you and I listen and now I'm not sure.'

'I don't have any say in what amenities are picked for the Bay,' Brade replied. 'That's a major planning decision.'

'But come on now, you're Dave Brade,' Simeon replied. 'A lot would say you *are* the Bay. You got your own ways of influence, haven't you?'

Cordial said: 'Don't stand there at the window in that garb, holding a can, Simeon. This is a different kind of neighbourhood.'

'So now you boys will be wanting a replacement to do Pillar,' Brade replied. 'You've got *your* middleman searching? Will anyone take the hit assignment after this, though? Hairy. God, I grieve about your costs, boys.'

11

They kept Kate in hospital for a second night. He found her even more restless when he visited. 'I'm lonely, Dave,' she said.

'Yes, me, too. But now and then in places like this they know what they're doing.'

'Think so?'

He kissed her on the forehead. Her chart at the foot of the bed said a fever and he felt it on his lips. Kate was fair-haired and fair-skinned and a small square of red had formed on each cheekbone. She still looked as Brade wanted, though – lovely, calm, full of good thoughts about him.

At home in the night he was awoken by the sound of someone light-footed moving about the flat. A re-run? Semprina on another call? He thought about going to greet her as before. Instead, this time he lay still, wondering.

He decided now it could be a someone not just light-footed by nature but *working* at light-footedness, a someone wanting stealth, secrecy. It might be a someone moving about not in an aimless, agitated way like Semprina the other night, but with purpose, perhaps at the moment towards the kitchen.

So, Brade adjusted. He told himself it might be the Reverend Cliffy Hale-Garning doing a search. Yes, he told himself and almost believed himself. Cliff still had his key. Possibly he had run out of booze and wanted to borrow supplies without disturbing Brade. Some nights, Cliff would naturally grow unnerved when recalling a life spent in places like Llandrindod Wells. At these times he needed quite a flow of drink to get him through to morning, plus a party if one was available, but at least quite a flow of drink.

Let Cliffy get on with it, whatever it was, by himself. If it *was* Cliffy. And if it wasn't Cliffy it would be Semprina, and she would call him in a minute. She knew she could always rely on a welcome from Brade.

But Christ, he had bad doubts suddenly, and then more doubts – worse. When alone he slept with the bedroom door ajar. Now, it was shoved hard fully open and banged against the wall. Whoever had done it stood far back to avoid retaliation. Brade saw nobody. Late, very late, he realised he should be upright after all and rolled out of bed on the side away from the door. An Anglepoise lamp stood on his bedside table and Brade bent down and disconnected the plug, then held the lamp with its heavy base upwards. This could give an effective blow, if he had time and could get close enough. The bed was between him and the door. When Brade went there, Cardiff High School had been a select sort of place and he was glad the headmaster could not see him now wearing the 1st XV rugby shirt in the dark and holding an upside down lamp that trailed flex. It was a kind of chaos, and the headmaster had always foreseen and feared future social break-up. 'Cliffy?' Brade called. 'I'm so glad you looked in.'

'Cliffy, nothing,' Semprina replied. She stood in the doorway, her right hand gripping a good-sized knife. By good-sized he meant at least a six-inch blade. Did he recognise it? From *his* kitchen? He had been right about the search, wrong about who was doing it. She held the knife pointing down safely to the floor on the seam of her jeans, but probably only for the moment.

'I still think of him as Peter Vincent,' she said. Her voice was loud and loving and crackled around the bedroom like a hard-backed house-fly.

'I can sympathise. This is the name –'

'Oh, great, you can fucking sympathise,' she said.

'The name that brings good memories back – the two of you together at your place.'

Raising the knife, she pointed it at his throat across the bed and he saw she was working out distance. Then Semprina whispered the four words, each of them very separate from the others, like a list of recipe ingredients, or items on a charge sheet. 'You. Can. Fucking. Sympathise.'

'I mean this sounds to me as though it could have developed into a very worthwhile relationship, something real.'

'Something. Real.'

'Such a tragedy,' Brade replied.

Suddenly she was speaking in a sickened whisper: 'Did you

string him up there? Oh, Dave, did you – kill him and string him up there?'

'Semprina, for God's –'

'When I say *you* I don't say you personally, not necessarily, but your people – the police, or some special friends of the police. Same thing. What I hear is – well, you spoke about a relationship. What I hear is a *relationship* between police and some people, crooked people, who wanted Peter Vincent on a rope. Jenkins – a college *relationship*?'

'Oh, all kinds of tales, Semp,' Brade said, 'stupid, poisonous tales.'

'Or even you personally,' she said. 'What's in it for you? A fortune? You're too seedy for promotion and too low on bullshit. What's with the lamp?'

'I brought him down.'

'Of course. That way you could muck up the evidence legit. This was a man who thought something of me for days, sheer days. In fact, more than a week.'

'A lot of us think something of you, Semp. A lot of us think a *lot* of you, Semp. You bring warmth and vim to the Bay.'

'He had genuineness and polish.'

'A fucking gun slinger with smart luggage, Semp.'

'I'm not talking just about giving me proper money, which he did, naturally. This was love. This was not just body contact.'

'A hired thug wanting lodgings and company while he lined up the target.'

'So I just come with the room?' she replied. It was shaped as a question but possibly not a question, more a sort of admission, the words dropping spent from her like dandruff. She might be saying, All right she had come with the room, but he, Peter Vincent or Clive Everton Indiment, had treated her as above this. And perhaps she was saying, too, that next time, if it happened, she might be offered by Cordial with the room again, and then that was all she *would* add up to, because there would never be another Peter Vincent ready to spot her value. She said: 'He would have bought me a ring.'

Though no lights were lit Brade thought he made out in her face that she had been hitting something pretty high grade and was just about on the harsh way down, most likely whiz or acid but perhaps even best grade charlie. She showed that sad sag of skin under the eyes as all the cheery tautness of a high began to die. And in her eyes themselves he saw the user's standard look of bitter incredulity and grief, because life was edging back to what it had to be. This was a bad segment of anyone's cycle and could produce fierce violence. Although he knew Semprina had respectably long spells of utter lay-off from all drugs, there were also these other spells.

'So where's your lady?' she asked. 'I thought I'd have to take on two of you.'

'Hospital. Urinary.'

'You shouldn't fret. It's routine.'

'Cordial told me.'

'Cordial *can* be a comfort now and then.' She leaned against the door frame, the knife still pointed towards him somewhere high – chest, eye, nose – her arm possibly just in reach if he swung the lamp. He could knock the blade away and perhaps in the same movement get the flex around her throat a couple of times and tightened until she lost all fight, nothing fatal, just enough. But Brade hated the idea of hurting Semprina. Hadn't she already been hurt so much? Didn't she already believe Brade was the shit of shits? Anglepoising would confirm it for her, and especially the flex. Even behind a knife and on a fast down trip her face still had some of that elegance men prized and paid for. It was very shadowed now but perhaps because of this seemed to take on a fine, pleaful frailty. He found it depressing to think that when she was older, into a property and marriage and a family, Semprina might recall the night a police officer wearing his schoolboy rugby shirt half strangled her with wire.

'So, does Glyndwr Jenkins know one of them?' she asked.

'He knows a business lad who might be coming to the Bay.'

'And then Bullfinch – he's in on it, some deal?' she asked. 'The talk. What chance for a docks whore against you crew?'

He hated to hear her speak like this, as if conspiracy was everywhere, destroying her little hopes. 'Don't put yourself down, Semp. Docks whores only do what all whores do.'

'For less. Unstatused.'

'Bullfinch in on what?' he replied.

'I'm not saying an engagement ring or wedding – of course not. But, Dave, a ring of definite value.'

'A fucking executioner.'

'To execute someone you didn't want executed – for private reasons? The business lad Jenkins knows?'

Brade swung the lamp in a quarter circle, not an onslaught, a mild, placating, conversational move, he hoped. 'Anyway, Christ, Semp – I mean, even if was true – Jenkins, Bullfinch – which it couldn't be and obviously isn't – even if it was, why come wagging the knife at *me*? I'm not them.'

'You're the one I asked to look for Peter Vincent. Next thing, I hear he's dead on a rope. I point you at him and tell you about the suit and hair and thinking and luggage.'

'Perhaps he was on the way to death when you asked me.'

She carved the air between them. 'And you knew it, did you, you sod? They already had Peter, did they, trying to squeeze stuff out before killing him? And you – you ask me questions about him and promise you'll be personally looking for him out of friendship.' She lowered the knife about twenty-five degrees to rest her arm, and after half a minute raised it once more. 'Or maybe you looked for him and found him.'

'It upset me to see him there.'

'Because you knew you'd helped put him there. You felt regretful and disgusting because you *were* disgusting and fucking unforgivable.' Semprina leapt suddenly on to the bed, standing and stabbing down with the knife towards his hand holding the lamp. Rage spit swung from her lips. This was a girl used to managing rough situations where a bed figured. Brade felt the blade rip his wrist and jar on the bone. He dropped the lamp. She jumped down off the bed alongside him and instantly had the knife up under his chin and tearing more skin. He could hear the blood from his hand hitting the floor, but only heavy spots, not continuous yet. Blood from his throat or chin ran down on to his chest and would be making a mess of the rugby shirt, though he could not bend his head forward to look. The knife pushed him back against the bedroom wall and she was a bit off balance and leaned into him for support. He had to try and prop her or she might lurch further forward and the knife would go right into his throat. Her face was against his and alight with the triumph of her attack, no sag now, no grief, no frailty. This was a girl avenging loss, loss of what might have grown from an eight-day straight-through cohabitation – and loss of half belief in a kind of friend, Brade. He could smell nothing illegal on her breath. With her jeans she wore a countyish sort of small check green-brown shirt which had a big dark rectangle of his neck blood on it now. 'You're going, Dave,' she said. 'You brought darkness to a great love.'

Kate struck her on the side of the head from behind with a full bottle of wine. It made that kind of heavy sound. The bottle did not break. From its shape, this was claret. Semprina gave a sad little grunt and the knife point slid away from Brade's throat. She fell to her left, in against the chest of drawers. Brade had glimpsed Kate just before the thump, but only as a fragment of an outline, because of the darkness, and because of that inability to turn his head to look properly.

'My temp's down and I discharged myself, Dave,' Kate said. 'Taxi. I bought the wine at an all night place, for us to celebrate. It's still OK.'

'It's symbolic,' Brade replied.

'Is it?'

'Wife annihilates tart. The past defeated.'

'You like symbols, don't you?' she replied. They bent over Semprina and Brade recovered the knife. More of his throat blood fell on her – on to her forehead, cheeks and shirt. It distressed him to mess up her face like that and he tried to wipe away the blood with his fingers, but more ran down his arm under the rugby gear sleeve and filled up her eye sockets. Kate went back to the door and switched on the light. Semprina was conscious but not strong. They got her into a sitting position against the furniture.

Cliff Hale-Garning came down from upstairs. 'I heard a bump, then another bump, Dave.'

'The door. Afterwards, the bottle.'

'Plus voices.'

'Semprina's enraged.'

'Kate, you're better?' Clifford said, turning to her.

'I wanted to be here,' she replied.

'Yes, I do understand,' Clifford said. 'I did marriage guidance work in Llandrindod Wells. Bed companionship – so important. I can probably patch you up.'

'Which of us?' Brade asked.

'You. You won't want to go to the hospital and answer all kinds of mad questions, I'm sure.'

'We've had enough hospital,' Kate replied.

'I'll stop the blood for you, Dave,' Hale-Garning said.

'Semprina thinks I've spoiled her life,' Brade replied.

'Poor Semprina. But not in Dave's nature, believe me, Semp,' Hale-Garning said.

'Never,' Kate replied.

Cliff disappeared briefly and came back with a corkscrew from the kitchen. He bent to open the claret. 'May I?' He made Semprina drink from the bottle. Kate brought four glasses and poured. They helped Semprina to stand and then sat her on the bed. Cliff undid her shirt and pulled it off. She had nothing on underneath. He went to the bathroom and came back with a sponge and towel and began cautiously to clean the blood from her, more efficiently than Brade had managed.

'Should *I* do that?' Kate asked.

Clifford continued with the sponge. 'I act only as a priest,' he replied.

It was sexual, of course it was sexual, but Cliff also gave the procedure an evangelical tone, like cleaning away a sinful past, or anointing. Probably he spent no more time on her breasts than he did on her eyes. Kate brought a sweater and after Cliff had wiped Semprina dry put it on her. He gave her another drink of the wine, this time from a glass. Brade went out to the living-room and brought some Bass cans to chase the claret and restore strength for him and Semprina. It was important to get a top-line burn going soon in their stomachs and veins.

Semprina revived and smiled. 'He was going to give me a true ring, you know, Cliff.'

'Who?'

'The dangling man,' Brade replied.

'That's a Saul Bellow novel,' Hale-Garning said.

'Oh, thanks. Do you think I don't know?' Brade replied.

'Yes,' Hale-Garning said.

'The dockside dangling man,' Semprina said.

'Oh, he was nothing but the heaviest of heavies,' Hale-Garning replied.

'I've told her that,' Brade said.

'All the same, no need to kill him,' Semprina said. 'Right out of order.'

'I'm certain Dave would never do that,' Hale-Garning said, 'unless there were absolutely pressing reasons, of course.'

'What? What the hell are you saying, Cliff?' Kate cried.

'You should really lie down, you know, Kate,' Cliff replied. 'This is a lot of exertion for you.'

'I can't think of Dave the old way now,' Semprina said. 'I think of him as to be killed because he might have killed, like an eye for an eye in the Bible.'

'That's very early. You should read on a bit, Semprina,' Hale-Garning replied.

Brade said: 'All this because of some fucking professional lout who –'

'But women don't care in matters of love,' Hale-Garning replied, shaking his head with bafflement. He had on the dark trousers of one of his suits and a collarless white shirt. 'I've offered myself to women and in the long run they've preferred rougher men of no piety. But I know there'll be others for you, Semp.'

'You think so?' she said.

'Of course, Semprina,' Kate said.

'You're so bonny,' Cliffy said. 'So dignified. There's a first aid kit upstairs, Dave. I have a lot of falls and cuts to take care of so it's always on stand-by. I believe I can save your hand and Adam's apple.'

12

From his days as a Balliol Open Scholar doing moral philosophy Jenkins still had quite a decent knuckleduster which he kept locked in the securities box at home, and he took this out now and put it into his pocket. God, but he would have preferred a pistol. There was a name running in his head. It had been since that talk with Beryl and Terry at the properties, especially Terry. Tonight, working solo, he would try to move a bit beyond the name to the man, Adrian Barnaby Garrant, elegant and talented fixer in the Bay, a consummate aid for any outside firm wishing to establish itself, or wishing to get rid of a nuisance figure, like

Indiment, or wishing to establish itself *and* get rid of a nuisance figure like Indiment. It looked as if Garrant had been picked above that other famous Bay middleman, Julian Corbett. God, yes, Jenkins would have preferred a pistol if he was going to do a bit of harassment on Garrant.

Before leaving, he went upstairs to say cheerio to Mair, who had just gone to bed and was reading aloud a Welsh translation of the Winnie the Pooh stories again. He wondered about Mair sometimes. But Jenkins loved this bedroom tableau. Women *should* be able to relax in such style – preparing to sleep propped on three excellent down pillows, rapt by a slim, more or less harmless book, while the man went out to his rough work. He bent to kiss her goodnight.

She tried to hang on to his mouth with hers, Mair's way of telling Jenkins he was genuinely wanted. That pleased him. Of course it did. Nobody should count on such desire, especially after that shambles with the skateboard. Just the same, he gently pulled back. 'I don't ask what the job is,' she said. 'Notice that.'

'Not much to it, as a matter of fact, darling.'

'I've learned. I've learned you wouldn't tell me.' She smiled. He thought of it as her Welsh smile, compliant, satirical, the smile of a subject people. Perhaps he did it himself sometimes. After all this would be a *black* Welsh smile, so possibly even more compliant and satirical. 'It's a tidying up call,' he replied. The name, Adrian Barnaby Garrant, would not say anything to her, even if he had meant to speak it.

'You won't be long?' she asked.

'Shouldn't be.'

'Is this off your own bat?'

'I'm a policeman. Things aren't like that.'

'I mean, are you meeting Dave Brade?'

'They let me handle items alone, you know, Mair.'

'Yes, of course I –'

'Just a bit of tidying,' Jenkins said. She worried about him and he liked that, too, loved it. Her devotion was exciting, and he always tried to give her his in return. He did try. But he wished she would skirt phrases like 'off your own bat'. Because Mair was North Walian, brought up mainly in Welsh, she did not always get English idioms spot on and would sound like a foreigner doing bloody well for a foreigner. Bilingual himself, Jenkins was *South* Wales bilingual, a different species, more cosmopolitan and niftier at taking what he wanted from both cultures, a born privateer.

He went back downstairs, fitted the knuckleduster on his left hand and dropped into a sparring crouch. Garrant's name, running in his head, amounted to a guess, a disturbing guess, maybe a good guess. What he had learned from those two at the properties was that he should be looking for someone big enough and rich enough to stipend and run a police officer, and hard enough and skilled enough to help with the death of a . . . of a hard and very skilled London assassin. And most likely hard enough and skilled enough to arrange Pedal Power's disappearance and death, also. Actually there were several names he could think of that would fit parts of the menu, but only Garrant's fitted the lot. Jenkins had done some work on the private index cards he kept boxed at home and confirmed this. He believed in index cards and clerking generally. Hadn't the Empire run on clerking?

In the sitting-room, he punched at nothing a few times and practised some footwork. Sluggish, he thought, and the punching gnatlike. There was a mirror on the wall and, watching himself in it, he decided he looked a push-over and deeply bureaucratic, less like a youngish Muhammed Ali than ever. *Tomorrow, that fucking moustache comes off.* It must be more than ten years since he had hit anybody with the finger irons, and there was probably something absurd about taking them with him now. Knuckledusters presumed a clean, cleanish, fist fight, but he might meet something more lethal and swiftly lethal tonight. This was not town-and-gown Oxford 1990.

He unhooked the finger irons and went to bring in his armoured vest from the boot of the car. It was supposed to stop anything fired from a handgun, anything fired from a handgun up to but not including a Sokolovsky. Jenkins had bought the vest with his own money. The issued one was sub-standard, meaning it might keep you from being killed but not unparalysed, and he did not want fifty years spoon-fed by Mair and read to in Welsh off her own bat. Jenkins stripped and put the armour on under his shirt. He replaced the irons for a moment and tried a couple more lefts, to make sure the vest did not hamper him. In Oxford ten years ago as a knuckledustered undergraduate there had been no body armour to interfere with the swing of a punch, naturally. Aggravation from locals was brutal then, if you knew where to find it. On dullish weekends he and Kim Pillar and a few others would turn offensive in pubs chosen entirely for their known hate of college boys. There had been a class aspect for Kim Pillar. He believed it a duty to prove the higher bourgeoisie would always hit shit out of proles. As a prole of proles, Jenkins had not really empathised, but used to go along as ... as what? Solidarity? Balliol solidarity? God, how had he acquired that so fast? And had it been a betrayal of where he came from? Chewy stuff. Probably he still felt some solidarity with Kim. Phoney? Obsolete? Strong? Pathetic? Definitely unwise. But it might be one reason he would be on his way soon to invite a risk or two, gunless.

Jenkins dressed again, then drove down towards the Bay and the Toledo club. Like Brade he lived outside the docks. These days most docks cops did. He had deliberately left the vest off until after his goodnights with Mair because when putting her arm around him as they kissed she would have felt the extra bulk and grown uneasy. Probably this was not a complication manufacturers of body armour considered. Although Mair boasted of asking no questions, she would have asked some then in that rich, vastly well-intentioned Snowdonia whine. The voice was not her fault, though. It was geography. At relaxed times it could be lovely, like gentle singing on a hillside, like incantations that could cure. Mair used to tell him that she and her husband had believed in complete openness with each other. Divorce must have been inevitable.

Jenkins felt nervous. As Mair had almost suggested, he would have preferred to make tonight's trip with Brade, preferably both of them vested, properly shoulder-holstered and armed, not just the knuckleduster. But perhaps Dave was already ahead on the crane man case, and it might be vital to try a bit of catching up. Jenkins needed to excel. This was in his fast-track soul, and more especially in his skin. As almost always with Brade, nobody could be sure how much he knew. In any case, Dave had appeared sick all day, unfit for such a trip, so Jenkins had doubly decided not to involve him. Dave seemed to be nursing wounds from overnight, possibly bad wounds to his wrist and forearm and perhaps elsewhere. And he was pale, might have lost a vat of blood. Obviously, these injuries were not something you asked about. Jenkins had hoped Brade would mention the damage himself eventually, seek discussion. But he did not, and the subject remained no subject. These wounds could have been picked up in secret inquiries Dave made on the Indiment case. He was entitled to his privacies, the close, selfish bastard.

And Jenkins was entitled to *his* privacies, Adrian Barnaby Garrant for one. Perhaps. Brade might have thought of him, too. Or might have been told about him. Garrant was white, fit, rich, influential, polished, probably as dangerous and influential as anyone in the docks. Adrian went to the Toledo for a while most nights and Jenkins would try to find him. Jenkins did not rush. He aimed to reach the Toledo just before midnight. It would be crowded then and the clientèle reasonably relaxed from one dosage or the other. This might be helpful. On the whole it was safer in the club when members had taken something aboard and lost their edginess.

Jenkins considered that if outsiders had looked for someone on the spot in the Bay to remove Indiment, Adrian Garrant must have emerged top of the likelies. This had been Jenkins' instant response when Terry was talking, and the index cards backed the idea. As for that second clue to identity given by Terry the other night, there had been hefty rumours now and then about low-rank officers who might take wages from Garrant to protect his businesses. Garrant's index card said this, too, though in Jenkins' special code. He adored codes – this notion of a language that was a language unique to him. Codes made him a one-man nation, no room for class or race. The card had Garrant's age as twenty-six. Adrian's only weakness was a shortage of cool sometimes, a tendency to turn wild-dog violent, though somehow he had never been convicted. *Somehow* never convicted? If you had police officers taking pay you could access a lot of somehows. The bullet-proof vest and knuckleduster were Jenkins' answer to the possibility of violence from Garrant, plus Glyndwr's unrequited yearning for firepower. That yearning was often the British detective's burden. His counterpart in the United States would never understand why someone like Jenkins on this kind of mission had to go gunless.

When he arrived at the Toledo, Jenkins saw Garrant at once on the far side of the bar amid some of his people. A karaoke was under way with A.W. Moss-Cober at the microphone singing 'New York, New York' to the backing in a cleverly adjusted Cardiff accent. Passion froth covered his top lip and offered prism colours under the lights. He had on a multi-striped blazer and navy trousers tonight instead of one of his agricultural suits. Some people joined in whenever the title line came, not just Moss-Cober's family and attendants, but the crowd generally. He seemed to welcome this, waving his non-mike arm to encourage. There was an unnerving look of good nature to him.

Jenkins stood for a while in the doorway of the karaoke room, getting himself seen. Brade had told him always to do this at the Toledo. 'Let them adjust to you, Glyn – nothing sneaky or furtive about the visit.' Even without the special risk of Adrian Garrant, the club could be volatile. This was sacred territory and members would bond and band to guard it, when they were not crippling one another in street wars. Eventually the club must disappear in the Bay rehash, but for now it stayed as strong as it had ever been. And so Glyndwr's fear and sudden disgust with that nice-boy moustache. And so his half regret that Brade was not with him. More than half.

Jenkins prepared to move deeper into the club. The faces that had turned towards him now, eye-frisking him, were mostly blank, not a welcome, not contempt. Brade and he would often look into the club at about this time for a drink. You could learn things, as long as you did not act as if you were there to learn things – and as long as you did not look and behave like a hunter. But tonight he *was* a hunter, and gave them extra, posing in the doorway for a few seconds more. He would have liked to get some comfort by touching the knuckleduster, but one thing you never did here was stand with a hand in your pocket.

Ah, guns, guns. At Dave Brade's rank and with Dave's bull-shitting, browbeating skills, he could apply for armoury pistols and stood a fair chance of getting them, although Bullfinch had last word. Dave might have been able to collect one each tonight. For Jenkins to ask on his own would have been tricky – at least a rigmarole, most likely a refusal. He did not believe this sprang from racism necessarily. No, simply, he was not Dave Brade. An aura matter.

Jenkins pushed gently through towards the bar, glancing

about without seeming to glance about, again on standing advice from Brade. Garrant did not appear to have noticed him. Simeon de Courville, on a stool at the bar, and wearing a yellowish suit, did: 'I saw you was looking about, Glyndwr, and pretending not to, that way you and Dave Brade have, so you must be here to look about for someone. Would Simeon de Courville expect you to disclose who that might be? He certainly fucking would *not*, Glyndwr. Do detectives on the force speak secrets to mere local magnates, no matter how long a friendship exists between them?'

'A routine pleasure visit, Simeon. I –'

'I hope Simeon de Courville is not one to say that because you was friends with some jumped-up fucker at Oxford now reappeared as a Bay tycoon this means you'll forget other dear friendships.'

Jenkins renewed Simeon's large gin, bought himself one and added a little tap water from a jug to each. Simeon's suit was silk and radiant. Against the bar's mock mahogany he gleamed with the warmth of sweetcorn on a wood platter. His tie was dark blue backing a strong, zigzag silver pattern, like electrocution in a comic strip: a tie to bully other people's eyes, and perhaps meant to offset all Simeon's sensible dreads. His eyes looked sombre and malign, which would be about right. Simeon's baldness was total except just above the ears and his scalp skin stretched as wide as a desert and made him seem solitary.

'The one thing Simeon de Courville would never say, Glyndwr, is that you and those above you such as Bullfinch don't give a wank about who put Indiment on the crane, seeing all of you wanted him taken out because if not *he* might of taken out someone cherished by you following Oxford, and cherished by them above you on account of fondness for his fucking *Terra Nova* project and the undoubted skim-offs for all of you deep into the millennium and, yea, unto the third and fourth generation. And yet this is the buzz.' He shook his baldness but slowly and with control, in puzzlement.

'I'm glad you'd never say any of that shit, Sim. And the one thing *I* would never say to *you* is you're so interested in the boy on the crane because you'd hired him for big money to finish this other boy, called Pillar, the Oxford boy. And yet this is the buzz.'

Now, Simeon's head skin flashed like a tapped furnace. 'From Brade you heard that. Brade, he's knowledgeable, meaning what he's not sure of he makes up. You fucking mad, coming in here, in the Toledo, *in the Toledo*, talking inflammatory and slanderous? It's not your home ground, Glyndwr. All right, you're black and born local, son of the soil, but don't think that keeps you intact for ever. Comradeship got limits. Ask Stalin.'

Yes, Jenkins realised he probably *was* mad, talking like that. Brade would have stopped him by a look or word. Dave was artful, first class at every side of detection. But he would never make staff rank. In any case, tonight Jenkins did not have to defer to Brade. Suddenly, against all the teaching, and against all the caution he had warned himself to use, Jenkins could not stand being smeared by muck like Simeon. Maybe such impulsiveness would one day push Jenkins' career under for ever, or put him on top. Brade did not do impulsiveness. That might be why he had moved as far ahead as he was despite everything. And it might be another reason he stayed stuck.

'You and Pillar, such intimates, of course,' Simeon said. 'He order you to take out Indiment? Sort of protecting your friend?' Mostly because of the suit, de Courville looked what he was, a gloriously dogged pimp with up-and-coming sidelines as the new Bay beckoned. He did periodic jail, though not for a long while now, and in any case always chased the cell blight from his face with holidays and a lamp.

'It got to be asked, Glyndwr – why you here alone? Coming with no hand-holder, have you truly got the Indiment case personal, then? Jesus, is that above board, in view of special interests – above board even for police?'

'Dave's sick.' He should by now be at home, recuperating. Brade had worn a magenta, roll-top cotton sweater under his jacket today, possibly meant to cover the wounds.

'And then Pedal Power gone,' Simeon said. 'Perhaps he saw something. They take him out.'

'Saw what?'

'That why you're here – Pedal?' Simeon replied. 'Concerned with Pedal and then with Indiment?'

'Are they linked then?' Jenkins replied.

According to Simeon's dossier the surname was genuine, so

his family might have meant something somewhere once, perhaps pre-Madame Guillotine. Even when seated he kept his back very straight. He had a small moustache which Jenkins thought might work better than his own, and which looked damned regimental. Of course, people said Simeon had once wanted to join the military police, but he must have mistaken a turning. Bald men often fancied a tight uniform cap. He said: 'Glyn, please don't think just because you're turning to Pillar, instead of to us, that Simeon de Courville would ever go in for bloody abattoir talk, saying we know where you and your girlfriend live. Even where she fucking works.'

'I'm glad you'd never say that, Simeon. It would sound uncouth from someone in such a suit.'

Moss-Cober still had the karaoke microphone and was beginning a main number from *The Desert Song* now, his accent changed no problem to sheikh-type. A.W.'s famous uneasiness with large rooms did not seem to affect him when he performed.

Simeon said: 'Not to mention, also, we knows where Brade lives, of course. Been there as a matter of fact. Oh, often.'

Jenkins moved away but did not go direct towards Adrian Garrant or Simeon would know too much. Now, Glyndwr did allow himself to fondle the knuckleduster in his pocket for a few seconds, like a talisman. He dawdled at the other end of the bar, watching Garrant while pretending not to. Marking time, Jenkins spoke for a while to the Bay's other most famous middleman, Julian Corbett and his unmanageable wife, Henrietta, and then to Brian Molsan and his happy live-in partners, Charmian Lewis and Jean Sinclair-Witt. Their talk did not grip him, though.

Suddenly, he heard someone calling out to him joyously, amiably, above the music. Adrian Garrant approached smiling, full of welcome, like somebody greeting a brother home from the war, or like somebody putting a new ally at his ease. 'Glyndwr, Glyndwr, one had an idea you would call in. So grateful. Mind you, I'd have sought you out if not. Things look brilliant for us jointly all the way ahead, don't you agree? Time we talked. But I don't know whether this is the best place. The din. Perhaps a look at some landscape?' He shook Jenkins' hand with unbeatable warmth. Jenkins tried to read from the hang of his ginger vicuna jacket whether Garrant was carrying anything leather-cradled over one tit.

Nimble and warrior-like Simeon de Courville suddenly joined Jenkins and Garrant, facing Garrant. For a second, Jenkins thought Simeon would try physically to break the handshake. 'Glyndwr, I hope you've asked all of them – Jule, Brian Molsan and now this object – especially this object – what they know about Pedal.'

'Pedal?' Garrant replied, chuckling chummily. 'Basil Endicott? *Should* I know something?'

'Jenkins, are you here to nail this sod, or to get into bed with him?' de Courville said.

'Do you mind, Simeon? Glyndwr and I are going to find some space. What say a little drive around, Glyn?' He giggled. 'I'm gonna take you for a ride.' He gave that a bit of Bogart.

'You'll go in a car solo with him?' de Courville asked Jenkins. 'So this has to be friendship.' Rage, betrayal, sorrow, despair coated his words. 'Does the bastard intermede in the Bay for your Oxford pal and his backers?'

Garrant leaned forward suddenly and took Jenkins' hand. Garrant pressed it against his own chest and at spots around his waist where a gun would have been if he was carrying one. Jenkins felt nothing but the excellence of the wool.

The two of them went out into the Toledo car-park. 'We'll wipe that gent out,' Garrant said. 'And A.W. and Cordial. Wipe them out *commercially*, I mean. Commercially, of course.' Garrant drove a big, ancient silver Daimler coupé. It was one of his quirks. They climbed into the car and left the yard. After a minute or two Jenkins realised they were going towards Collingdon Road and the properties. 'Intermede, Simeon calls it,' Garrant said. 'Yes, that's not a bad word, I suppose. Kim Pillar and the "backers" have asked me to keep an eye on you, Glyndwr. By which, naturally, they mean nothing sinister. They do mean guard you, protect you, make sure you stay around. I was glad to take on the task. They value you hugely. And so they should. Irreplaceable. For instance, Glyn, they don't really like to hear of you endangering yourself by visiting these unofficial flophouses in the night. You can meet all sorts – druggies, drunks, boys on the run and desperate, boys looking to score against an officer out alone.'

He stopped the Daimler near the filthy little ruin where the poet Terence lived, and where Pedal Power had lived. 'Anyway, has Kim had a word with you about all this, Glyn? The arrangements? As you know, there are two liaison experts that people from outside can use in the Bay. One is Jule Corbett. The other, mine estimable self. As middlemen go, Jule has gone – has burned out, Glyn. He's done fine work, but it's in the past and he's sliding now. Plus, he's wife-dominated, of course. That bustling Henrietta. I noticed you chatting to Jule in the Toledo, and I thought it very slick – keep folk uncertain of your links.'

'Pillar told you to talk to me?' Jenkins asked.

'His chiefs. They wanted me to tell you what I said – that they prize you, want you properly looked after, Glyn. They realise you might be a bit torn at this stage – absolutely natural. They have faith, though. We all do.'

'I came to the Toledo because I thought you could have had something to do with the man on the crane,' Jenkins replied.

'Oh, Indiment. A barbarian. A killer. I can't regret that whoever got him got him when they did. And you probably feel the same, Glyn, though it's clearly not something an officer can say. Not as of now. This boy was paid to do Pillar. It rated as a service, whoever took him out. Ah, here's Machen.'

The sound of the car must have reached him and Terry came out from the property and stood gazing at them. Garrant rolled down the driver's window and beckoned. Terry approached. He looked scared, confused. Jenkins could see why. Comfortable in the car they would seem to Terry like a couple of pals, everything parcelled up between them on the quiet. Didn't Terry ask last time whether Garrant had sent him, though without mentioning the name? 'Seen anything, Terry? Heard anything?' Garrant said.

'Nothing.'

'Mr Jenkins would want to hear, if you'd seen anything for yourself or even been told anything. Well, you know this. He's been around here asking you himself, hasn't he?'

'Nothing at all,' Terry replied.

'I thought not,' Garrant said.

'Have you seen Pedal?' Jenkins asked.

'No, only the bike,' Terry replied.

'That's a mystery,' Garrant said.

'Yes,' Terry replied.

'I still want to know if he told you anything,' Jenkins said.

'When?' Terry asked.

'About the crane – getting the dangling man dangling,' Jenkins replied.

'Nothing,' Terry said.

'He'd given you a name, for fuck's sake,' Jenkins replied. 'You and Beryl.'

'Not at all,' Terry said.

'He could turn up again, you know,' Jenkins said.

'Well, I hope so. Beryl and I do hope so. I've got his bike.'

'Then he'll talk,' Jenkins said. 'To Dave Brade or me.'

'I expect so,' Terry replied.

'I said before, you could be liable for withholding,' Jenkins told him.

'Nothing to withhold,' Terry replied.

'Do you want to look out Beryl as well, Glyn?' Garrant asked.

'They're frightened,' Jenkins replied.

'I expect so,' Garrant said.

'Of you. Things will change if we find Pedal himself,' Jenkins replied.

Garrant closed the window and they drove away. 'I think that whole Indiment situation is shut down, don't you,' he said. 'Obviously Kim Pillar and those above Kim Pillar will be pleased, Glyn. They'd want to feel you were pleased as well, I'm sure.'

'Pedal Power could change the lot,' Jenkins said.

'I accept that. Kim Pillar and the boss men, Ardnell and Fonnet, accept that.'

'And?' Jenkins asked.

'Yes, they accept that if Pedal ever did turn up he could change the lot, badly,' Garrant replied.

'Are you saying he never will turn up?'

'I'm glad we had that little exchange with Terry.'

13

At the Toledo Julian Corbett and his wife Henrietta had watched Jenkins leave with Garrant. 'Oh, ho,' she said, 'an alliance forming there? Will you get left behind, Jule? Jenkins is on Garrant's payroll?'

'I don't think so.'

'You mean you hope not.'

He hated it when Henrietta was in this kind of mood, aggressive, determined to diminish him. He did not understand where these destructive fits came from. 'For all we know, Jenkins was taking him in for something,' he replied.

'Did it look like that?'

No, it did not. She was right, it had looked like friendship. 'Jenkins wouldn't put a hand on his collar in this sort of place.'

Henrietta drifted away to talk to Brian Molsan and his partners, Charmian and Jean. Simeon de Courville approached Corbett. 'You saw it, Jule?'

'What?'

'Fucking what! Jenkins, Garrant – cahoots. Don't you spot the linkage? There's Pillar and Jenkins, those college pals, and now Jenkins reaches out and joins Adrian to the network. Isn't it bloody lovely? You can see why we want you to get active for us. My feeling is you've done nothing so far about finding us a lad to step into Indiment's shoes.'

Indiment's shoes hung close together and useless over the former Bute Dock East, and Corbett did not believe he would find someone else willing to risk that kind of treatment. Corbett did not want that sort of risk for himself, either. Simeon was right, and Julian had done nothing to recruit a replacement. 'This process takes a while, Simeon – the shortlisting and weeding out.' It angered Corbett to have first Henrietta and now Simeon talking to him as if he slumbered while his career faded. He would look for ways to do Pillar *and* possibly Garrant, but he would do it as he wished and as the opportunity came, not because he was nagged by Henrietta or Simeon and his chums. He would do it because Pillar's firm had looked for a middleman in the Bay and had rejected him, Julian Corbett. He would do it because Adrian Garrant was moving too far ahead.

'I heard you had a grand project of your own going, anyway, Sim – the Jim Driscoll restaurant,' Corbett said. 'That will knock the *Terra Nova* into nowhere, surely. I thought perhaps you weren't so bothered any more about getting Pillar seen to.'

'Yes, I'm fucking bothered, and you ought to be fucking bothered, too. A.W. and Cordial and myself don't blame you completely for what happened to Indiment, but we blame you a lot,' de Courville replied. 'It would be wise to try and find us some comfort, which means finding a new operator, Jule. Oh, we talk about the Jim Driscoll, but it probably won't never come to nothing, will it? A fucking crazy idea – the kitchen in the ring. It's just to keep us in the picture, just to make sure the *Terra Nova* people get a fright – so they don't think it's easy, in the bag. But it could be, if they got the police with them, couldn't it? Can the Jim Driscoll compete with that, even if the Jim Driscoll made sense?'

'I thought it a quite wonderful idea, Simeon,' Corbett replied, 'and –'

'You thought it was shit and on that I *don't* blame you at all,' de Courville said, 'but you wanted something that seemed to say you did not need to help us knock out the *Terra Nova* main man. You *do* need to help us, Jule. I'd hate for A.W. to lose patience in you. You know what he can be like.'

Henrietta returned: 'Who?'

'What I say is, such a loss if the old Toledo gets flattened in the redevelopment,' de Courville replied. 'A community hub, oh, definite. Love the robe, Hen. This is a colour so right for you.'

14

Brade was enjoying a recuperative night at home trying to interest Kate in his videos of *Prisoner: Cell Block H*, when Clifford came down to the flat, deeply uneasy about Semprina and insisting he and Brade should go to the Bay and find her immediately. Although he worded things carefully so as not to suggest blame of Kate, he feared that Semprina's injuries from the wine bottle attack might be worse than had been obvious. That was his tale. Brade thought there could be more to it than this. Did he sense a lingering special affection in Clifford for her? Perhaps it began when he drove her home the other night and was confirmed when washing her breasts and speaking so miserably about the rejections received from other women. He wore full church gear. In cassock and hat he looked brilliantly typecast for someone called Clifford Hale-Garning.

At first, Brade resisted Cliffy's suggestion. He wanted to stay with Kate and felt tired and weak after the knifing. But he had already suffered anxieties himself over Semprina and during much of the evening between videos his mind turned to her. She might walk into terrible hazard if she kept on inquiring about Indiment's death. This was a dirty, unchartable area. She lacked the training and the tact to move through it safely. Her behaviour had grown hysterical. Semprina was a fine wholly honourable girl and Brade could sympathise with her grief at loss of a relationship, but to come after him like that with a Kitchen Devil . . . It must be seen as extreme, even if she believed he was idling on the case, or had been told to idle. And, as he loaded *Cell Block H* episodes, he had wondered where else Semp's mad sorrow might take her. Would she get noticed by the people who did Indiment or had him done? Perhaps he should go to see her, tell her to lie a lot lower, for a while at least. He had settled with himself that he must speak to her very soon – tomorrow or the day after.

This did not satisfy Hale-Garning. Cliffy came down carrying bandages, a stainless steel kidney dish and ointment. He would minister to Brade and re-dress his wounds. He did not want Kate bothered with this. She must rest as much as she could. It upset him to hear she intended going back to work soon. But it was plainly Semprina's state, not Kate's pregnancy or Brade's injuries, that troubled Clifford most. In fact, a few hours later, when they eventually did find Semprina, Brade wondered whether Hale-Garning had received a personal, dark, God-given premonition, despite the way Cliffy sometimes spoke of Him.

'As soon as I've treated you we'll call on her, Dave,' Hale-

Garning said, mildly fingering the neck cuts. 'I know Kate would like us to see she's well.'

But Kate could be damned tough. 'She had it coming.'

Cliffy tried to ignore that. He boiled some water and put it into his kidney dish. Perhaps he knew what he was doing. If anyone came in and saw the garb they might think he had started last rites. Brade loathed the kidney dish. It seemed wrong with a biretta, from a different game. Brade said: 'Find her tonight, Cliff? Oh, look, I don't believe it's as urgent as –'

'I hoped she'd still be here,' Clifford answered. 'I'd like to be sure she's not gravely hurt – I must know as a divine. No passing by on the other side.' His voice became weak, confessional: 'And I must know as a man.'

'Yes, she *is* a responsibility.' Brade tried to nod, but the pain stopped him. 'Gone home,' he said.

Hale-Garning's big, triangular impious face was very close to Brade's during the neck work. Most days Cliff looked angry, even savage, like someone holy on a Coeur de Lion crusade, but at this point only tenderness and concern showed. These were for Semprina, not Brade, and, yes, he thought that reasonable. 'And – and – and, Dave, making things worse – now, please don't take this personally – but making things worse, the police seeming – I say *seeming* – seeming to do nothing.'

'Fuck off, Hale-Garning,' Brade replied.

'Yes, fuck off,' Kate said. 'Does Dave tell you how to sing canticles?' She could be gloriously combative, as well as tough. Brade loved her for the instant loyalty.

'This Indiment death is complicated,' Brade said.

Cliff at once held up both hands, signalling apology and surrender. Perhaps he was afraid Brade would grow offended and refuse to go to the Bay tonight. Used bandage trailed from one of Cliff's hands, the slight line of mottled off-white against his dark clothing like a strand of fat in venison. '*We* know this, but such a girl as Semprina – in some senses a girl outside the law – a girl such as that is bound to fear conspiracy against her, isn't she – police and big-time crooks? She feels abandoned.'

Brade's neck was soothed by the ointment. 'This is a girl longing for permanence,' he replied. 'Suddenly, it seemed available. And then, even more suddenly, her chance of a true relationship, a permanence, is snatched away.'

Hale-Garning made a bandage pad and swabbed Brade's wrist with water from the kidney dish. He put balm on the broken skin and began rebandaging. 'Any luck and you'll have this arm well into old age. I've mentioned both Semprina and you to God. I don't say cathedral prayers wield special clout just because they *are* cathedral, Dave, but a cathedral *is* a cathedral, after all. Oh, can we go to her now? She is needy, so needy.'

But Brade still tried to insist tomorrow would do. 'It's likely to be very –'

'Suppose she didn't really recover and had to get medical attention – doctor, even hospital. Suppose the circumstances are publicised. There'd be rough questions for me, Dave, from those beautifully shaved church hierarchs again.' He put on a sacerdotal bleat. '*What was I doing out of my flat so late and a tart present?* I must head off that inquisition.'

Brade pulled down his shirt-sleeve over the new bandage and buttoned the cuff. 'You performed a Samaritan act, Cliff, that's all.'

In his eagerness, Hale-Garning made an involuntary step towards the door, towards the Bay. 'Say we can take her some support now.'

'They don't like men calling at their own place.' But, yes, he was coming to recognise it might be necessary, might be wise. Brade found his apprehensions grow more acute and blacker as he listened to Cliff.

Hale-Garning said: 'People will see my garments and dog collar. I'm simply a vicar visiting.'

'So late? And people know *me*. Anyway, she probably won't be there but out tomming to make up for last night.'

'Oh.' He looked appalled at this, possessive, betrayed, then managed a bit of recovery. 'If she is, it will mean she's all right, not badly hurt, and I'll be content to leave it at that.' Hale-Garning stood in front of the ice-floe picture, head lowered, grey hair glinting palely. It was desolation.

'No, I don't believe you *would* be content, Clifford,' Kate said, her voice suddenly gentle and approving. 'You fancy her, don't you, you good, lonely, old carer? So much touching concern. You – you want to offer her the permanence Dave mentioned. It's like that? You consoled her with the thought that she'd land someone else after Indiment. And you – you're the man?'

It was the moment that Brade decided he must take Hale-Garning to the Bay at once.

'But this is lovely,' Kate said.

Brade pulled on his shoes and crossed the room to switch off *Prisoner: Cell Block H.*

'Oh, thank you, thank you,' Cliffy cried.

There was nothing to thank Brade for. He took Hale-Garning to a tragedy.

'Dave, I've never known anyone so entirely Christian as you,' Cliff murmured in the car as they went towards the docks. 'It's an age since you had anything going with Semprina yourself, yet you still take a respectful, kindly attitude to her in her present distress. I admire that. This is the Gospels.'

Proud of the testimonial, Brade drove in contented silence for a time. Then, fear ravaging him, he said: 'You must protect her, Clifford. You can do it, I know. Stop her digging – into the Indiment situation and into the docks thing altogether. She wouldn't take this kind of warning from me. Thinks I'm implicated.'

'Are you?'

'We'll park here, not too close,' Brade replied. 'Neighbours notice a car more than people, especially *my* car.' They could get no answer when they knocked Semprina's door. It was what Brade expected. All the same, his unease soared. Jesus, had he been casual, lazy, even callous? But he said: 'There, Cliff. Semp's out fraternising, she's fine. No lasting hurt.' Hale-Garning knocked again and then again, without result. Brade said: 'OK, if you're still bothered we'll have a drive around her beat.'

'Oh, once more, thank you, thank you,' Cliffy replied.

In Tyndall Street, not far from the Cardiff Bay hotel, they spotted a couple of Semp's colleagues, Erica and Louise, chatting at the corner, waiting for takers. Brade drew in near them and spoke through the car window. They had not seen Semprina tonight. 'What's all the activity, Dave?' Louise asked.

'Don't tell me your people and you have suddenly learned how to move, Dave,' Erica said.

'I heard Semp might come revenging,' Louise said.

'We talked a few matters over, yes,' Brade replied. All his wounds were hidden.

'Oh, but where is she? Where?' Hale-Garning said.

'Pastor, don't ever let them update that outfit you're wearing,' Erica replied. 'It's *intense*. Look, your rev, does it *have* to be Semprina? Louise is really into churchmen and she'll do it the Italian way, no premium.'

Brade drove back towards Semprina's place. They knocked again. 'You're jumpy, Dave,' Clifford said. 'My God, something awful?' Brade brought out his bit of plastic, worked the door and once more went in through the familiar little hall. Hale-Garning followed after closing up behind them.

In Semprina's sweet-smelling, spruce living-room Brade's flashlight beam illuminated someone Brade of course recognised at once as Basil Carl Endicott, known as Pedal Power. He was seated tidily in an armchair, hands together before him, no cycle clips on, wearing his old beige, belted raincoat and slightly tattered but still impressive tan brogues.

Hale-Garning had followed Brade into the room and said: 'Oh, excuse us, sir, do, but we were concerned about Semprina. You're a . . . a guest of Semp? We felt it necessary, wise, even, to break in – in case she was in, well, difficulties. Have we disturbed you?'

Brade went nearer. As ever, Pedal's beard looked nicely tended. Brade had often admired it when Pedal was talking minor secrets to him, and exclusively to him. Pedal would not be talking to Brade any more. He had been shot in the back of the head, probably only once, but enough. His face hung forward bending the beard up a bit on his chest, like the nose of a crashed aircraft. There was a little blood behind him on the chair, though only a little.

'What, Dave?' Cliff said.

'He was brought here and arranged.'

Hale-Garning looked closer. 'Oh, God.'

Brade moved towards the bedroom and found he did not want to move towards the bedroom. Semprina was on the floor by the top of the bed wearing jeans and a striped blouse, half sitting, half slumped and propped between the bed and the wall, her head fallen forward like Pedal's. He saw a round, slightly stained Elastoplast stuck to her scalp and partly covered by the hair-do. Cliff came very slowly forward and stood by him, looking down at Semprina. He would have seen the Elastoplast, too. Bending to her, he spoke something close against her ear that Brade did not hear. Brade thought it sounded fervid but not a goodbye, an avowal. After a while, still staring at Semprina, Cliff addressed Brade in more like full tone over his shoulder: 'There's another wound? Not the blow Kate gave?'

'Of course there is. Shot. The same as Pedal.'

'I've lost her, *we've* lost her.' Cliff put his arms around Semprina's shoulders and hugged her gently, hungrily. 'It's the kind of damn thing God always does. He answers my plea that the bottle should cause no long-term hurt but then comes up with His own special bullet.'

Brade heard heavy knocking at Semprina's door and some shouting, male and female. Neighbours must have seen the torch beam this time. Brade switched on the bedroom light. The left sleeve of Hale-Garning's cassock was wet with blood and he had a patch of it on his forehead and on the biretta.

15

'A tart and a tramp? This is one person?'

'Two,' Kim Pillar replied.

'So, what are they to you, to us?' Probably this was supposed to sound like a challenge, even a dismissal, but it did not. He heard the beginnings of a shriek. His wife knew these deaths spoke something to them both, and the certainty terrified her.

'Obviously, it's appalling and sad,' he replied, jubilation in check. 'But a plus, too.'

'How are you involved, for heaven's sake? A *plus*? Two low-life killings? How? My God, Kim, isn't it time to run now? The three of us – *run*. If you're getting pulled into things like that? Please, darling, let's go. France. Spain. Mexico. The pound's high. Let's use one or two, wherever they came from and however. Let's stay alive so we can use some. Oh, do let's get the child clear of all this.'

The morality of the money did not seem to matter to her any more, she was so scared. He leaned forward and kissed Jane lightly on the forehead. 'Of all what, darling? We *are* clear. No, I'm not involved. Not in the least. That's the beauty of it.'

'Beauty?'

'As I say, appalling. But it's changed things in the Bay. I'm strengthened, hugely strengthened.' He meant it and felt he must force some of that strength upon her, like good food on a picky child. Was this the way their relationship would dwindle under all the stresses – daddy, daughter? It had not started like that, but perhaps she was slipping behind. '*We're* strengthened, love. They see that. Believe me, all my colleagues see that, and Dominic and Geoffrey especially. Definitely not the time to run.'

'Your *colleagues* don't trust you. Dear Dominic Ardnell and dear Geoffrey Fonnet think you took them for more than one and a half million, remember?'

'Oh, trust. Trust is . . . But I don't rubbish it, of course not. Trust can be crucial. Wasn't I brought up on it?'

'I wouldn't be surprised,' she said.

'But who trusts anyone much in this game, Jane? They recognise power, though.'

'Power.'

It enraged him, the way she gave words back decked with irony, dead with irony, but he never turned really rough with Jane. 'Well, all right, power's a big, flashy word,' he said.

'You're a big flashy achiever.'

'Call it strength – as I said first of all.'

Jane's voice slumped to a blurred whisper. Her eyes were three-quarters shut, as if she feared to look hard at what he said. 'Jesus, Kim, you're not telling me you, you personally –'

'Not involved. Haven't I promised?'

'And *that's the beauty of it*,' she replied. '*Why we don't need to run*.'

Written down her talk would slavedrive italics. He said: 'Why they've asked us to host this thing here in Maidrew. They'll fix and finance the catering. Or the company will. We host. It's responsibility, Jane. It's status. I've moved up. They recognise it. They're willing to come in like guests – like visitors to a stately home.' He whooped with laughter and did one of his pirouettes, then another. Afterwards, hands clasped behind his back, he paced about for a while with a slight, modest, aristocratic stoop, as he imagined a marquis might in his grounds on days he opened the property to payers. Pillar wished he had been born noble and landed, with no need to meet people like Dominic and Geoffrey, let alone work alongside them. It had not happened. He knew Jane always wanted to believe in him, just the same. Kindness said help her do it. She was stuck with him because of the child and the prospects. Poor Jane.

'They think Maidrew is theirs,' she replied. 'Their money. They'll price the place for when it has to be cashed.'

She could be shrewd. 'I *am* the Bay, as far as they're concerned now – Dominic and Geoffrey,' he said.

'You still want to be?'

'The two deaths are absurd, a daft spasm, last throes of violent, old, local villainy. Dominic and Geoffrey had another lad down there, you know, a docks-born magician. Or they thought so – middlemanning supposedly, smoothing things for me and the company, using his homegrown knowledge, handpicked. He's gone haywire. What you'd expect. A provincial. A very clever artisan, I gather, but an artisan.'

'*He* killed them?'

'Absolutely, though no charges yet. There will be. Anyway, we don't need charges. Dominic and Geoffrey are sure. They'll probably switch to another guy in the Bay now for that kind of work, a Julian Corbett, but it doesn't matter. They've learned I'm the one they really have to rely on. This idiot was trying to stop any poking into an earlier job he'd handled. He'd done it damn well, real flair. We thought. He didn't say there'd been complications, a witness. Of course he bloody didn't. Suddenly he's into saving himself – himself, himself, himself. The witness is gone and the tart for trying to see too much. He doesn't care where inquiries might lead. This is someone linked direct work-wise to Dominic and Geoffrey, no intermediary. He could be a true embarrassment if he's caught and talks. And, even if he's not caught, this bastard never considers the impact on developments down there from the extra aggro he creates – my *Terra Nova* project. In these embryo months that concept has to look clean and honourable above all. He's lost balance. Frantic. Naturally, Dominic and Geoffrey want him cut adrift. At once. It's late. It's panic.'

'Cut adrift.'

'My words.'

'You'll know what they mean then.'

He grinned. 'The thing about these dreadful deaths is they bring us all closer, Jane.'

'But not *the handpicked magician* in the docks. He has to be cut adrift.'

'The company partners – and wives. *Much* closer. It's why they want the dinner here. Dominic believes family participation is healthy for the business – a nice openness. As far as there can be, that is. Their wives, you, me, that pair. It's good, Jane. It's an advance. It's security. And what we deserve.'

'They'll forget the 1.6 million?'

'They've begun to see I have to run things solo. I – we – might have told them that, but they had to be forced to recognise it by events.'

'But *cut adrift*. How?'

'He'll never give trouble. Not once he knows Geoffrey and Dominic have lost belief in him.'

'Who *cuts him adrift*, Kim? And even if he's cut adrift couldn't he still talk if he's picked up for the deaths?'

'These are dinners that usually rotate – Geoffrey's place, Dominic's place,' Pillar replied. 'Previously, I wasn't even invited.' Hurriedly he corrected again. 'That is, you and I weren't invited. I wasn't even officially told they happened.' He beamed. His optimism was genuine and unfoolhardy, based in reason. 'Then, suddenly, love, we've got parity. We're part of the circuit. I'm seen as not just a partner but a *senior* partner, with Dominic and Geoffrey. I can *feel* it in the way they talk to me. Remember Fredo in *The Godfather* wanting "respect"? We've got respect, Jane. In a sense the 1.6 million has become a laurel.'

'A laurel.'

'Don't.'

'What?'

He spoke gently, but he spoke: 'It's like church responses. Except you're pissing on me. These ideas take some grasping, yes, but they're not mad, Jane. The 1.6 – the fraud as they see it, and *only* as they see it – but the scale is enough to give status. If it *was* deception, it would take some ability, guts. Now that they're suddenly looking around for a saviour they know they need someone big.'

She softened but still did not swallow it. 'Whereas, *I* need someone alive and safe, Kim, able to help bring up our son.'

He did not mind deep family stuff from Jane occasionally. 'The catering – wine and drinks as well as grub, plus the serving, all laid on,' he replied. 'No cooking. Not even a drawing of corks by us.'

'You'll have to live down there, if they're getting rid of the local guy?' Jane asked.

'Not getting rid.'

'Dispensing with.'

'Perhaps we'll all shift there for a while. Would you like that? The Bay flat is fine, and more secure. You've felt . . . well, exposed here.'

'Yes, we're sitting in open ground. But they'll like that, Dom and Geoff. They'll want Edward and me to stay, I think. They'll want distance between you and us. As long as they've got the child and me tucked up here they've got *you* tucked up there. You can't run. That's basic thinking, now you're even more valuable to them. Now you're *big*.'

'I've told you, running's nowhere in my head, love. We'd be rubbishing our future.'

'I'd call this a banquet, a true banquet,' Dominic Ardnell said, his voice a clarion, 'and could the setting be more splendid, splendid and fitting?' He did not stand and yet it was the opening to a kind of speech. People had gone quiet. Pillar liked it. He enjoyed the hear-this tone and the heavy rhythm of the repetitions, but produced by someone folded down in his chair, bent over the remnants of the meal, as if crushed – what Pillar meant about changes. The dead-beat oratory was Dominic trying so hard to cling on, but sliding, sliding. They had fucked up at the Bay with Garrant, he and Geoffrey. They knew it. Of course they knew it. They had had a choice of middlemen, if they needed a middleman at all. And they had picked the wrong one, Garrant, not Julian Corbett. They were ashamed of the mistake.

And they were nervous, afraid the shit ripples would wash over them. These were two who liked to stand well back and play legitimate. But rumour had Glyndwr Jenkins focusing on Garrant. Dominic and Geoffrey would not like that, the possibility of a black coming at them with questions. It was true what Kim had told Jane – more than ever, they must realise how much they needed him. He was beautifully unconnected with Garrant and the murders. He was beautifully unconnected with the death of Indiment, too, even though it was laid on to keep him in one piece, so they said. And Kim Pillar had that unique Balliol bond with Jenkins. Pillar could turn out even more useful, now matters might get troublesome.

'I'll tell you what I see when I look around a room like this,' Dominic declared, 'I see style. I see it in the gorgeous Regency furniture, I see it in the silver on this fine table and in the linen, I see it in the proportions of the room itself, I see it, if I may say, in Kim's lovely wife. This is what Kim is known for, above all – style.'

'Yes, oh, yes,' Mary Ardnell cried.

'This style is what he will bring to our enterprise at Cardiff Bay, has already begun to bring. But Geoffrey and I recognise it is a kind of cruelty for us to ask Kim to leave this magnificent set-up and those in it – Jane and their lovely son, Edward – even for limited spells.'

'Hear, hear,' Geoffrey said.

'Cruel indeed,' Angela Fonnet muttered.

'And yet we *do* ask him, I fear,' Dominic said. 'Demands of business – business which will benefit us all in time. We *do* need him as what I might call a temporary permanence at the Bay, especially now. Perhaps I should have realised it before. Well, no question I should have. I will say this, though, folks – Geoffrey and I do regret having to be disruptive even for a short while in Kim's superb household, and we are very conscious we must limit that disruption.'

'Thank heavens, Dom,' Angela said.

Pillar glanced at Jane down the dining-table from him. He longed to see contempt in her face for Dominic's performance, and for the support performances. Kim hoped for the start of a smile from Jane, or at least harsh merriment in her eyes. He found only a frown. She was concentrating on Dominic's words, yes, searching them, but not for loud show – for threat. She looked weak, weaker even than Dominic. Pillar longed to prop her. She seemed obsessed and, of course, he knew what the obsession was. Jane never stopped thinking about their child's safety. It scrambled her brain, made her incapable of understanding that these two, Ardnell and Fonnet, were harmless now, whatever they had thought they were before. As obsessions went, concern for one's child was definitely a worthwhile one, but motherliness could not run the shop.

Dominic said: 'We would never expect or ask that Jane and their fine son should also have to quit this home, not for even the briefest of periods. Perhaps in one way we are self-interested. Fact is, we're sure Kim will operate at maximum effectiveness in the Bay as long as he knows this wonderful base to his life is still here, itself operating at maximum effectiveness under Jane's management, and ready to receive him at weekends and so on when he feels he can slip away from the Bay for a few days without bringing risks upon any of our interests.'

Pillar could agree with some of what Dominic said. The room did have style and pointed to style in Jane and him, too. Yes, he'd always had his special way of doing things, presenting things. Besides the furniture and silver on display, there was the high ceiling and the paintings, not prints, which he and Jane had spent months and a lot of money hunting at galleries. Mostly they were abstracts with vivid patches of colour and bold shapes – imperfect, intriguing circles and rectangles. None of the artists represented here now had been known to Pillar and Jane when they began their search, but they followed their taste, picked out these works on the walls of the galleries or in illustrated catalogues. They were bought for what they were, not on name. Pillar felt pleased at that. These pictures gave a flavour. He and Jane had created it. Dominic was big-time, his dinner jacket classically cut, but his features were lumpy, unpolished, back-street, and Pillar thought he looked out of place in what Ardnell himself had called a splendid set-up. It was particularly true because of the cowed way he sat over the remains of his meal. A faulty circle might be fine in art, but the ramshackle spread of Ardnell's features seemed just fucking déclassé.

Pillar said: 'Your remarks are generous and they are much appreciated, Dominic, both by Jane and myself. What you point out about Maidrew and the solidity it offers is gloriously true, but we have wondered whether it wouldn't be even more of a help in my work at the Bay to have Jane and Edward close to me there, at least for a while, a ready support.'

Geoffrey, sitting opposite Pillar, leaned forward and said at once in that breathtakingly honest Geordie accent: 'Believe me, a mistake, Kim. We *have* discussed it, as you would imagine, Mary, Angela, Dominic and myself, and, while we could all see superficial attractions in the arrangement, we were surprised to find ourselves absolutely agreed at the end – unanimity is not our long suit, no indeed – but, yes, four to nil – we agreed that to take Jane and Edward to the docks flat would not do. You see, they would become as if part of your job there – no doubt a very comforting part, but that only, and definitely the less for it. They must have their own role, and it is here they play it best.' Geoffrey, plump, large-headed and unworldly-looking, nodded the large head a couple of times without losing control of it and smiled in turn at Jane and Kim.

Angela, twenty years younger, tall, dark, with good, sharp features and the warmest of voices said: 'How, how, could anyone seriously think of quitting such a spot for some dockland flat, even temporarily, unless compelled by work calls, like Kim? Oh, take my word, Jane, it would not be fair to you or your laddie.'

'Never,' Mary said. She was alongside Jane at the table and put a hand on her wrist with true comradeship. 'It's totally understandable that you and Kim should want nearness. I hate it when Dominic has to go away.' She was about thirty-five, Ardnell's age, tall and brawny like her husband, her longish face a bit too mobile, as if she might be on something strong, or had been on something strong, had stopped it, but still enjoyed phantom twitches.

The caterers had been asked to leave the room for a while. Pillar went to the long mahogany sideboard and brought brandy and glasses. He was conscious of Dominic watching him non-stop and of Jane watching them both.

'On top of which,' Geoffrey said, 'there is at present a certain obvious danger in being at the Bay. I'm sure this is only transitional, and the success that Kim will achieve is guaranteed to make such menace blessedly obsolete very soon. But I think short-term, we have to cater for it. With protection provided by the company, and using his own admirable influence on the police, Kim can easily handle such risks. Perhaps the most grave of them was, in fact, dealt with a little time ago. I'm proud to say we very quickly saw the need for that. It would possibly complicate this situation unnecessarily, though, to expose Jane and the child – perhaps especially the child – to such tensions.'

'Two absolutely nobody people slaughtered like that, Jane,' Mary said. 'Are they animals down there? My dear, you're so well out of it in this delightful country spot.'

16

At home, there was a letter for Brade from Pedal Power, starting as Pedal's letters always did, *My dear Dave.*

It was written on very high-calibre lemon-coloured notepaper with an embossed address in bold black at the top of page 1, and came in a beautifully substantial lemon-coloured envelope with very little muck on it and a second-class stamp. Occasionally, Brade did get letters like this from Pedal, usually to suggest a quiet meeting somewhere in the Bay. Pedal had obviously taken a good supply of stationery with him from home when he left and kept it uncrushed and clean in one of the baskets tied to his bike. Such stationery was meant to give status to the writer, of course, and majesty to what was said. But for this writer status through notepaper had not been easy lately, even when he was alive. Pedal wrote small and there were five sheets each covered on both sides in Biro. This broke pattern. Usually, he sent a single page, with one sentence on it, sometimes ink, sometimes pencil. The letter was postmarked noon yesterday, about twelve hours before Clifford and Brade found Pedal and Semprina. Brade had left home for work before the mail arrived this morning so did not see it until Kate handed it to him in the evening. She seemed completely fit again now, eyes bright, but not fever bright, the red patches gone from her cheeks. He kissed her on both of them, to celebrate, then for longer on the mouth.

My dear Dave . . . Pedal had begun like that from the very first of his letters to Brade – how he must have addressed business contacts and ships' masters he knew well when running the chandlery. For use between equals. Pedal always behaved as if Brade and he were socially level. That had seemed important to him. These things hung on. Brade never objected.

My dear Dave,

I write at unusual length because it might not be possible for me to meet you and convey 'face to face' what I have seen. I trust that what I am about to say will not seem melodramatic or panicky, but it could be that by the time you receive this letter I shall not be in a condition to meet and talk.

One is aware that most of the information I have been able to provide for you over the months has been comparatively minor. Cycling about the Bay attending to one's commitments one is unlikely to become privy to plans for large-scale organised crime! You have been civil, patient and generous. I think that now, though, I may have something worthwhile to offer you. Regrettably, it could be posthumous!

On the night of Thursday the 24th, while returning late to the properties from a pleasant evening with a friend in the 'tinkers'' caravan encampment on Collingdon Road waste ground, I happened to look across to the crane on the other side of the former Bute Dock East. Imagine my astonishment, Dave, when I saw a man climbing out on the jib of the crane. At first I thought a possible daredevil prank but then he passed a rope over the pulley wheel at the end of the jib and returned with some agility to the ground, bringing the end of the rope with him. Although it was dark, there is enough lighting at this spot for me to see reasonably clearly what took place. The lighting was also sufficient for me to make what I think was a reliable identification of the man (see later). I now noticed that a body lay on the dockside, near the crane. I could see it was male and in a suit and collar and tie. (We, of course, now know this was Clive Everton Indiment.) The man who had climbed the jib bent over this body and appeared to be binding the figure on the ground in some way which I could not make out. A little while later I saw that he had been fixing a noose around the other's neck. He began to haul the body into the air. At first it was suspended aslant and bent, with its feet skidding on their heels across the dockside, a terrible sight, degrading to any human being. I saw the body's legs and hands were tied. In a way it was a relief when the figure swung out, hanging upright now over the water with a kind of awful dignity, and was raised to about 40 feet above the dock. The man ceased hauling and fixed his end of the rope around a bollard. I would estimate the time to be about 3.30 a.m.

As soon as I saw the man on the jib I had, of course, hidden myself and my bicycle, realising that to witness such behaviour was dangerous. Cycling about the Bay one does learn caution. Now, the man went behind the crane and emerged immediately with a wheel-chair. He ran, pushing this along the side of the lake towards the Pier Head and possibly to a car parked near the cinema complex. I certainly heard a vehicle start and pull away, sound travelling well over water, particularly when everything was so quiet, because of the hour.

I waited for a while, wishing to be certain that the man had definitely left, and was about to proceed on my bicycle towards the properties. Imagine my horror when I saw coming up Collingdon Road a car with its headlights on and travelling slowly. It seemed to me that it was engaged in a search and I immediately hid myself and my bicycle once more, this time at the back of the former Osmond machine shop. The car pulled up near the heaps of debris where I had previously been concealed and waited for several minutes. I believe the heaps were being scrutinised, though nobody left the car. I gained the impression that I and possibly my bicycle had been observed from the other side while the man was hanging the body. I could not see the wheelchair in the car but it might have been of the folding type and stored in the boot. I assume this was how Indiment's body was brought to the crane from the vehicle.

The car moved off, but still very slowly. It stopped a little further up the road, as though for another scrutiny. It seemed to me that it might systematically search both sides of Collingdon Road, and would eventually come to the former Osmond machine shop. I therefore moved back with my bicycle to the heaps of debris, since these had already been examined. I hid there again and shortly afterwards the car did in fact stop at Osmond's and there appeared to be another examination. I had been fortunate.

Again the car moved away, this time faster, as if about to leave the area. It had begun to get light and I heard vehicles elsewhere in the Bay as the day began. However, in view of what had happened previously, I could not rely upon the car's final disappearance, and remained where I was. Possibly I slept a little. At any rate, I suddenly became aware that dawn had really arrived and when I looked across the former dock to the crane I observed a man standing beneath the body. This one was black and in a while I recognised a police officer, your colleague Glyndwr Jenkins, well known and respected in the Bay. Of course, my hiding position was on the wrong side of the debris now, since I had been concealing myself from someone searching from Collingdon Road. Mr Jenkins was staring across the former dock. I immediately changed the position of myself and my bicycle, but it might have been too late. Perhaps Mr Jenkins has informed you of what he saw. He continued to watch for a time and then turned away and ran towards the leisure complex car-park, maybe to fetch something from the vehicle. While he was gone I left my hiding place and returned by bicycle quickly to the former 221 Collingdon Road, one's current accommodation. As you will probably have been informed by him, he came to the properties next evening looking for me, wishing to discover what I had seen. I felt it would be unwise to tell him and left with my bicycle. I shall determine soon where to lodge for this very difficult interim period. I am writing to you now from behind the old bonded warehouse, where a piece of three-ply waste provides a useful portable desk.

May I now approach what I regard as the main information in this letter, and, Dave, I do see it as being of some monetary value, if I may say, the labourer being worthy of his hire, even when the labourer is but an informant. I believe the man on the jib, and seen subsequently in the searching car, to have been Adrian Garrant, a figure well known in the Bay, as you will appreciate, powerful and dangerous and with the physical fitness needed for jib climbing, hauling etc. The car was a blue Peugeot 406, not unlike one I previously owned myself, its registration number R 016 GPK. It is true that Adrian Garrant normally uses an old Daimler coupé, as an adjunct to his supposed 'image'. I imagine he would not wish any vehicle so distinctive to be used in this kind of work.

As you probably know, my wife still lives in the family home with her new 'partner'. In the event of my not being available to collect, Dave, I do not wish any of the fee that you might think this information merits to go to her, if you please, but all of it should be paid to the campaign for establishing a new mud habitat for wader birds displaced by the Bay barrage. Loss of a habitat is a terrible thing, about which I now know a little. My bicycle and the possessions attaching thereto should be divided equally between Terence Machen and Beryl Costo in or around the former 213–227 properties Collingdon Road with the recommendation that if they use the stationery for correspondence they should, of course, block out the printed address. Terence may wish to use the paper only for poems, in any case.

Thank you for your attention, Dave, and I much regret should any funeral expenses fall upon the public purse.

B. Carl Endicott

Brade telephoned headquarters and asked for a check on the Peugeot. He was told it had been stolen on the 23rd and found abandoned on the 25th in the north of the city with a folding wheelchair in the boot. The chair did not belong to the owner or his family and had itself been stolen – from Casualty at the University of Wales hospital on the 21st or 22nd. Brade wondered why the chair had not been left behind at the crane. Perhaps Garrant, if it *was* Garrant, feared the wheelchair might then have been restolen from there. Did he want it properly returned via the recovered car to the National Health Service? All sorts of people had all sorts of weird, marginal scruples, even someone like Garrant.

Raging Bullfinch required a visit to Semprina's flat. Bullfinch did like to think of himself as hands-on. He wore one of the four or five bespoke London-made dark suits he bought when promoted and was rumoured still to be paying for. He was also rumoured to look around for help in paying for them, and to pay for other items in his bright lifestyle. Jenkins had not seen Semprina's flat, either, and wanted to come. He and Brade went in Brade's car. Bullfinch was going on direct to some function later and used his own vehicle with a driver.

On the way, Brade said: 'Are we getting any movement on Indiment, Glyndwr?'

'Not a thing,' Jenkins replied.

'My God, we're still at damn basics, like how the hell did they move him down there and out on the end of the jib?'

'Quite,' Jenkins answered.

'Where the devil are the witnesses?' Brade said.

'You've got one, have you, you sod?' Jenkins replied. 'Or had one.'

'I wish I'd got down there earlier,' Brade said.

'You did,' Jenkins replied. 'I told Bullfinch.'

'Even a few minutes before there might have been something to see,' Brade said.

'But this is always the cry in our job, isn't it, Dave?'

Bullfinch was already at the flat when they arrived. Touching the armchair lightly with three fingers of his surprisingly long, elegant hand he said: 'Endicott found here, right?' Then he walked into the bedroom, small nose questing: 'Semprina here. *Semprina*. Remind me of her real name, Dave.'

'Ann Chapple,' Jenkins replied.

'And your report says that when you discover them you're with a vicar?' Bullfinch replied, sharp blue eyes very sharp. He led back into the living-room.

Brade said: 'The Reverend Clifford Hale-Garning was concerned about her.'

'Yes, that's also in the report. But has it been properly explained?' Bullfinch replied.

'What, sir?' Brade said.

'Why the cleric was concerned about the whore.'

'This is a clergyman with wide sympathies, sir,' Jenkins replied. 'Across the so-called class spectrum. I've met him. Impressive.'

'And the whore had an injury to her head,' Bullfinch said.

'She died from one,' Jenkins replied.

'Apart from that, apart from that,' Bullfinch said. 'The scalp plaster.'

'There *was* a wound, yes, sir,' Brade said. 'This was what troubled the Reverend Clifford Hale-Garning.'

'But how did he know about it?' Bullfinch asked.

'He's in touch with a great many sources, in the nature of his work,' Brade replied. 'Someone could have said, "Semprina's got a plaster, father." Folk do talk to him. It's one of his assets as a minister. He is much esteemed.'

'He's what's known as a people's priest,' Jenkins said.

'I'm told he does fucking slob jobs around the cathedral because they can't kick the sod out or force him to retire,' Bullfinch replied. His face was plump and boyish, but full of resolve now, resolve to reach the truth.

'It's a fact there's envy of his way with ordinary folk,' Jenkins said. 'I've heard him described as "Christ-like" – his humility, ease with parishioners, decency. This would obviously set up brotherly envy and hate among his higher-placed colleagues, the kind you might run into socially, sir. They'd put the apostolic shit around.'

'He shags tarts,' Bullfinch replied.

'Yes, that's exactly the kind of slander, sir,' Jenkins answered, 'the kind of slander those top figures would spread. Good on you for spotting it, if I may say. No evidence of this at all, I believe, Dave?'

'None,' Brade said.

'How did she get the original wound, and how did Hale-Garning know about it?' Bullfinch asked. 'Who stuck the plaster?'

'These are probably not matters one can ask a priest, sir, on account of confidentiality towards his flock,' Jenkins said. 'An extension of the confession box principle.'

'This prostitute was not in his flock,' Bullfinch replied. 'Hale-Garning is at the cathedral. The whore was a docks whore was a docks whore was a docks whore.'

'I adore the Gertrude Stein pastiche, sir,' Jenkins answered. 'Literature's always got there first, hasn't it?'

'I believe the Reverend Clifford Hale-Garning saw the whole city, and, indeed, beyond, as potentially his flock, sir,' Brade said.

'"Go ye into all the world and preach the Gospel,"' Jenkins said. He grew weighty. 'Hale-Garning is a very literal, Biblical man. I remember saying to Dave after the first time he introduced me to Clifford that this seemed a very literal, Biblical man. Remember that, Dave? And no worse for it. Indeed, no worse.'

'Did Holy Joe give her the wound himself, for instance?' Bullfinch said. 'Some perverse sex antics? Where, one asks, was her head actually placed when it received this scalp injury? There are erotic procedures in which the woman's head could be anywhere and inadvertently injured. And so, subsequently, when the dick excitement's down, Hale-Garning gets guilt spasms and scared?'

'There's a neatness about this living-room that is a testimonial to Semprina, I feel,' Brade replied. 'Even when Pedal was in here dead, his beard askew, that was still the most telling impression I had upon arrival.'

Bullfinch stared about very favourably, taking in the light, leafy wallpaper and framed prints of Paris scenes. 'Yes, a nice place and a credit to her. What I have to fucking worry about, Brade, is whether you were here for crowd pleasure with her, the three of you – Endicott, the priest and yourself, and something goes wrong. All right, you're married now, but there's unwholesome sex stuff in your past, yes? You can't leave it? What occurred here would be well within your ballpark. Do you need the other men in a gang bang to be costumed before you're turned on – one wearing church robes, the other in rag-picker gear? A pistol for kicks?'

'Sort of Russian roulette with trimmings?' Jenkins asked. 'You know so much of the world and its quirky ways, sir.'

'I've had Press queries from London,' Bullfinch replied. 'This is serious. Some major investigative cow, Susan somebody. On *Six Days*. The tale's around, one girl three men – a priest, a derelict and a senior police officer – the various wounds. She's heard the priest has been caught with an inflatable doll at least once, probably on his way to your place, Dave. Susan Fiston. Notoriously meaty by-line. They've also heard Endicott might have a fink connection with you. Was joint use of the girl a kind of binding ritual between you, and/or in lieu of cash payment for him? Don't you ever think of your health, for God's sake? These newspaper sleuths are sniffing. They just don't expect a police officer to be taking part in a kink night with a tramp and a sex-sick priest. They're all keen to smear the Bay project and this kind of sordidness is perfect. It's the sort of smelly publicity that could do the development bad and long-lasting harm. The *Terra Nova* project, for instance.'

'You have an interest there, sir?' Jenkins asked.

Bullfinch gave him a bit of a blue-eyed stare.

'I mean, interested in it as a fine concept,' Jenkins said. 'Obviously.'

'Exactly. There's already resistance, because of what people call cheapening of a piece of history,' Bullfinch replied. 'I certainly do not see it this way, but anyone can understand that group sex and killings involving a policeman, a raver cathedral priest and a vagabond are not good for the valour image. One has been able to fend this journalist off so far. But she'll persist. Perhaps others. I feel I am entitled to know, Dave, whether, in fact, you had some part in these deaths.' He waved a hand to show generosity. 'I certainly do not say deliberate killings. I say simply a three-into-one party that went a little astray. Or were there more people here, others who got clear? One knows such things can happen. If I have the truth I'll be better equipped to deal with these damned inquiries from the papers, you see.'

'Why, here in fact *is* the Reverend Clifford Hale-Garning now,' Jenkins replied. 'We've met occasionally at Dave's place.' Semprina's front door was pushed gently open and Brade saw Cliffy there holding a credit card which he had worked the lock with. He must have picked up this minor skill by watching the other night. Hale-Garning was in quite youthful mufti – jeans and a denim waistcoat over a roll-top navy sweater. He looked appallingly old, his big face loose, eyes clouded by unkempt memories. 'I found I could not stay away,' he whispered. 'This was a scene of such sadness, and yet of . . .'

He seemed unable to get an ending to the thought.

Raging Bullfinch did not wait. He said: 'I'd like to ask you, Reverence, whether you came down here with Mr Brade and the tramp for a team shag that went off-key a bit? And then what about the scalp plaster?'

'A mystery,' Hale-Garning replied, 'wasn't it, Dave? Who would wish to injure such a dear kid like that?'

'How was it you came here with Mr Brade at all?' Bullfinch asked.

Hale-Garning half spoke, half sang: 'There were ninety-and-nine that were safely laid. But one . . . one was away from the Shepherd's care, you see?'

'I can believe you've laid the ninety-nine,' Bullfinch replied.

'We mentioned your flock, Clifford,' Jenkins said.

Hale-Garning went into the bedroom, leaving the door open. They could see him standing at the spot on the floor where Semprina had sat, dead. He didn't weep but, even from where he stood in the living-room, Brade could tell Cliffy had begun to tremble with pain and loss.

'How did you even know this hustler?' Bullfinch called.

Cliffy quarter-turned and spoke over a shoulder: 'Yes, it was a wondrous thing to have known her. This was a girl who could take all the rottennesses of life and make them whole again, whole and wholesome. I think she would have done it for my life. I believe she might have saved me.'

Bullfinch gasped and his head dropped a little. He didn't speak for a while and then said: 'I feel I stand near a tragedy I fail to understand. I feel I am an intruder.'

'No, no,' Hale-Garning replied, turning completely now and coming from the bedroom, 'I am grateful for all who witness my sorrow. It's a feeling to be cherished, to be proclaimed, to be honoured.'

At home later, Brade found himself worrying about Hale-Garning. The rage with the world which had often appeared in Cliff's large pointed face and given it zest had been replaced by something feeble, something close to despair. Of course, Brade himself was also saddened by the loss of Semprina, but for Clifford this killing seemed to bring the death of hope, a hope destroyed before it even had time to reach proper form. That was what his words to Bullfinch had meant. Cliff's loneliness would continue now, and the tonic wine and a farcical blow-up doll were never going to dispel it. To Brade, such grief looked terribly liable to slip into full depression, and he decided it was unwise for Cliffy to be by himself too much in the Llandaff flat. Kate agreed at once that they should put him up for a while. In the evening, Brade called on him and suggested he should lodge in their spare bedroom until the main shock passed. Hale-Garning immediately accepted. He obviously craved company. He craved an audience. Brade hurried back down to arrange things. He removed all the sleeping pills and the Paracetamol from his bathroom cabinet and hid them, then moved a big framed photograph of Captain Scott in a high-necked uniform with epaulettes from the sort of sideboard and put it on the bedside table in Hale-Garning's room to help him think fortitude. After half an hour Cliffy arrived with some gear in suitcases. 'I could have shown her a life, Kate,' he declared several times. Clifford picked up phrases from TV drama and parishioners. 'And she would have brought me purpose.'

'You *have* purpose, Cliff,' Kate said. 'I hear all the time what a vital role yours is in the Church in Wales.' She had a lovely warmth and kindness which Brade found exceptional in a girl of twenty-five, and in a girl who could occasionally turn very hard.

'Oh, that sodding smooth-pawed crew,' Cliffy replied. 'I must find who did it to her, Dave. I must trawl the Bay, listening, learning.'

'Not now. Leave it to us. It's hazardous.'

'Us?'

'Me. Jenkins.'

'You don't look convinced, Cliff,' Kate told him.

'Dave, I do believe you want to put all these matters right, whatever people say. But you're not the whole thing, are you, not in control? That damn Bullfinch is above and he's in on something, isn't he, the evil-eyed lout.'

'I believe you truly moved him, eventually,' Brade replied. 'He had a revelation.'

'Revelations are ten a penny on my beat.'

17

'Kim, I hope we're not the kind of folk who would ask someone polished like you to act the hit man and take out this mad sod Garrant,' Dominic said. 'We're disappointed in Garrant, I have to admit . . . well, obviously. We should have gone for Julian Corbett, despite his bloody loud wife. Corbett's father-in-law's a local chapel minister. This is connections, Kim, this is status. I don't know how we didn't see that from the first. However, the present problem is Garrant. But this doesn't mean we'd expect you personally to finish him for us, although he has to be finished.'

'Fast,' Geoffrey said.

'Luckily we did a thorough survey of Garrant a while back before we took him on.' Dominic gave a big comical wince. 'Oh, sure, you're thinking it wasn't *so* fucking thorough or we'd have known he'd break up the way he did at the first bit of pressure, killing nobodies like that. Well, all right, we *could* have done better on the psychology side. But I meant more concrete stuff – his movements, lifestyle, his protection and back-up. Geoffrey's got all that in note form and charts. We can look at it soon. The research shows him gifted, determined and energetic, but it doesn't reach recent incidents, incidents which sadly cancel all we thought before.'

'Our notion is, Kim, that you invite him here. This would be a social/business meeting and maybe he'd decide not to bring all his guard squad. He might consider it rude to turn up with a swarm of thugs. Even people like Garrant can show sensitivity. We're sure he'd be eager to meet you, colleagues within the same organisation, as it were. You're a name – through the black cop connection.'

'Get the fucker here, Kim, if possible alone, and we can handle it from there on. No need for any involvement by you. In fact, best not. We keep you out of such banalities.'

'He'd be done actually here, on the premises?' Pillar asked.

'This is a beautiful old building, good stone walls,' Dominic replied. 'Sound is not going to travel.'

They were in the Bay flat drinking Château Lynch Bages from a good stock in the utility room cupboard-cellar. Pillar had moved down and reinstalled himself a couple of days ago. Jane and Edward remained at Maidrew. As they were leaving after the pleasant dinner there, Dominic and Geoffrey had promised to call on him in the Bay as soon as he was settled, and now early in the evening here they were. Oh, Jesus. Pillar had come to feel much less sure he could manage them than when he spoke to Jane. It was different seeing them in the Bay. The scope of Maidrew and its grounds thickened his courage. Although those acres worried Jane, he loved them, took stature from them, found a line to history and timeless grandeur through them, and believed himself and his family worthy of the succession. Now, in dockland . . . Christ, he was only living in dockland at all because they had asked him to come. Told him to come. Told him to come because he was talented and indispensable, yes, but still told him to come. Now, he could be mistaken for an employee, not the senior partner he described himself as to Jane. When these two walked into the flat they behaved as if it belonged as much to them as it did to him, or more. They held the lease, paid the rent. A job cottage. Jane had said Dominic and Geoffrey would regard Maidrew as theirs, too, because they considered it bought with their money, the arrogant pricks. Perhaps they did think of it like that. Pillar never would. Maidrew was his and hers and the boy's. These two had no rights to it and were not going to get any rights to it. This flat was different, though.

Geoffrey put a cardboard folder on the mahogany side table where the ship's bell and that fine model of the *Terra Nova* still stood. Possibly the folder contained Garrant's dossier but it remained closed for now. 'We've tried to think of other sites, believe me, Kim,' he said. 'Disposal from within a multi-tenanted building is always difficult, and we're very conscious that you have to be seen as wholly taintless in the run-up to these project negotations. In fact, of course, the *company* has to be seen as taintless, and that's our very reason for deciding Garrant must be removed. The trouble is, he keeps himself pretty well shielded, and did long before Indiment. He pays some low-rank police for at least blindeying and possible aid. Maritime House, his home in Stuart Street, is a fortress and our profile shows that when he's at the Toledo with his wife, Lorna, or at the racing or out bowling he has a team close, minders, executives. Now, he'll feel more than ever he's a target, if A.W. Moss-Cober, Cordial Max and de Courville have him down as a likely for that death. And he knows they will. They had proper money in Indiment and genuine aspirations.'

'Fucking brutal aspirations,' Dominic said.

'That as well, yes, but they were all committed to the ploy. Naturally they'll feel vindictive. Somehow we must separate Garrant from his chaperons. The beauty of it is, he'll trust you, Kim. He'll quite reasonably expect your thanks because he did Indiment to keep you safe. We can use that trust. Trust is a lovely commodity. It delivers people on a plate.'

'But we can see how jumpy the bastard is if he kills two nothings to silence them, the floozy and the cyclist,' Dominic said. 'We're going to have to play him with total subtlety.'

'*He* kills those two to keep them silent, and now we have to kill him to keep *him* silent,' Pillar replied.

Dominic had a happy chuckle. He was sitting in a Queen Anne wing chair, re-covered with pale blue tapestry, and this did all it could to make him look temperate. 'Yes, you'll often notice a circular element in our kind of work,' he said.

'This is very much an unfortunate digression from our purpose in the Bay,' Geoffrey said, 'and by no means of our choosing. However, we cannot move forward securely while Garrant and his mouth are still potential damage. It might not be so bad if he went abroad, but he won't.'

'He thinks he can take care of anything at all, the big-headed jerk,' Dominic replied.

'But disposal *is* possible, of course, given some organisation and luck,' Geoffrey said, 'as long as we get him alone. Emergency stairs here? And there's a good deal of deep water around.'

'All the same, I wish it could be somewhere else,' Pillar replied.

Dominic had left his chair and was standing bent over the *Terra Nova*, admiring the delicately made models of East Siberian sledge dogs on the deck. He had one of them in his hand. Straightening up, he faced Pillar, the clutter of his riff-raff face worse than Kim had ever seen it. 'Sure you wish it could be somewhere else, you fucking dreamy ponce,' he said. 'Christ, we're even thinking of handling this ourselves, our very selves, that's me and Geoffrey in person. We are people who always stay away from that kind of involvement. Maybe now it can't be done. But you, you want to be far from it all, don't you – the mess and the risk and the organising? You skim 1.6 million and see no need to help us pull it back. That's what this will be, taking out Garrant – it's how we make sure our scheme here gets to be real and gets to earn.'

'But you've said you don't want me tainted, Dominic,' Pillar replied.

'We don't want you tainted and we don't want you acting like none of this is to do with you. If dear Garrant starts telling what he knows, the project is sunk. Then the chance of getting back the money you thieved is sunk. And we might be sunk ourselves.' Dominic threw the dog back with no consideration on to the *Terra Nova* deck and went and took his seat again.

Geoffrey moved his enormous head about seriously. He was standing at one of the big windows, glancing down now and then towards the mock dock. 'If I may say, it *is* hurtful, Kim, this apparent lack of commitment on your part – especially when Dominic has striven to look after you and yours, regardless of the 1.6. I don't only mean having Indiment wasted, then brilliantly displayed to deter replacements. But also by consenting to put his parents in at Maidrew and ensure your wife and child are taken proper care of.'

'What?' Pillar said. 'When? Jane wouldn't allow –'

'Ah, forgive me. You didn't know?'

'How could I fucking know?' Pillar yelled.

'Jane hasn't telephoned?' Geoffrey asked.

'Will they let her?' Pillar said.

'We were fortunately able to arrange it more or less at once,' Geoffrey replied. 'Today, as a matter of fact. We worried about Jane and little Edward alone in such a spot – very beautiful but also very remote, Kim, impossibly exposed. Dominic was so concerned he thought it worthwhile asking his mother and father whether they could take these duties, and to their huge credit they accepted, despite the brevity of the notice.' He did a replica chuckle of Dominic's: 'I don't suppose many boys will be able to look back on their childhood and say there was a butler in the household.'

'I'm not making a big thing of this – not looking for a lot of gratitude, Kim,' Dominic said. 'It was just something I had to do.'

'Dominic is like that,' Geoffrey said. 'So much that is unadvertised.'

'Get Garrant here,' Dominic told Pillar.

'Sell it as a tête-à-tête,' Geoffrey said.

'We can be around. He needn't know,' Dominic said.

'You'll definitely deal with this personally?' Pillar asked. He was restless and would have felt safer moving about, but he made himself stay seated.

'You could make some kind of presentation to him, for saving you through the hanging man,' Dominic replied. 'Say a Rolex or a chain and good gold medallion. He's into medallions, isn't he?'

Geoffrey went to the mahogany table. He replaced the East Siberian dog at its voyage post on the *Terra Nova*'s deck, then opened the folder and consulted some papers.

'Whatever the gift is it can be recovered later,' Dominic said. 'Immediately. People are easy to take when they're receiving something of worth. At maximum trust. As Geoffrey says, we can use that – must, it would be dereliction not to.'

Looking at a paper in the dossier, Geoffrey said: 'Yes, he likes medallions. Astrological motifs. And Celtic legends. He has a watch, of course, but not a Rolex, if this is up to date.'

'Make it a Rolex,' Dominic replied. 'What the fuck do we do with a Mabinogion medallion after he's gone? I don't imagine you'd wear it, Geoffrey. Nor me. I've still got the chest for it – haven't let myself go. But myth gives me colic. And as for Kim, well Kim's had enough from us, already.'

They left to drive on over the Severn Bridge to see a boat-builder between Avonmouth and Bristol later that evening who would adapt a vessel to look more or less like the *Terra Nova*, once there was planning consent. Immediately they had gone Pillar went out to a public telephone booth and dialled Maidrew. He did not feel confident about the line to the flat, and never felt confident about mobiles. A man answered: 'You have reached the Pillar residence. Mr Pillar's butler speaking.' The voice was heavy and very precise, like a flunkey in a comic play.

'This is Kim Pillar. Put my wife on.'

'Mr Pillar himself? This *is* a pleasure, sir, if I may say.'

'Is she there?'

'Of course, sir.'

'Put her on.'

'Certainly, sir.'

And in a moment Jane spoke. She sounded bright, bubbling with spirit. 'I'm fine,' she said. 'Edward's fine. We're all fine. Are you fine? The grounds look fine.'

Listening to it, the joyful warning gibberish, Pillar knew how stupid he had been to think only of the phone line to the flat. They had fitted a recorder for calls in and out of Maidrew, or, more simply, someone was on an extension. What else were butlers and housekeepers for? 'Yes, fine,' he replied.

'Edward misses you. We both miss you.'

'And me you two,' he said. 'You've got some new help.'

'Yes,' she replied, 'help.'

He walked back towards the flat. The street was empty, clean, well lit. Neat little Noddy-style marina houses clustered around the big old converted warehouses. Was this really once a working dock? He could see why the feelings of someone like Brade about the development would be in such a mess – he'd love the new cleanness and yet sentimentalise the lost vigour and wealth, though Brade was too young ever to have seen it at the full. Pillar would bring Jane and Edward here. The place had a future. He would take them from Maidrew at once, regardless of anything the alleged butler might try or his wife, or Dominic and Geoffrey. Pillar could make Jane and the boy secure here. Once he had done that he was back to prime power in the company. Jane would still like to run, of course. She would want to run even more so now. But that was not the way to do things. He saw money in prospect here, proper, continuing money, even if he had to first clear the 1.6, and he might find a way out of that. He saw a position to be built in the Bay. He could handle it. He could handle it once the hostages were picked up and safe. Sod that self-educated pleb, Dominic. Sod that petit bourgeois charmer, Geoffrey. Sod Dominic's mum and dad, if that's who they really were, the sudden lodgers.

He turned around, went back to the telephone box and dialled Glyndwr Jenkins' home number. Pillar might need help to bring Jane and Edward away. The butler and housekeeper were possibly not the only people Dominic had placed there. And, in any case, perhaps the butler might have additional skills to a noble telephone manner. This should be the kind of trip Glyndwr would enjoy, rekindling former loyalties. Glyn might still have the finger irons. Pillar felt entitled to ask him to come, felt almost obliged to ask him. This expedition would have the same flavour as some of those happy violent Oxford sorties. And it could not be more legal – nothing to offend a cop. He would be helping a man recover his family. There was grandeur to it, and grace. Glyn would appreciate this.

A woman answered the telephone, speaking what Pillar took to be Welsh. When he asked for Glyndwr she said in English that he was out. 'Is he working?' Pillar asked.

'Most probably. Who wishes to know?'

'Would you know when he'll be there?'

'Could be any old time,' she replied.

'I'll try again fairly soon.'

'Should he call you?'

'No, I'm out and about,' Pillar said.

'Mobile?'

'Yes, mobile.'

She snarled something, then asked: 'Mobile number?'

'No.'

'Shall I tell Glyndwr what it's to do with?' she asked.

'Oh, it's not urgent.'

'It's not urgent, but you'll call back soon?'

'Fairly soon, yes. But, no, not urgent. I expect he gets a lot of calls,' he replied.

'Are you afraid your number's bugged?' she asked. 'I assume you're not on it.'

'Bugged? Oh, dear, hardly,' he replied. 'I'm not at that level yet. Goodbye.'

18

Because of security, it always took a while to arrange a meeting with Adrian Garrant in his home, even for Brade. He would make a request by telephone and someone would ring back and suggest a time. Occasionally, it might actually be Garrant in person who returned the call, but generally Robin Hewlitt or some other sidekick. If the proposed time turned out unsuitable, Brade was entitled to say so. Then there would have to be further discussions and consultations of the diary by Garrant and staff at Maritime House, his place in the Bay, and ultimately they would telephone again with an alternative. They always *did* ring again. Garrant believed in protocol. He liked things to be done with graciousness and hated swearing.

As a business he would by now be about equal with each of the main three, A.W. Moss-Cober, Cordial Maximilian and Simeon de Courville, though Garrant probably did only drugs and some enforcing and ran no girls. Garrant would definitely feel comfortable competing with any of the three on their own, but since they merged he most likely saw himself as suddenly dwarfed and very vulnerable. To improve his base, he might look for an understanding with one of the big outside interests keen to invade the Bay. They all craved to recruit a good middle-man, which would mean either Adrian or Jule Corbett.

Garrant was still only in his mid-twenties and possibly more adaptable than A.W., Max or Simeon, less committed to the Bay's established crooked patterns. As part of this realignment, had he already begun to take on work for an incoming firm? That would explain the showy death of Indiment. Nobody disputed Garrant's rough talent, probably more suitable for that type of job than what Corbett could offer.

Of course, Brade might have run into Garrant almost any night at the Toledo, but that would placard things. And, also of course, things would have been different if it was a matter of arresting Garrant. Then, Brade would simply go in at the house mob-handed, never mind the gates and alarms, and pull him out. Brade often dreamed of this, had actually prepared drawings for himself of how it would be done. They were carefully hidden and might stay hidden because to date nobody had ever established enough against Adrian Garrant to nail him. Increasingly he looked unbeatable.

'Dave,' Garrant cried. He shook Brade's hand with both of his in long drawn out friendliness, the sort of greeting an old man might give another at a funeral, as if holding him safe from the grave, for now. 'Naturally, I've heard about your trouble – this cast-of-thousands sex production that went a degree off-script. I thought you might come seeking help. I mentioned it to Lorna. And whatever I can do I will. She absolutely agrees. Within the law, that is, obviously. You'll probably understand our respect for the law.

'I want to assure you, Dave, that no matter what extremes took place at Semprina's I'm convinced you, personally, would have nothing to do with actual deaths, not deliberately. Sex thrills get more difficult as people grow older, I know that – don't at all look forward to it! – but regardless of how unkempt and boisterous your needs, Dave, I, speaking for myself, and for Lorna, and for the majority of the colleagues I've had a word with about this, do not believe you individually would be conscious party to a snuff script. Whenever this notion is put to me I reply, *Not Dave Brade, no, no, no, never. Dave's married now. Different. The magazines and tarts – all that finished.*'

They drank tea from what looked to Brade like top china, decorated with panels of flowers and fruit in mild colours. The cups were wide, for conveying full aroma. Brade loved such quality material. These cups gave a flavour of true civilisation even though Garrant was present.

He said: 'Dave, I expect you're thinking of a lawyer and want to be put in touch with some of mine. As a matter of fact, I've already alerted them – though without committing you. Dave Brade is old enough and seasoned enough to make his own choices, I hope! And, in any case, the Police Federation probably supplies advocates for a distinguished officer like you who's slipped up a trifle and inadvertently caused heart failures.'

'Adrian, I have a witness who puts you on the fucking jib when Indiment was strung up,' Brade replied.

Garrant laughed pleasantly, as if not surprised that Brade switched subjects. 'Now, Dave, looking at your personal situation, I believe I can see what would trouble any lawyer asked to take on your defence. To him, this case will seem to have all the standard features of a hundred other disastrous multi-sex capers. That is, two practitioners of a certain age and status – you and the cathedral priest – oh, but the priest was an unfortunate factor, Dave, because everyone knows they're *so* inventive and determined when it comes to uses of the human frame – but, anyway, you and the priest, on the face of it totally respectable figures, indeed eminent, and then two victims of rock bottom social significance, a whore and a vagrant, about whom nobody is going to bother much. Lawyers will fear a jury would recognise these elements and see only culpability in you middle-class people. But I might be able to lead them away from such downside factors. Oh, they won't want to upset me, nor, if I may say, any dear friend of mine, Dave, in case they jeopardise their fat fee relationship with my outfit.'

Brade said: 'The witness categorically identifies you.'

'Who's that then, Dave?' Garrant asked quietly. 'Someone willing and able to testify?'

'This must have been big money, Adrian, or big prospects – I mean for you to handle an exposed, artisan job yourself.'

Garrant spoke sadly now: 'People working for me here didn't want to let you into Maritime House today. They said you would not be coming to look for my help but to probe and allege. I overruled them. Oh, I said this might be the *police* way but it was not *Dave Brade's* way. I said you had trouble and when someone as age-old in the Bay as you had trouble it was a duty for other Bay figures to get supportive.' He frowned and gave a small groan of betrayal. 'And now you start doing just what Robin and others warned me of. But I'm the kind, Dave, who would rather show too much faith than too little. You've been knocked off balance by shock and you're into desperate scape-goating. Well, I can understand that, can forgive it, more or less.'

'You've been offered a slice of some incoming firm, Adrian?' Brade asked. 'They'd never insult you by suggesting only a wage for such work, not Adrian Garrant.' Brade waved an arm slowly: 'They'd know about this, the kind of place you run. You must have been promised a long-term share. Why did they want Indiment taken out?'

Garrant laughed again for a while. 'I see how it's going, Dave and why you're here. Smart. I'm supposed to have done Indiment for future favours and then I do Pedal and Semprina for silence? Semprina was poking into Indiment's death, wasn't she, because she fancied him, loved him, even? And I suppose Pedal was your grass. He's your witness? Your witness and whatever else you and the Rev. used him for, used both of them for. You want to put the deaths on to me, do you, Dave – just as my folk here said you would? That way you protect yourself and your holy friend.'

'You thought you might have been spotted and went searching.'

'Indiment was put there during darkness, yes? Naturally. Who'd do a rope rigmarole like that in daylight? Where was this witness? How did he see so clearly? And if it's Pedal, what use?'

Garrant owned a large place in Stuart Street, not far from the new Welsh Assembly complex. Brade used to wonder sometimes, which had the more clout, Garrant's roost or the Assembly. In late Victorian times, when the docks began to boom on coal, Garrant's property had been erected as a rooming house for seamen between ships. Takers dwindled later because port trade shrank, and the building became a Christian mission hall. That use faded, too, and the building stood empty for decades until Garrant bought it at a nothing price and lavished some of his early profits on alterations and refurbishment. Brade hoped it was deconsecrated first. Now, Garrant, Lorna and their children lived in the upper storeys, with wide views out to the barrage and the Channel. On the ground floor Garrant had a strong room and offices and accommodation for his security people. There was a big yard in front of the house with ornamental gates on to the street. In any move to take him in, Brade reckoned the gates would have to be rammed. One of his drawings showed a personnel carrier, with bull bars at the front, bursting through. It had thrilled him to do that sketch.

He and Garrant were alone in the fine long front lounge. Rain beat at the two picture windows ruining the twilight outlook, but Garrant went and stood at one of them holding his cup and saucer and peered out. 'I like a bit of weather. We are all Bay people and we love the place, even its harsher sides. My own feeling is that folk like you, me, Glyndwr Jenkins, we all want to see this wonderful new concept thrive. Although we'll have different ways of ensuring it, that's the common objective. Forgive me, but I tend to regard you and Glyndwr as – not as *associates* of mine, that would be presumptuous, improper even, but as – oh, let's say as like-minds. And so it comes as a shock when you or he approach me with hostility. I expect you know he tried the same kind of questions. Well, probably you sent him, although he didn't mention anything about a witness. I believe I was able to satisfy him on these matters and I hope I can do the same with you. People I'm in touch with value Glyndwr. They value you, also, but there's a more personal link to Glyndwr. I feel a duty to make sure Glyndwr does well – not merely because he's black and refused to let this hold him back, but because . . . oh, because he *is* Glyndwr.'

Garrant was in a short-sleeved, green and yellow striped open-necked beach shirt, jeans and black moccasins. A large gold medallion with astrological or folklore symbols on it hung against his chest. He wore his dark hair long, with a wide wedge of it down across his forehead. There was almost always a look of half-puzzlement on his face, as though he felt shocked at what the world confronted him with, and more shocked that he had learned so fast how to handle it. His features – nose, chin, eyebrows – were neat and rounded and helped a lot with the appearance of general pleased wonderment. His eyes contributed to that, also. They were grey-blue and could probably turn hard, but as he listened to Brade they remained warm, respectful, injured and apparently baffled.

'You're in danger from all sides, Adrian,' Brade said. 'I wouldn't think the people who commissioned you to do Indiment will approve two follow-up killings. They're bound to trouble the scene. Businessmen crave stability.'

The wonderment and shock in Garrant's face grew radiant. He went and sat in a black steel-grid frame chair which looked to Brade like the 1950s. 'You'll really stick to that story, will you?' he replied. 'Oh, I can see why. If you manage to get this version around it takes the trail away from you and your loving cleric. And I'm put up as a general target. Someone else might do your work for you.'

'You've annoyed outsiders as well as A.W. and so on,' Brade said. 'And Clifford Hale-Garning is heartbroken about the death of Semprina.'

'What are you here for, Dave? You're selling protection?'

'I'm here to ask you if you killed three people and to warn you you could soon be dead.'

Garrant had not gone the whole road and furnished Victorian to suit the building but seemed to be getting back to Coronation times style. Talking of stability, some people, even people as young as Garrant and his wife, found comfort in recalling those hopeful new Elizabethan days. Brade himself was in an armchair with thin metal legs and wide, flat laminated wood arm supports. He reckoned you might have sat in such a chair if you were waiting for someone in the Royal Festival Hall forty-odd years ago, and if you'd kept your weight down enough not to fear busting the legs.

Garrant sighed: 'To save yourself you plait a case against me, and then offer to stop the consequences for a fee. Brilliantly opportunist, Dave. But, yes, all right, I might be interested. You've got nothing, nothing beyond a witness who can't appear, and who wouldn't be able to say anything against me if he could, but, all right, yes, you'd probably still be able to do me bad damage, or get others to. I don't question your power, Dave. You want to talk terms?'

Brade stood and put his cup and saucer on a wooden drinks trolley with solid white wheels. 'You'll always think along those lines, Adrian. The tale goes you already stipend some officers.

But, no, not that. Look, sordid deaths in the Bay are bad for investment. It's like the mucky past elbowing its way back. I don't want a fourth and I'd like to settle the other three.'

A door opened at the far end of the room and Lorna Garrant came in. She was tall, energetic, dark, about twenty-four or five, like Garrant, though with no comparable look of surprise in her face, only confidence and attack. Her features had some boniness, but the bones were in the right places, and Brade thought of her as beautiful. Probably they would rate as a beautiful couple, in fact, and, Western movies apart, Brade had never seen anyone moccasins suited better than Garrant. Brade had read that well-structured faces like Lorna's aged well. Even if they didn't nobody would know for quite a while.

Garrant said: 'Dave wants to stick not just Indiment but Pedal and Semprina on to me, Lorna.'

'Robin said he would,' she replied in a big assured voice with only a touch of Cardiff to it. 'We admire you, Dave – all of us, even Robin – your cheek and tenacity. The Bay needs someone like you.'

At home, Clifford brought Brade a telephone message he had written in capitals along the top margin of an old *South Wales Echo* front page. WOULD MR BRADE KINDLY MAKE CONTACT WITH SELF, A.W. MOSS-KOBER IMMEDIATELY, PLEASE, IN A PERSONAL CAPACITY? Brade was not certain how to read this. Who 'in a personal capacity' – Brade or A.W? Was Moss-Cober saying, 'Come yourself, not a subordinate'? Or did he want to tell Brade that he, A.W., would be keeping this meeting private from his own associates, Cordial and Simeon de Courville? Had something come adrift in their alliance and in the sparkling plans for their Jim Driscoll boxing restaurant?

'Is it safe for you to go alone to see this man?' Clifford asked.

'A.W. doesn't do violence himself. He orders it.'

'How do you know he'll be alone?'

'He says in a personal capacity.'

'You believe that, Dave? Please, take me if you're going out again. Night approaches. Surely it would be better if I were with you, concealed, but ready to intervene should matters turn bad. Plus, I want to tell you of my pain.'

Brade would have liked to keep an eye on Clifford non-stop, but impossible. Perhaps, after all, it had been a mistake to bring him down to this flat. Almost at once, Cliff had grown troublesomely dependent on Brade's company. In fact, Brade was alarmed by the degree of collapse. Why didn't prayer and Cliff's beliefs do something for him? He dreaded to be left, and Kate was now back at work at her car rent business and could not look after him.

Hale-Garning suffered further anxieties. The orgy rumours detailed by Garrant and Bullfinch had apparently reached Church high-ups. 'They'll send me back to Llandrindod Wells to do marital counselling, Dave,' Clifford had cried several times. He feared that a task force of clergymen would come for him while Brade was out. From the side of the window, now, as Brade phoned A.W. Moss-Cober and arranged a meeting, Cliff made frequent concealed surveys of the street, for fear the flat was watched. Instead of robes, he wore football gear all the time – a red and black striped shirt, black shorts and goalkeeper's cap – so he could never be smuggled away forcibly among vicars pretending he was simply one of their group.

But Brade could not have him tagging along to job meetings. 'No, you stay, Cliff. And please don't go to the Bay, investigating on your own account. It's difficult there at present. You mustn't. Continue to man the telephone. This is vital. You'll be a sort of Control Room here.'

That seemed to comfort him a little. He wanted to contribute. His face picked up some of its old cragginess and fight. 'I'll open the door to nobody. Might women ring?'

'I doubt it.'

'I'll speak well of you if they do, Dave, and if they mention you going to tarts I'll deflect it. Some women can't tolerate men who fancy whores. I'll tell them I'm in holy orders. This can make a recommendation worth more.'

'Thanks, Cliff.'

Like Brade and most other prominent Bay folk, A.W. Moss-Cober lived outside dockland, of course. He had a handsome

Edwardian terraced house in what Brade always thought of as another resonant and proud part of Cardiff, Roath. The streets of the area were named after glorious battles – Agincourt, Blenheim, Waterloo, Balaclava, Ladysmith, Mafeking. They were tumbled together, as if someone had put all the best items of British history in a bag. *And* there was a great general. A.W.'s place stood in Marlborough Road, red-brick, double-fronted with a pillared porch and a boot-scraper. A polished metal plate in the front door gave the house name as Sanctuary. This was wholesome and meaningful. Brade hoped A.W. had christened the place himself, not merely inherited the name when he bought.

Moss-Cober opened the door in person. But, yes, Cliff could be right, of course. There might be other people here. This was a big place. You could hide a team until it was needed. While Brade was still in the porch, Moss-Cober said: 'I understand better, Dave. We spoke before in your homely flat, but I see a completed line now. It's Pillar, the first Oxford boy, who gives the instructions to Jenkins, the second Oxford boy, who passes them on to the Bay boy up for bids, Adrian Garrant. Jenkins and Garrant have been observed. This offends natural justice, Dave. Surely, I have to discuss such matters with you in person.' For an evening at home he wore not his outdoor thornproofs but what Brade thought could probably be called a smoking jacket. It was a double-breasted three-quarter length coat in brown velvet with elaborate black woven loops for buttoning. With this he had on tan slacks and tan slip-ons. He took Brade into the front sitting-room containing a three-piece russet-coloured moquette suite – a bit like Brade's own, but more solid-looking – and a long, low teak sideboard where several beer flagons had been lined up. There were still-life watercolours on the walls in plain, broad frames. They looked amateur but all right if you liked blues and yellows. Brade wondered whether A.W. had done them himself, or one of his family.

Moss-Cober filled German-type tankards with hinged lids which he brought from a sideboard cupboard. Brade thought this was the wrong type of drinking vessel in a road with such a name, but he went along, made no query. Upstairs someone was playing with real love what he took to be a flute. Woodwind done well always wowed Brade. Listening, he could feel that life's foulnesses need not win. A.W. had several children at local schools who must be teenage by now.

'And which one is that?' Brade asked, pointing through the ceiling towards the wonderful sound.

'I'm as interested in music as the next man. Mine could be said to be a creative household. It's karaoke that's probably my own forte.'

'Some have the gift, A.W. Nobody can explain why. Yet flair is not the whole matter, I'm sure. Practice, practice, practice, like ballet.'

'In the Toledo,' he replied.

'The club's reputation for karaoke helped make the Bay development viable. It's not properly recognised.'

'And while I'm giving Toledo people several numbers the other night – e.g. from *The Desert Song* – I see Jenkins in obvious friendship with Adrian Barnaby Garrant, Dave.' He stared for a moment towards one of the watercolours. 'I have now to use the word conspiracy. I don't think any of us would have done that on our visit to your flat, but things have darkened.'

'Garrant?' Brade replied. 'Have I got it right – the lad with the place in Stuart Street? Do you think he's involved in Bay development matters then, A.W.?'

'This was witnessed, the comradeship. You might think I was so caught up in *The Desert Song* I couldn't watch their meeting accurately. Simeon, entirely uninvolved in the karaoke, will confirm. He once considered entering the military police and knows how to assess evidence.'

'People,' Brade replied. 'Simeon's always had a lovely interest in people, whether his own girls or girls run by others, or even in the punters.'

'All right, you'll tell me that if there was anything real between Jenkins and Garrant they would not make a show of it in the club. But they believe they're above normal precautions, Dave. They think they're sovereign. Garrant, plus those he represents, in alliance with Jenkins see themselves as unassailable in –'

The door was pushed hard open. Brade had made sure he sat facing it. He half stood now, then relaxed. A fair-haired, thin, bustling girl of about fourteen dressed in a Catatonia T-shirt, green track-suit bottoms and plimsolls entered the room pushing a world globe on its wheeled metal stand. 'We've got to show the export routes from Colombia for the drugs class in school, dad,' she said. 'Give us a hand?'

'*Anti*-drugs class, Fiona,' Moss-Cober replied.

'Don't be pernickety, now. How shipments get to the Bay via Europe. For the local angle,' she said. 'Where in Europe, dad?' She placed the large globe close to where A.W. sat and put her finger on Colombia.

'Mr Brade's the one to answer. He knows everything about the Bay. He runs it.'

'He's in business there?'

'Now, there's a thing to ask about a police officer.'

'Oh, *that*,' Fiona said.

'On the whole I'm in favour of schools tackling the drugs topic,' Brade replied.

'I prefer drama,' Fiona said. 'That play we're doing about the woman Pope et cetera. Some real laughs and shouting. You do Isabella again, dad.' It seemed farcical – Brade, expecting an attack, was about to see some amateur dramatics. Was he? Arm raised and her head jutting forward, she took a pose that Brade thought *could* have been like a woman Pope, or as much that as anything else. She began talking what must be a speech from the play to A.W. about Vatican-type work as a woman would probably see it – consecrating bishops and having her feet kissed. A.W. stood up from his armchair holding the German tankard and also assumed a theatrical stance before answering. Brade did not know the play. It seemed a scene they had gone over with each other quite often. The girl's performance was striking, full of good bite and intelligent noise. A.W. was not too bad, either, his voice flexible, probably because of karaoke skills. His dossier said that before the hyphen arrived one part of the Moss-Cober family had been in music hall or revue though Brade could not remember whether it was Moss or Cober. When Fiona and A.W. finished their scene Brade put down his tankard and applauded, but the girl went abruptly from the room without returning to the globe and her drugs task.

A.W. said: 'You see. Can I afford merely to watch, Dave, while this filthy police-backed confederacy establishes itself in the Bay? My commitments grow. A son looking for a flute future and two other children intent on genuine business or professional lives –

say the theatre or a vet. This is specialised training – maybe even years in Bologna, Italy, where they really know flutes. You'll understand that I can't stay passive when I've now actually *watched* relations cementing between a detective and an outlaw. Certainly it was open. This was to advertise that disgraceful line of complicity I've spoken of – a warning to us, to Simeon and me, and therefore to Cordial. This was the most brazen statement yet that they believe their project, the *Terra Nova* smack and coke emporium, is unstoppable, irresistible, uncatchable, far, far out in front. Why I requested this interview *in person*, Dave, is to ask whether you, you, Dave Brade *in person*, not just the general police body – to ask whether you, Dave Brade in person, are part of it, this dirty backing for the *Terra Nova*, and therefore anti the Driscoll commemorative restaurant, and joined with them to kill it before birth?'

Brade said: 'I've always liked the –'

'Garrant is amused by us,' A.W. replied. 'Despises us. When I say "us" I don't mean self and colleagues only but all those with regard for the integrity of the Bay. I'd like to include you in that, Dave. Truly.'

'Thanks, A.W.'

'He's taken out for his own reasons, obscure reasons, at least three people, Dave.'

'Is it certain he did your man?'

'Which man, Dave?'

'Hanging man.'

'Oh, I've heard you and the Rev. are supposed to have made that mess of Semprina and Pedal Power. I'd be inclined to doubt that.'

'Thanks, A.W. Ridiculous, of course.'

'As far as you're concerned. I don't know about the vicar. But I've got to ask you, Dave – is there a kind of magic wall around Garrant? You're part of that? You weren't at Oxford, as I gather, but you could still be part of it. How this would distress me I needn't tell you. This would be that chaos we all dread.'

A.W. had taken some beatings in jail or during his long commercial career in the docks and you could see small areas of permanent displacement near his eyes and on one side of his nose. Yet by will-power or muscle exercise he had managed to bring his features to almost a balanced unity. These days his face looked admittedly not distinguished but kindly now and then and like something whose sections might belong together. Such a face deserved its occasional spells of sanctuary. In his own sitting-room he seemed blessedly free of the terror of large spaces that had stricken him since his cell days.

A.W. said: 'The flute. The lady Pope in *Top Girls*. None of this was laid on just to touch your sympathies, Dave. I hope you understand that. It's how the house always runs. You could say culturally vibrant. The other girl's into ladies' snooker as well as animal welfare. Of course, if you want to compromise all this, even destroy it – yes, it might go as far as that – if this family is of no importance to you or, even worse, a target to be wilfully demolished by a compact with outside influences and a gangster like Adrian Garrant – if so, that is your privileged choice, clearly.'

'Now, listen, A.W., don't you or Simeon or Max fucking well try to waste Garrant,' Brade replied. 'I hear he knows he's a bit exposed. He'll have protection, extra protection. I can't have more carnage.'

'That's what I mean. You've warned him? You look after him? For it to be someone local like Adrian makes things worse. One knows the man. One has observed and, yes, admired his career so far. He has taken on and at least matched Julian Corbett, an achievement. This familiarity with Garrant means one can focus hatred very exactly on him. He is not some vague, undefined exterior menace. Garrant has a shape, a history, Dave, a shape that can be undone, a history that can be obliterated.' He stood: 'It's been lovely talking to you and putting on that moment of theatre in your honour with my daughter. Like a Command Performance.'

'A privilege to be an audience, A.W.'

19

He had brought a spanner with him from the car, a spanner small enough to go in his pocket. He would have felt absurd carrying it like a cosh. He was not Bill Sykes, but a business partner in a good company, a man wearing office clothes even now. Also, it might frighten Edward to see his father toting a lump of metal as weapon.

In the dark, Maidrew looked squat and unkempt. It was a house that needed sunshine. At night the property seemed to fold down scruffily on itself, like a sleeping wino. Pillar had always thought this and thought it again now as he approached on foot through the beech and elder woodland in the south-west of the grounds. He could see the Maidrew frontage occasionally when the trees thinned out for short stretches. It was just after 3 a.m. He was alone. At the Bay flat he had given up the idea of inviting Jenkins on this outing after all, and did not try him by phone again. Perhaps his partner would tell Glyndwr someone called, and she might be able to describe the voice well enough for him to guess who. Possibly he would ring Pillar to see what it was about, or even turn up at the door. No answer now, either way. It had been idiotic, sentimental, a throw-back to think of bringing Glyndwr.

He used to tell Jane that if they had first inspected Maidrew in the small hours he would never have bought, and the joke was not all joke. On a bright afternoon its stonework, long narrow windows and gravelled forecourt would sparkle, making the house appear what it was and what he wanted, a beautifully set, middle-rank, late-Georgian emblem of wealth, a time-hallowed residence for someone on the up. Without that glow, Maidrew seemed stunted and drab and neglected, about to slip into decay. If you went closer you'd expect to find a door off its hinges and goats in the kitchen.

Pillar did begin to go closer. God, he wished he knew firearms and had one aboard. Instead, he was a company thinker who did not know firearms but did know several men who knew firearms and had some. Until now this had been enough. Once in a while he had been required to turn these hired experts on to company enemies, and that was as near as he ever came to the brute side of the firm. As near as he had ever wanted to. Orders and then eternal ignorance of their results were his function.

And night manoeuvres now. He tried to keep to a slender path through the wood, perhaps a gamekeeper's route once, when Maidrew *had* gamekeepers, and now more or less overgrown. Brambles tugged at his trouser legs. Occasionally he had to force his way through bushes and undergrowth. Despite everything, though, he felt glad he had come. He remained sure he must bring Jane and Edward out and set them up with him in the Bay. Then he could resume work on the *Terra Nova*.

For a while back in the flat this resolve had wobbled, and there were a few terrible poltroon seconds when he favoured running. He had thought he would go back to Maidrew and snatch Jane and Edward, yes, but then get abroad, stay abroad for at least months, write off the project. Fuck the project. Could it rate against Jane and Edward's security? The escape fund was still adequate. Jane would not resist. Resist? Didn't she long to go? Pillar had been sure he could dispose of Dominic's father and mother if they tried to obstruct. And naturally they would try to obstruct. It was why they had been installed. Too bad for them. He would fight to reclaim his family and take them far away, eventually start something brilliant and new, and without Dominic and Geoffrey, of course.

Now, he thought the first part of that plan was necessary and the second weak and stupid – weak and stupid and wasteful. Those two could not scare him into retreat.

He was nearing the end of the woodland and the protection it gave and must work out soon how to manage the last hundred and fifty yards or so to the house. He stopped behind a beech, watching Maidrew and wishing he had night glasses as well as a pistol. Perhaps Jane was looking out from one of the windows. She would expect Pillar to come for them as soon as he discovered they were prisoners. For the moment he had to stay hidden. She might not be the only one looking out. His concealment would have to end very soon, though. Whichever way he picked for the final lap, it would entail getting across open ground of lawns, gardens and forecourt, or the paddock and yard at the back. Perhaps the back was a little better. Even if he had a gun, what would he do – wave it about as he tackled this final bit, like a lion-hearted subaltern leading troops over the top?

He was not lion-hearted, not always – not always even honourable. Perhaps his yellowness had spread further than the wish to bolt abroad with Jane and Edward. He realised there had been instants – very fleeting, hardly perceptible instants, but definitely there – instants when he considered doing a bunk alone. He had feared it might be impossible to reclaim Jane and the boy. Describing these warders at Maidrew as his father and mother could be a macabre Dominic joke. Perhaps they were hired people skilled at all sorts of heavy work. Even if they *were* Dominic's parents they could be skilled at all sorts of heavy work. That was the kind of parents you would expect for Dominic. There would almost certainly be guns around, and he had realised then what he was still aware of now, that more than two people could be guarding Maidrew and the surrounds. In the Bay flat, viewing the difficulties like this, Pillar had considered clearing out to the Continent on his own, though unquestionably with the intention of coming back for Jane and Edward one day when things grew more relaxed. Surely they would not be in danger once Pillar had gone and could no longer be pressured through them.

Neither of those miserable escape reactions had lasted, thank God, but as he edged on again towards Maidrew now he felt an almost crippling shame at recalling them, and especially that selfish, solo plan. Disgusting. Not typical. God, no. He had come for them, hadn't he, and would move them to the Bay?

He knew this patch of woodland pretty well from strolls with Jane and the boy, but he went gingerly, his eyes all round. That did not signify much in the dark, though. If Dominic and Geoffrey expected him to come for his wife and child – and, of course, like Jane, they *would* expect it, knowing him, his love for them and decisiveness – if they expected him to come they would not simply garrison Maidrew. Perhaps men had been placed in the likely approach routes, such as this rectangle of woods. Dominic and Geoffrey could hire special staff. Pillar moved from the cover of one fat tree to another, paused, squinted about and listened, then moved on slowly again. He knew this might be absurd. He could be standing on the wrong side of the tree and utterly exposed to attack from behind. But, oh, Christ, it was just something you did when creeping up through woods. Those jungle war films.

He had no flashlight. A fall could mean noise. And he wanted no damage to his legs or feet. There might be some sprinting to do finally, probably carrying the child. He had left the Mercedes on a side road half a mile away. He thought that about right. The car was near enough for Jane and Edward and him to reach quickly once he brought them from the house. But he had needed to make sure the engine was not heard at Maidrew when he first arrived. Car sounds carried in the country late at night.

He reached the last of the trees. The lawns and flower beds began now. Briefly, he sat down with his back to another beech to rest and decide on the final bit. Although he was strained and tired he felt athletic enough, clear-headed enough, and he tried to apply to this exercise what he knew about strategic thinking. This he was trained in. After Balliol he took a master's in Business Administration at Bath University and corporate strategy was a course. True, there had not been too much in the classes about how to wipe out someone like Adrian Garrant before he could talk, nor about how to get your family back if business colleagues made them hostage. But the general message from the course still gripped him. It said what all organisation-man courses probably said, that nothing mattered more than advancement and improvement of the firm you worked for. Pillar had accepted this at the time and accepted it now. It was in his nature, it was his core, and he would probably have believed it even without the seminars. This was why he had come to Maidrew tonight, and why he would not turn back. He still believed he must hold together the partnership with Dominic and Geoffrey, despite their crude, threatening action against Jane and the child. He could deal with that, *would* deal with it, even make a plus of it. This was something else from the strategy course. You looked for ways to turn threats into pluses. The reverse take-over gambit. His determination was solid now. He believed he could undo this gross, panicky little ploy by those two and still keep the business intact. It must not disintegrate.

He stood up and did another systematic eye search of the façade, working slowly from window to window and taking in the roof this time. The company, the company – you looked after the company. The company was Dominic, Geoffrey and himself. Those two would provide the capital for the *Terra Nova* scheme, and were irreplaceable – shitty, but irreplaceable. The *Terra Nova* scheme was brilliant, and his, and had to work. And it could work, as long as he personally operated it. Once he had Jane and Edward safe he *would* be able to operate it personally. All that prime power would be his again, with Dominic and Geoffrey hammered and subordinate. Were they much more than pathetic, flawed money-bags who could be taken for 1.6 million by a partner, and who inhumanly tried to pressurise Pillar through his wife and child? Pillar's power would be especially secure if Garrant were dead. And he would be, had to be. Any leaks in the interrogation room and the company was finished. This, at least, Dominic and Geoffrey had correct. The present episode was about more than a man saving his wife and child. It *was* about a man saving his wife and child and re-establishing his authority in the firm, but it was also about providing for the end of someone who could imperil the partnership if he were not instantly seen to. These were two parts of the same mission. And it was because Garrant's death must follow at once after Pillar reclaimed his family that he had decided he could not bring Jenkins. To let him deep into Pillar's private anxieties seemed too risky when the next anxiety must be how to fix an execution. Glyndwr was bright and very quick at sensing and spotting. Jenkins had been a friend and perhaps still was, with all the loyalties this brought. Now, though, Jenkins was also the police, with all the loyalties *that* brought.

Pillar stepped out from behind the beech and started to march openly towards the house, head up. This was how they used to behave in those Oxford days, he and Jenkins and a few others. When looking for a fight they would simply stroll direct and confident into one of the pubs where undergraduates were hated, nothing furtive or hesitant – the quick way to tell the other customers they were due a thumping. Pillar longed for the simplicity and bravado of those days. He never showed yellow then, and he wouldn't now. He quickened his pace, staring all the time at Maidrew. He had the beginnings of a smile on, a smile that said, *Watch me, I'm a winner.*

Suddenly he dropped to a crouch and, turning, stayed down like that and scuttled back to cover behind the beech. Jesus, what fucking bollocks that had been, the Memory Lane stuff. This was not Saturday night piss-up and punch-up time. This was a defended house and the lives of his wife and child. This was possibly firearms, and possibly people who knew a lot more about violence than Pillar did, possibly even Dominic and Geoffrey themselves. He left the beech tree again but did not repeat his one-man gung-ho assault on the front of Maidrew. Instead, he abandoned the path and began to pick his way laterally across the woodland rather than following its length. This was even harder, slower progress, but he would eventually come out at the rear of Maidrew, and remain hidden most of the way. Although the last part of the approach to the house was exposed, here, too, a few outbuildings would provide some concealment, and the wood came up closer to the back of the property. He would sneak in, if he could, not go for glory at the main entrance. Glory and the career he had picked did not mix. Just the same, he hated having to skulk like this around his own property. An insult. Tenacity and opportunism had helped him corner the funds to buy this home, qualities much pushed on the MBA course.

When he reached the rim of the wood at the back of Maidrew he saw a light burning on the first floor in what should be Edward's bedroom. He waited again, hidden by the trees. Perhaps Jane left the light on all night as a comfort, if the boy was frightened by changes in the household and the presence of strangers. Pillar listened for a child's crying or Jane talking but could make out nothing. He grew impatient and very jumpy. Soon it would be dawn.

Another light suddenly appeared, perhaps on the stairs, and a moment afterwards the kitchen door into the yard was pulled open and Jane came out carrying Edward in both arms. She had on day clothes and so did the child. Pillar wanted to yell in relief. She must have spotted him from a window and come down quietly with the boy to rendezvous and to flee. He did not yell but moved out a little from the trees and called her name twice very softly. She heard at once and turned towards him. He thought she shook her head slightly, very slightly. Because of the darkness and distance he could not be certain. He went towards them, walking quickly, resolutely.

The door opened again and Dominic and Geoffrey emerged at a dawdle and stood behind Jane and the child, one to each side. At the same time, Pillar picked up the sound of an approaching car, perhaps more than one. 'Kim,' Dominic called, 'you wanted to see Jane and the little fellow were all right, did you, and isn't that natural? Natural and creditable. Well, here they are – Jane a little peeved at having been pulled out of bed in the middle of the night, but I said it would be a kindness to you and that you would wish to return as soon as you could to the Bay. I mentioned that you had our plans to look after down there, our funds also – well, 1.6 million just to start with. These responsibilities meant that you certainly could not be absent from the Bay for long. And so Jane agreed this small-hours get-together. But it must be brief. In fact, I'm afraid Edward has already fallen back into slumber. What an asset! Why, here's mother now with your car.'

Dominic's big BMW, driven by a bald man in his late fifties, entered the yard followed by Pillar's Mercedes. An elderly woman with a cigarette in her mouth was at the wheel. Both cars stopped, their headlights on Pillar.

'I thought it easier if you didn't have to hike it all the way back to your vehicle,' Dominic said. 'Luckily Jane had a Mercedes key. You can leave immediately, you see.'

The woman climbed out of the car and left the driver's door open and the engine running. She made a welcoming gesture, inviting him to replace her in the front seat.

'Jane,' Pillar said, 'is everything –?'

'Everything's fine,' Dominic said. 'Well, of course it's fine. Aren't she and the boy safe at home? I'm glad you've left the door open, mother, for an airing. We don't want Kim dead from passive smoking.'

20

After they had made love in the morning Mair said: 'There was an important phone call.'

'When?' Jenkins asked.

'Last evening.'

'Important how?'

'This was a man wanting you urgently. A commanding, very *unlocal* sort of voice. Clearly not someone who would disclose any matters to me or my Welsh-accent sort. Terse with me.'

Often during, and briefly after, sex Mair liked to behave like an eternal nothing. She seemed able to get off on that as well as enjoying it for a while post coitus. Apparently, this was her way of acting out the condition of Wales, what she sometimes called 'a subject nation', an 'English colony even after devolution'. She drew vast excitement from the fiction that she must be continuously on tap and heat for a conqueror. This made no sense, since Jenkins was also Welsh. But it was not about sense, it was about getting there.

In any case, Jenkins was never going to be as *truly* Welsh as Mair. She could chart her family back at least a century and a half to farmers in the foothills of Snowdonia. Her mother had inherited a huge Bible where the ancestry was laid out in a genealogical table on the flyleaf, nearly up to Chronicles class. In contrast, Jenkins' lineage as a Welshman was short. His skin proved it. At some point in his ancestry was an invader. Invaders took. She adored being taken and at the best moments, which were admittedly terrific, would howl words of thrilled servitude, though for some reason not in Welsh. This morning with her legs wrapped hard around him like straps on a suitcase she screamed: 'Oh, what, what are you doing to me?' The brilliant make-believe was that this triumphant foreign aggressor brought bed behaviour she had never met before, not with her ex-husband or other partners, nor through sex manuals eyed secretly as a kid in Betws-y-Coed.

'Educated voice?' he asked.

'Oh, entirely.'

'Businesslike?'

'A "Do this and he doeth it" voice. Boardroom.'

'He told you nothing?'

'Would he? Who am *I*?'

Mair went for love-making in the mornings. The night was too routine and mutual. Sex around dawn was supposed to demonstrate she must be always on call for the victor, proclaimed that no time was her own. Exploitation she lusted for. It gave her pathos and the tragic grandeur of a crushed people. After the frenzy of her surrenders she would continue for minutes to treat Glyndwr as member of a ruling clan – for instance, someone worthy of mysterious, weighty calls from mysterious, weighty strangers. She had delayed mentioning the most recent until doing her down-trodden bit. This would make her feel she was no more than a go-between, the native runner, message in a cleft stick.

And a fucking slow-running native. Jenkins did not object to the fantasising, knew she was still the same warm, raw, ego-maniac, nasal, loving, lovable woman regardless, but he would have liked to hear about the call sooner. 'No number?' he asked. The tone Mair described sounded like Kim Pillar.

'He said he'd ring back.'

'He didn't?'

'No.'

'Did you try to check him by dialling 1471?'

'I did not feel it was my place to snoop.' Mair got out of bed, showered and started to dress for work. Still lying in bed, Jenkins watched what he could of this. As ever he delighted in the energy and grace on display, and in her tall, lean, fluent body. He worshipped her long neck and the symmetry of her knees, which were at about his eye level. These knees had been handed down, knees perfected lifetimes ago by forebears scaling damned tough slopes to get sheep in. With extreme decisiveness she pulled on her very pricey, Belle du Jour Paris-bought knickers. Unlocal. Her spell as Celtic plaything was probably over, most entrances sealed off. 'In any case,' she said, 'every bastard who rings you has always done 141 and made tracing impossible. I don't bother. Why should I ruin my head against a brick wall? You seem troubled.'

He thought that the phrase should be *run* one's head against a brick wall, but ruin was stronger. English gained from all kinds of input, including North Walian. He said: 'Not troubled, curious.'

'I can't make the buggers talk if they don't want to.'

'You're not at all to blame, Mair.'

'Who do you think it was?'

'Puzzling.'

'You're another bugger I can't make talk.' It was a snarl and yet real sadness came through. He knew she often felt distanced. Did he need to be so secretive with her? Did he strain her patience and loyalty? That would be cruel and idiotic, wouldn't it?

'Shortlist of twenty possibles,' he said.

'Don't kid me you know twenty educated people.'

'Perhaps I'll hang on here a while in case he does ring back,' Jenkins replied. Or most probably he would drive to Pillar's flat in the converted warehouse.

Mair had not put her skirt and blouse on yet and stood close to the bed gazing down at him where he lay on his side, looking at her. A tuft of fair-to-auburn pubic hair curled out around the silken gusset, perhaps a design fault. Of the knickers. 'Oh, my God, you want me yet again. It's outrageous,' she groaned.

'I do.' He made sure nothing in his voice even hinted at a question, but then asked: 'Is there time?'

'What do you care about my time?'

He had been wrong. Her serf mood was still busy or had bounced back. 'I meant the office,' he replied.

'What do you care about the Wales Tourist Board?'

'True.'

She took off the Belle du Jours and then her bra. For a couple of seconds she remained standing there, not a pose, an offer of tribute.

'God, Mair,' he said, 'you look such a prize.'

She got into bed and began to lick his chest all over. He had not known how good that could be until she showed him a few months ago. He doubted whether this flair was something passed down to her from history like her knees. While she did it, she needed Jenkins to stroke the underside of one of her arms, her armpit and a breast, a slow, very regular movement going on a long while. For up to ten minutes life was reduced to nipples – enlarged to nipples if the alternative was getting to her job at the Tourist Board or calling on Pillar.

'Who would have thought you were so gentle,' she said.

'Not always.'

'No, not always or where would we be?'

'Only for ever on the way to something,' he said.

'Mind, on the way to something can be brilliant, especially if one has already been there once or twice lately already.'

'Was it once or twice?' he asked.

'Let's avoid data.' She turned on to her back. 'We could end the gentleness now.' She welcomed him on top of her with a great fatalistic tremor. 'I always knew something like this would happen to me,' she said.

'How?'

'It's a sort of folk thing – yes, folk foreknowledge.'

'Did it tell you it would happen so often, though?' Jenkins asked.

'Let's avoid data?' she replied. 'Data and gentleness.' Not long afterwards she cried out: 'How can you do this to me, Glyndwr?' but he did not answer. He did not know how he could do it to her but was grateful he could. In any case, he was not interested in more talk.

At the Bay apartment block, Jenkins announced himself on the building's security screener and was invited up. The Mercedes stood parked in the yard. It was mud-streaked: some overnight rural driving?

'A private talk, Glyn!' Pillar said. 'I'm glad. I've thought a few times about ringing you to propose a meeting but then I wondered whether that was proper. Would I look like a businessman touting for favours from a police officer? I can't deny that the police attitude to our proposal might turn out crucial.'

'This may be Bay City, but it's not *Chandler's* Bay City, you know, Kim.'

'Of course I know. Would I want to be part of anything like that – corruption, violence? Just the same, I have to be careful not to embarrass you. So, I didn't call, wouldn't. But now here you are, unprompted, obviously feeling the need of a chat yourself. My hesitancies are resolved for me. Splendid! Early for a drink? Coffee?'

'Fine,' Jenkins said, sitting down on a green damask sofa. He did not have many kinks but if there was one material he liked under his arse it was damask. Any colour. 'Kim, you ought to get out.'

Pillar, on his way to the kitchen, stopped and turned, perhaps genuinely startled. 'Get out? Of this flat? Why?'

'Of the Bay.'

He seemed to think about that for a minute. 'This is Brade talking?' Pillar remained standing near the model of the Scott ship, mild, attentive. He was in jeans and a blue sweatshirt. He looked antiseptic and haggard, as from a recent bad time. 'Brade sent you? He still has power to do that, despite all these rumours? My God, Glyn, a senior police officer in disastrous sex games. The Press on to it, I heard, but afraid of libel, to date. Some ace woman investigative reporter, I gather – Fiston, Susan Fiston of *Six Days*. That's the rumour.'

'Suppose you wanted to quit your business involvements here immediately, could you?' Jenkins replied.

'Could I?'

'Are you tied in somehow? A debt, for instance.'

'I hope I'm free to do whatever I like.'

'Yes, *I* hope you are,' Jenkins said.

'I'm a partner in a company. I have responsibilities. I don't know if that's what you mean. I have obligations in the Bay. In this very special sense I don't think I could "get out", as you put it, even if I wished. I'd be letting down too many folk. As with any business company there is interdependency of people at the top.'

Jesus, the claptrap. Jenkins would have liked to moan and froth. Although Pillar wanted to recall and trade on those all-pals-together Oxford days, he spoke a business lingo that held Jenkins off, cold-shouldered him with its corniness. In ten years people learned new outlooks, crap phrasing. As concealment, Pillar had put up a company prospectus around himself. Jenkins felt he was ruining his head against it. 'You don't *need* this fucking awful restaurant project, do you, Kim?' Jenkins pointed at the model. 'You're already at least comfy? Why take on such risk? I'm not sure we can protect you. I'd like to because you're you but . . . And then your family.'

His face tightened. 'What?'

'Where are they?' Jenkins replied.

'Maidrew, of course.'

'They're all right?'

'Maidrew's our home. This flat is just a cottage with the job. And so my family are where families ought to be, at home. Certainly they're all right. Why not?' For a moment he began to shout, then forced himself to become matter-of-fact again. 'They're fine. Of course.'

Two 'of courses'. Everything so supremely ordinary and settled. Christ, what had happened to the woman and the boy?

'We decided, Jane and I, that they'd be better off there, at least for now,' Pillar said. 'I'm going to be chasing around setting up the *Terra Nova* and wouldn't really have much time to give them here. Perhaps when the project is under way they can move in for a while.'

'You see them?' Jenkins asked.

'Of course, of course. I'll be able to get there most weekends.' He continued into the kitchen now, shutting down the topic.

But Jenkins stood and called after him: 'When were you last there?' Pillar might not have heard. Or he might have. There was no reply and Jenkins did not repeat the question. The topic seemed to hurt Kim. *Of course* it did. How easy would it be to find this house, this *home*?

When Pillar came back it was with coffee in mugs on a silver tray. Jenkins said: 'So where *is* the famous Maidrew?'

'In royal residence Land Rover country. Wiltshire. Near Melksham.'

'Lovely.'

'Yes, it is. A therapy to get away there.'

'Open?'

'How do you mean?'

'Parkland around it? Woods? Acres?'

'It's in grounds, obviously,' Pillar replied. 'A small estate.'

'A wall? Alarms?'

'No wall. My God, the cost.'

'Not even around the house?'

'The house is famous for its views,' Pillar said. 'Alarms would scare Jane.'

'You must have had some real coups to raise that kind of money. Stables, paddocks, wine cellar?'

'Nothing enormous.'

'Which – the cellar or the coups?' Jenkins asked.

'I did a few good deals, yes. For a couple of years under Thatcher and Major it was hard to fail.'

'That's what I mean, you could quit. You've got Maidrew and a pile in the bank, I expect. Just sit it out. It's not disputed money, is it?'

'Sit what out? Am I the kind to give up, Glyndwr? You know Kim Pillar. Play the full eighty minutes.' He giggled. 'Wow, hark at the headmaster – but it's true, I don't chuck in.'

'You know what I mean when I say disputed money? Some cornering of company funds. Alleged. Always happening.'

'A wonderfully forward-looking concept like the Bay – it's a tonic, even to an outsider,' Pillar replied.

'People feel envy, hatred.'

'Which people?'

'The big trio. Perhaps others,' Jenkins replied.

'Which big trio?'

'Oh, you know, don't you, Kim?'

'No, who?'

'The team who think you'll rip off their markets. Cordial, Simeon, A.W. The three who hired Indiment to do you.'

'Well, if you know that –'

'I don't *know* it,' Jenkins replied. 'Not as a court would require me to know it. I only know it.'

'Well, I *don't* know it, not in any sense.' He drank some coffee and spoke from behind the raised mug. 'For God's sake, Glyn, this was a professional assassin, as I understand things, like Edward Fox in *Day of the Jackal*. Don't you see it's ludicrous to think anyone, or any three, would hire a hit man to dispose of Kim Pillar? I'm not de Gaulle. I'm someone looking to start an eatery.'

'Mair gave me a voice profile of a man like you who rang the flat last night,' Jenkins replied. 'Was there an emergency, Kim? It's over?'

'What emergency?' Pillar asked. 'No call from me.'

'I want to help you. The only way I can is to tell you to disappear from the Bay. This pair, your partners, can they pressure you somehow?'

'Pressure? Why say that?'

'Because I've heard of them and they're the kind who pressure. Because if you were free you'd read the signals and move off. Because you know your *Terra Nova* has only a forty to sixty per cent chance and you'd almost certainly do better somewhere else.'

Pillar gave his eyes integrity. 'It's a fine scheme and wonderfully meaningful in the Bay context, Glyn. I've never been more committed to anything. And you'll remember from far, far back that when I get an *idée fixe* it couldn't be more *fixe*. Do you recall when –?'

Fuck recall. So, a bit late in the meeting, Pillar was going to try the old mates rigmarole out in the open. Public relations. 'Your partners will be damned pissed off with Garrant, I should think,' Jenkins replied.

'Garrant?'

'Killing those two so they couldn't name him for Indiment. This could lead back to your colleagues. My Lord, Kim, they might expect you to get rid of him, or at least help. Have you been given orders?'

'Which two?' Pillar asked. 'You mean the people Brade and the vicar were involved with? "Name him for Indiment"? What's it about, Glyn? And Garrant? Should I know him, of him? I'm still behind on names here. That's why it's so helpful to talk. How do you mean, "get rid"?'

'Don't let them push anything like that on to you. He's formidable. We haven't been able to touch him so far.'

'Anything like what?'

'Or, if you can't leave, you should move in with us,' Jenkins replied. 'Just till we see how things shape. Mair wouldn't mind. She loved your telephone style.'

Pillar looked confused, almost appalled. 'That's incredibly kind of you, Glyn.'

'I feel . . . I feel a bit obligated. People have you marked because we knew each other, know each other. So, my fault, in part. You could carry on with your work if you have to, and you wouldn't be on offer, like a target. This place is known everywhere after that presentation.'

'Yes, so kind, but I really can't, Glyn.'

'You *have* to stay here? Is the flat crucial to some ploy?'

'Really, couldn't impose myself like that, not even for old times' sake.'

21

Now and then Kate worked through lunchtime at her office, and today Brade had bought a Chinese takeaway for him and Hale-Garning. They were eating together in the flat when Brade heard through the part open window what he took to be the sound of a skateboard in the street and then someone calling his name. He crossed the room and looked down. A woman of around forty-five waved. She had on a khaki balaclava helmet, a long raincoat, or perhaps two, and glistening blue and white trainers. He recognised her and the gear. Or he recognised the gear first and then her.

Cliff joined him at the window. He was in a jumpy state again and wanted to be close to Brade continuously, like a dog just back from the kennels. Grief for Semprina downed him. Also, he was still obsessed by dread of a priestly attack. He knew, *knew*, that his towering status as holy maverick had led his bosses in the cloth to doom him. Staring at the visitor he asked, 'Who is she, Dave? They wouldn't draw the line at disguise. A balaclava. What's behind it?' While they ate he had listed colleagues in the Church who wanted him at least retransported to Mid-Wales sticksland, and if possible defrocked. Hale-Garning wore the sleeved vest and multi-coloured beach shorts he probably slept in. There was still a kind of dignity to him but a special kind.

Brade returned Beryl Costo's wave, inviting her up to the second-floor flat. He knew her as a friend of Pedal and Terence Jerome Machen. Brade tried to keep a contact with all the folk in those ruins. Some of them needed looking after, and they saw things, heard things, just as Pedal did, though few of them were prepared to tell as much as Pedal. Perhaps they were wise.

She put the skateboard under her arm and disappeared through the apartment block's main doorway. Brade went out to meet the lift and brought her into the flat. 'Terry is talking to someone we think you should meet,' she said. 'Could you come to the Bay right away? We asked one of the girls for your address and your phone number, but Terry said for me to see you in person because one never knows what sort of jiggery pokery there might be on a detective's line. He'll keep talking until we arrive, although it's taken me ages to get out here, even on the board.'

Hale-Garning snarled: 'Mr Brade can't just drop everything and go to the properties.'

'You're the vicar?' she replied.

'A clergyman.'

'You've been mentioned in general dockland chat, too. Well, obviously.'

'Mentioned?' Brade asked.

'As to blame.'

'Dave, I implore you, get rid of –'

'We believe none of it, Terry and I,' she said. 'We *know* what happened.'

'Terry?' Clifford asked. 'Terry What? You keep speaking of him. I know a Terry in the Church. Gushing rancid lout of vast envy.'

'This will be Terry Machen, won't it, Beryl?' Brade replied. 'A neighbour from the properties.'

'Terry's first class with conversation, ask Glyndwr,' she said. 'He'll keep this reporter interested until we get there. Putting her right, naturally, but also just occupying time so you can defend yourself in person, Mr Brade. She came on the trawl to our dwellings. People think they're meeting the nitty-gritty when they meet us – one down from slumming.'

'Reporter?' Hale-Garning asked.

'Not just local,' she replied.

'Oh, hell, have I drawn the London Press?' Cliff said.

Costo strolled about the room, brisk in her fine trainers, almost flashy, the skateboard still under her arm. Perhaps she was reminding herself what it used to be like living in standard accommodation. She smiled now and then, but Brade could not tell whether it was from pleasure at returning to furniture, carpets, pictures – even *his* kind of furniture, carpets and pictures – or relief at the knowledge that she needn't stay long. She said: 'The reporter told us she wants to look at the killings and so on in their widest turn-of-the-millennium context.'

'Jargonising bitch!' Cliffy remarked.

'She's got all the tripey rumour about Mr Brade and the sexual practices with Semprina and Pedal,' Costo stated. 'And about you, if you *are* the said man of God.'

'Of course I'm the fucking said man of God,' Hale-Garning replied. 'Who in the cathedral sent you? Terry Dace? You're here to frighten, poison and disrupt, aren't you?'

'Her name is Fiston,' she replied. 'What's called *investigative*, you know. Turning over stones and bleating loud about public interest.'

'From *Six Days*,' Brade said.

'You know her, Dave?' Clifford said, his voice all at once squeaky with suspicion.

'A heavyweight sheet, not the tabloids,' Costo replied.

'I'd better go and see her,' Brade said.

'In the properties?' Hale-Garling demanded. 'This is lunacy, Dave. You'll be unprotected.'

'From what?' Brade replied.

'All we have is this woman's word.'

'Beryl is reliable.'

'I, too, must come then,' Hale-Garning said.

'This is a strictly police matter, Cliff,' Brade replied. 'Confidential.'

'How, how can that be, Dave? My career is involved here, my reputation. We are confronted, surely, by a high conspiracy against Clifford Hale-Garning.'

Costo turned her fattish, motherly face towards him and spoke considerately: 'Fiston's interested mainly in Mr Brade.'

'Do I believe this?' Clifford asked.

Costo removed the balaclava and raincoats. She did this slowly and possibly against her will, an act of politeness only, as though discarding the items put her back into bourgeoisville. Beneath the coats she wore denim dungarees and a navy cardigan. She placed the balaclava and coats on a straight-backed chair and her skateboard underneath, where she could keep it in view.

'I'll find some food for you,' Brade said.

'Any kind of meat,' she said. 'Kidneys, sausage, steak, liver. Coffee rather than tea. No cereal. Laver bread?' She went to the raincoats and brought a fork and tablespoon from one of the pockets. Her wish to get back urgently seemed to have been suspended at the prospect of a meal.

'And we'll fill a carrier bag to take to the properties,' Brade replied. 'What does Terry like?'

'Bulk,' she said. 'He's a poet, but he loves pork pies and saveloys. As to beverages, Sauterne, or at a push, sherry.' She glanced about. 'As a matter of fact I used to live not far from here myself. I grew out of it, that's all. The double glazing and school run. Perhaps one day I'll go back. Oh, God.'

After she had eaten, Brade drove the two of them to the carpentry works in Collingdon Road where Terry Machen and the journalist waited. At once Hale-Garning shoved his Christian warrior features towards Fiston and said: 'Madam, have you allowed yourself to be made an instrument of by a malign, scabrous, playful cabal within the Church? If so, how can you reconcile it with your responsibilities as a member of a supposedly free Press?' He wore his dog collar and a dark suit now. His voice was strong and heavy with mourning.

Terry said: 'I have given no name because it was Pedal's wish no name should be given, but, as to the buzz, I've told Ms Fiston it's impossible that you, Reverend Hale-Garning, and Mr Brade should have –'

'Oh, it's Adrian Barnaby Garrant, isn't it?' Fiston replied. 'I'd heard of him, naturally. A crooked colossus. One came to the Bay to look into the sex slip-up rumours and associated corruption tales, yes. But the slightest inquiry revealed these were nonsense. And then there is Terence, so informed, so convincing, so graphic, even without giving the name. Upshot – it has to be Garrant for all three. He must be exposed. If I do that, you'll have to take him in, won't you, Mr Brade.'

'You should be careful,' he replied.

'Obviously, I'll talk to him and put what one has discovered,' Fiston said.

'I don't know about that,' Brade replied. 'This man runs an operation.'

'Is allowed to?' The voice was at least unsuburban and possibly upper-class, languid and sure, the kind of voice servants once jumped to it for.

'You can't print anything,' Brade told her. 'There are no charges.'

'Why are there no charges?' she replied.

'How dare you!' Cliff cried. 'That's twice. Are you suggesting Dave has been paid to go easy?'

'Someone somewhere might have been,' Fiston replied. It was said with matter-of-factness. Cliffy's rages did not reach her. She would be about fifty, square built and with a square, small-nosed face full of what could be intelligence or vanity or the determination to plump up her pension fund. She and Terry sat facing each other on benches nicely constructed from piles of bricks and timber taken from a Collingdon Road flydump. The reporter was in a dark green blouson-style wool jacket and brown cord trousers. She wore brown suede boots, scuffed but good quality, right for the properties. A carrier bag with provisions in it was against Terry's bench, the necks of two bottles sticking out. Brade experienced a pleasant atmosphere of primitive comfort and plenty. They had stopped at an off-licence to buy him the Sauterne.

'We're working on all three deaths,' Brade said.

'It's too late when there are charges,' Fiston replied. 'Everyone knows then. Press Office handouts. One aims for exclusives. Besides, the law won't let us report any more than there *have* been charges. I want to tell the whole tale.'

'I say again, a powerful lad who will look after himself,' Brade replied.

'Yes, I heard,' she answered. 'I regard it as my job to take on powerful lads. Don't you, Brade? What else is a worthwhile Press for?'

'Don't hit us with that shit,' Cliffy replied. 'A worthwhile Press is one that's worthwhile for the owners.'

It was a good sunny afternoon and the wrecked building had plenty of light reaching in through window and door spaces where the boarding up had been torn away. Slates from part of the roof were gone and sunshine penetrated there, too, slowly shrinking storm-water floor pools. On such days the decayed workshops had a sort of rough chicness uniquely theirs, and Brade could see why Costo and others might tire of life in Llandaff and escape here. Irksome domesticity and house-proudness could probably have no place in the properties. Himself, he was happy in Llandaff now, but only thanks to Kate.

Terry said: 'Perhaps we could assist in your hunt of the guilty man, Ms Fiston – we, the people from the properties.'

'United we, too, are powerful,' Beryl Costo declared. 'Pedal's gone, yes, but there are others.' Brade watched her swing an arm like summoning reserve regiments from the adjoining shells.

'Magnificent of you, Terry, Beryl,' Brade said, 'but too dangerous.'

They all grew silent for a while, charmed by the setting. Shadow patterns changed thrillingly around them as clouds obscured the sun then moved clear, and when remnants of the door and window boarding shifted in the breeze. Particles of broken glass among the floor debris glinted happily for seconds at a time before lapsing again into dullness as the light went. This would be one of the most select addresses in the road, despite its partial loss of roof, and Brade thought Terry Machen smart to have chosen it for his conference with the reporter. Surroundings could impart weight. Sad the place would have to go soon, as redevelopment progressed, but Brade felt delighted that during these final months there was life here and important transactions. Old dockland still had a brilliantly constructive role. The flashing fragments of glass amid the rubble seemed symbolic.

'But I, where am I in all this?' Cliffy cried, stamping his black lace-ups angrily on the littered floor. 'Am I not a target? Can you really tell me, Fiston, that no envious, godly Church in Wales coven contacted your paper seeking my destruction? Think now, try to recall. Most likely it would come as a spiritually defunct, slimy voice on your telephone, probably anonymous, nominating me for extinction. The sod would possibly refer to me as Hale-Garning, but perhaps also Clifford, Cliffy, Cliff or the Llandrindod Dickhead.'

'Nobody like that has spoken to us,' Fiston replied.

'So why not?' Cliffy demanded. 'Does that holy mob think all of a sudden I'm negligible?'

22

Maidrew had a spot on the Ordnance Survey map and Jenkins found the estate in the early part of the evening, then waited for nightfall. He did not take the car close. In the country vehicles and vehicle noises might be noticed. Things were not right with Pillar's family. Jenkins had sensed his way to this conviction, guessed his way, hunched his way. He needed surprise at the house. When it grew dark he began walking. He had the knuckleduster with him.

What he might do here rated as good policing, he reckoned. It meant restoring Pillar's wife and child to him. That could not be seen as wrong, surely. If this restoration was needed, and if he could manage it, Jenkins would be able to do more than ensure the woman and child's safety. Once Pillar recovered them he might agree to quit the Bay. Jenkins should be able to persuade him to seek a hiding place for the three abroad, or at least somewhere else in Britain. From talking to Pillar and observing him and filling in the pauses at the flat Jenkins judged that he did not know how to get his wife and son back for himself. Or he might have tried and failed. Oddly, at times Jenkins felt he could be treading ground that Pillar had trodden very recently. Perhaps people expected Pillar to try and had him watched, were ready to get Maidrew fully guarded if he left the Bay. They would not be watching Jenkins or expecting him. He thought he owed Pillar this much. They had always looked after each other in pub scraps. But, God, how maudlin and macho and powerful this relationship was. It had boundaries, though. Jenkins wanted him gone, if possible for ever. The Bay would have a better chance of peace then. Good policing.

He approached on foot through a wood of mainly beech and elder to the south-west of the house. For most of the time he could make out a slender path even in the dark. Brambles tugged at his clothes. Occasionally, when the trees thinned, he glimpsed the building. Jenkins knew history but he did not know architecture. He thought Maidrew would be late Georgian, maybe even Victorian. When did ten-pot chimneys arrive? The coalfields must have been hard at it by then. About 1840?

There was a grey, squat look to the mansion in the dark. He liked a bit of height in old places, so they could get themselves noticed on an horizon, shout their survival. Maidrew skulked and lurked, no elegance. It was not right for Pillar. He loved display. Neon was his element. Didn't he clang a ship's bell before he made that *Terra Nova* speech? Jenkins wondered briefly whether it was worth saving the wife and child of someone dim enough to buy a dull, aged tip like this for probably hundreds of grand, even if only to get rid of him from the Bay.

Then he pushed on towards the edge of the wood for a proper gaze at Maidrew and to think about access. He was pretty good on locks. No alarms, according to Kim. Lawns and flower beds began now. This last stretch of the approach would be hopelessly exposed if there were someone watching. Would there be? It was about 3 a.m and Jenkins saw no lights. But he still thought Pillar had seemed frightened and defeated, and it would be wisest to expect opposition and round-the-clock alertness. Why the fuck was he here, otherwise – a black man doing the white knight turn because the white man couldn't? Perhaps Pillar's wife would be looking out, expecting Kim. He and Jenkins were about the same build. She might spot someone moving in the trees, imagine it was Pillar, grab the child and come to meet him. She would not be able to make out his face, its shape or colour.

All the same, he decided it would be stupid to try anything in full view and, leaving the path, began to force a way towards the back of Maidrew, across the wood, rather than along its length. In the rear there might be outbuildings to give cover over the last stretch. Or was he just trying to put off the time when he must come out from cover? Progress became difficult and slow. Why hadn't he been trained in jungle warfare?

At the back, several first-floor lights were visible through curtains. He had just reached the last trees to the rear there and, still concealed, fitted his knuckleduster while watching the lights. It would be perhaps two bedrooms illuminated and a landing. In a moment he heard what seemed to be screaming from that part of the house, and he thought he saw something move fast and in a downward arc across one of the curtained windows, like a blow with a pole or stick. The cries might be those of a child. They did not last long, or not as he first heard them. The screams seemed to get part stifled, or possibly they changed into something else, something more helpless and liquid, as if the child were choking and fighting for air. Jenkins stood dazed for a few seconds, and then decided he must get into Maidrew at once, whether he was seen or not. Christ, it had been wrong to pussyfoot. He stepped towards the edge of the wood, but, just as he began to move out, someone pulled a rear door of the house hard open. He heard it before he saw it. There were still no lights downstairs. A woman appeared carrying a child wrapped in a blanket. She stepped forward, staring about. He heard the child retching repeatedly. 'Kim,' Jane Pillar called in a loud whisper.

He did not answer, waited to see whether anyone came out behind her.

'Kim,' she called again, slightly louder, slightly more anxious. 'Darling, I saw you at the front again. Didn't I? Did I? I knew you'd come back. Oh, where are you?' Suddenly she began to run towards the trees, but not the spot where Jenkins stood, and not as though she knew where she was going. She acted as if she had to get out of Maidrew immediately, it did not matter to where, as long as she escaped and could hide herself and her baby in the woodland.

'I'm here,' Jenkins said, getting into view.

She stopped.

'I played rugby with your husband,' he said.

'You fucking *what*?'

'At Oxford.'

She remained still for a second, her mind working on these testimonials. She had been holding the child with only one arm but now put the other around him as well, more protection. The blanket looked soaked, stained. In the dark he could not make out colour either, only the wetness. She said: 'Yes, Kim spoke of you. You're the high-fly cop? He sent you?'

'Along those lines. What's the matter with the boy?'

'He's swallowed blood. I got some of it out. A *lot* of it out.'

'Whose?'

'Don't worry.'

'Whose?' he asked.

She began to walk towards him. The child still coughed and gasped. She was in khaki trousers and a brown leather jacket. 'Aren't there people watching you?' he asked.

'I've dealt with them,' she said.

'We go back through the wood,' he replied.

'Yes.' She walked faster. Soon they were into the trees. 'I've had to leave so much jewellery there, but the best stuff and all the cash is wrapped up with Edward. Watch we don't drip trinkets in the undergrowth, will you? Are you here as a friend or the police?' She asked it without venom, a request for information.

'It's tough getting through the wood,' he replied. 'Perhaps I should carry the child and loot.'

'Kim trusts you anything up to fifty per cent,' she said, handing him the bundle. 'You could take the brass knuckles off, though.' The blanket was soaked, sticky against his wrist. He could see now that the wetness was blood.

23

'This is merely what we could call a round-up get-together, Dave, Glyndwr,' Bullfinch said. 'To define where we're at.'

'Immensely helpful,' Brade replied.

'Plus, however, something . . . something, yes, significant I can bring to you.'

'This is great, sir,' Jenkins replied.

They were in Bullfinch's office at headquarters. Occasionally, when the meeting lost some of its traditional malice and grew dull, Jenkins found his mind slipping back to last night's car journey from Maidrew with Jane Pillar and the child. No, NO. His mind did not *slip* back to the trip home. He *sent* it back, and re-relished the sporadic conversation between him and Jane. He had a high-grade memory for words. Hadn't it helped him to his good Second at Oxford, which should have been a First, the footling, hair-splitting fuckers?

After about an hour in the car, Edward had seemed to recover and began breathing easily. She cleaned him up pretty well at a services station. They bought sandwiches there to eat *en route* and afterwards transferred her jewellery to the carrier bag the food had come in. The rug they dumped on to the motorway through the passenger window. Edward had slept the last part of the drive on her lap wrapped in an old coat which Jenkins kept in the car.

Listening to Bullfinch now with a particle of his mind, Jenkins recalled the comforting moment when the baby slid into quiet, easy sleep. Bullfinch was saying: 'At my rank one can feel a little removed from the *actualité*, as it were. Preciousness may set in. From time to time I need to be reminded of street-level pressures.' He spoke with a loud, grating nostalgia for the nitty-gritty. It was a fine Bullfinch show.

'Hard to think of you as precious, sir,' Jenkins said. 'Your instincts reach out, far out, sensing the currents with remarkable delicacy.'

'Obviously this is an aptitude that comes with my post, or one would be simply a peaked cap clerk.'

'That *will* be the day, sir!' Jenkins cried, tacking on a brilliant laugh.

'Even so, one does profit from contact with lads of your sort,' Bullfinch replied, 'and one is grateful for the patience you show to someone whose circumstances have become willy-nilly a little rarefied.'

'Our role is to feed our findings upwards for overall appraisal by the leadership,' Brade said.

And Jenkins thought Bullfinch did look full of leadership today, small blue eyes aglint, flat gold cufflinks well forward from his suit sleeves. He had lovely poise and even some consideration for subordinates until difficulties began. The suit was navy pin-stripe, one of four famous, bank-breaking London outfits custom-made after his last promotion, at least Jermyn Street and possibly Savile Row. Of the four, this suit above all gave Bullfinch thrust. Somehow, its majestic darkness and the emphatic quality of the stripes could make you forget some of his flakiness. The other suits were also good in their different modes, but this was the one he wore most. It parcelled him best, the waistcoat proud, high and possessive over his bony chest. Barristers' clerks and juke box marketers wore such suits. Bullfinch knew about image. Perhaps he had been on a course.

'But, as I promised . . . well, happily, there are a few occasions when *I* can supply some matters for *you*,' he said, 'in a kind of repayment.'

'This is grand, sir,' Brade said.

'Rare, but it does happen,' Bullfinch replied.

'Certainly not the first time,' Jenkins said.

'Here, then, is an instance,' Bullfinch answered, his head a little to the side, cheekily, proudly. 'It's something in which we can all take pleasure and perhaps some credit. On the face of it, this may seem to be not a strictly police matter, unconnected with crime and crime prevention. And yet, I feel it is, and in fact could hardly be more so.'

'That's good enough for me, sir,' Brade declared, 'and I'm sure for Glyndwr, too.'

Bullfinch was seated at his littered desk but leaned forward over it and became soft-voiced and confidential: 'As I understand things, the team behind the marvellous *Terra Nova* notion are so excited and comfortable about prospects here now that they have asked Kim Pillar – as you know, their main man in the Bay – yes, they've asked him to move his family down and really settle in. Become a part of us, an integral part. In fact, they are already installed.'

'Wow, this is quite a testimonial to the development, sir,' Jenkins said.

'I think so, Glyndwr,' Bullfinch replied. 'It testifies to long-term confidence rather than mere carpetbagging.'

'When did this happen, sir?' Jenkins asked.

'Only last night,' Bullfinch said.

'Congratulations on hearing so quickly,' Jenkins replied.

'Perhaps to your and Dave's surprise, one does have certain personal sources of information,' Bullfinch said. He ran a hand down and then up each of his lapels. Jenkins had seen him carry out this gesture in the suit at previous meetings. It asked whether anyone in such tailoring was likely to be short of high talents and all-round influence. 'I have to tell you that I feared – indeed still fear – feared and fear that recent events here – the deaths of Indiment, Semprina, Pedal Power Endicott – feared and fear such violence might begin to discourage investors,' Bullfinch continued. 'And particularly I dreaded what effects the kind of sickening rumour attached to Semprina and Pedal might have. This is what I mean when I say the *Terra Nova* decision does reflect on crime and policing. These people believe in us, regardless.'

'I'm damn glad to hear you describe it only as rumour, sir,' Brade replied.

'Persistent, fucking credible, and fucking awkward rumour, Dave,' Bullfinch said. 'But it has not deterred Pillar and his partners. They must feel – as I do myself – that these admittedly worrying incidents are simply features of a disturbed transformation period – horrifying, certainly, but only stirrings from the Bay's grim past, in no way indications of how things will be in the future. They have confidence we can maintain a decent and safe environment here, despite this outcrop of savagery and the total failure so far to detect who is responsible.'

Brade said: 'I –'

'I don't speak with any wish to condemn,' Bullfinch replied, 'and certainly with no suggestion that you have something to conceal, Dave. At this stage.'

'Grateful, sir,' Brade said.

'Some might allege you are up to your unclean neck in at least two of those deaths, Brade,' Bullfinch replied, 'you and your priest chum, and I would have to listen to the allegation. Not to be brushed off. But one is a professional and would ask, where is the evidence – evidence as distinct from speculation and likelihood?'

'I know I can always trust you to take my part, sir,' Brade said.

'Oh, what else is my role here?' Bullfinch asked. 'For *all* my people.'

'This is a consolation,' Jenkins replied.

'I'd like to bring in Adrian Barnaby Garrant as a possible for all three killings, sir,' Brade said.

Bullfinch looked appalled and gave his desk a slap. 'Garrant? I'd ask about him what I would ask about you, Dave – on what evidence? Is this going to look like a mere tactic, to take the attention off yourself?'

'Pedal Power might have seen him,' Brade replied. 'I had a letter. He probably spoke to friends.'

'To friends? To other tramps, you mean? Impressive. And hearsay only, anyway,' Bullfinch said. 'Useless. A fucking letter from the crem. A dead alleged witness who confided in dossers. Forget it, Dave.'

'Only to talk to Garrant a bit,' Brade replied. 'For clarification.'

'Forget it, Dave.'

Bullfinch began to describe the gorgeous Bay future as he saw it, and particularly how enlightened policing would provide secure and fitting conditions for wonderful proposals such as the *Terra Nova*. Jenkins wondered again whether Bullfinch was on a salary from Pillar and his partners. Perhaps one of them had been in touch to tell him about Jane and Edward's move. The message would probably not mention they were coming only because Jane had managed to break out from Maidrew. The message would try to get a smile on to the face of disaster. It would not mention either that Jane had needed to beat Dominic Ardnell's father unconscious with a poker while he bent considerately, suspiciously, over Edward in her bed, nor that Jenkins had provided the escape wagon. They would not know Jenkins had helped her, he hoped. This was to stay a secret between him and Jane and the child. Did Bullfinch fear Garrant might say something difficult for the *Terra Nova* team?

'. . . which is why I see the *Terra Nova* plan as so much more right for the Bay, so much more *authentic* and, yes, sexy, than this retaliatory, banal idea for a Driscoll restaurant by A.W. Cober and confederates,' Bullfinch said.

Perhaps, after all, the *Terra Nova* concept *would* one day get to be more than a concept. Certainly Jenkins no longer aimed to fuck it up. He wanted it, wanted it. That trip back from Maidrew did things to him, deep things. A good while before they reached the Bay, he had stopped wishing that Pillar would leave the city for ever – stopped wishing he would disappear preferably abroad, and preferably to somewhere further than Europe, somewhere it would be a drag and expense to come back from. Less than twenty-four hours ago this had seemed a brilliant and workable piece of creative policing, and led him to help spring the hostages. He had imagined saying: *Bargain: I've restored your wife and baby, Kim, so you do something for me and quit our ground, you* and *the mock* Terra Nova. *I'm assuming you, you personally, had nothing to do with any of the deaths, so a flit would be entirely legal.*

Now, the idea had come to seem negative, painful, mad. If Pillar disappeared for ever Jane would disappear for ever with him. The possibility depressed Jenkins. He did not know what she would think of it. Perhaps she still wanted to go. Just the same he would work at stopping them, holding them.

It had been somewhere between Maidrew and the Severn Bridge in a night rain storm, when Jane suddenly asked: 'But how did you know we were jailed there?'

'I didn't. I guessed.'

'Kim tried to get us out.'

'I'd expect that. Kim doesn't roll over.'

'It would probably be best if he didn't know you turned up and managed something he *failed* at,' she said.

'I didn't manage it. You did. I'm only the chauffeur.'

'Yes, well, just the same, he wouldn't like it.'

'He'll like having you back,' Jenkins replied.

'We'll stay silent about this part. Please.' The last word had been not much more than a whisper, and irresistible. 'Only Dominic Ardnell's mother and father were there. Dominic and his pal Geoffrey think they have Kim bottled up. Well, I suppose they *have*. Had.'

'What did you mean, when you said "dealt with"?'

'They're not young. They were holding me against my will, weren't they? Aren't I *entitled* to resist?'

'How will you explain to Kim about making it back to the Bay?' Jenkins replied.

'I've got cash. I hired a car. Take me to a Cardiff taxi firm. I'll do the last bit like that, in case the flat is watched.'

Jenkins had begun to feel then that this was a notable girl. He could see why Kim had chosen her and wanted to hang on to her. In Bullfinch's room now Jenkins would have liked to reminisce a good while longer about Jane and their journey. But his mind was dragged back. 'And then a further fragment of information I can give you both,' Bullfinch stated.

'Really, sir?' Brade answered, his face vivid with cod gratitude.

'Fiston,' Bullfinch replied.

'Fiston?' Brade asked.

'Susan Fiston,' Bullfinch replied. 'I've mentioned her before.'

Brade said: 'I feel I know the name, sir, but can't –'

'An investigative journalist,' Bullfinch answered. 'It's what they call themselves in their damned arrogance, as if to announce that we're not the only ones who can investigate. A heavyweight paper.' Bullfinch always kept his desk untidy. He was probably aware that people thought of him as prim and fussy, an insignia'd charwoman, and would be determined to correct that. He pulled out a folder from under a heap of documents and opened it. Jenkins saw newspaper cuttings. 'I've been looking at some of her previous work. It's formidable.'

'Is she coming here?' Brade asked.

'Imminent, according to our Press Office,' Bullfinch said.

'To what purpose, sir?' Brade asked.

Watching him and noticing the infinite blankness of his face now, Jenkins had the idea that Brade knew most of this already, or more than most of it, and probably much more than Bullfinch. This would be normal. 'The Bay does seem to fascinate the media,' Jenkins said. 'I expect in some ways it's a good thing – gives the city prominence.'

'Does the city *want* prominence because it houses a senior police officer and a holy Joe who could be mixed up in pervy sex deaths?' Bullfinch replied. 'That's why this woman's coming.' He stood, square-built, fat-faced but fit-looking, and came round from behind his desk to stand nearer the chair Brade sat in. 'What I can't afford, Dave, is for this woman by her own subtle means, to prove – I say to *prove* a connection between you and the two deaths, perhaps the three.'

'Afford, sir?' Jenkins asked.

'It would pollute the whole Bay development.' He lightened his voice, was able to sound mild, humane, even pitying: 'Tell me now, Dave, tell me and Glyndwr, how gravely are you involved? I asked Glyndwr, your friend, to come in as well, hoping that this would soothe, convince you it was a time for the full truth. Do you now feel this, too, Glyndwr?'

'What?' Jenkins replied.

Bullfinch muttered: 'Fuck you, Jenkins. Feel that it is a time for the full truth.'

'I should think it's always that,' Jenkins replied.

Last night under questioning in the car Jane had eventually given him the full truth about how she got out of Maidrew. 'Tell me what happened to Dominic's father,' he had asked.

'I did what I could,' she replied.

'How?'

'We have proper antique fire-irons at Maidrew, to suit the period, you know. Heavy.'

'How heavy?'

'From behind,' she said. 'Well, of course. This is a woman attacking a quite hefty man – oldish but hefty. I told him I'd taken Edward into my bed because he was ill. The cagey thug didn't really believe it, but eventually came to look. He was nice enough to do that. Prick. I got him while he'd become caring, half caring, anyway. Pretty bald so no mat to protect his skull. Only one *real* blow.'

'What's that mean?'

'Only one that did damage. He went down then. Fell on Edward. Listen, his blood all over Edward, like red fingers, throttling him. Collapsed on top of him in the bed, this ageing ape on top of *my* kid in bed, bleeding all over him.' Jane had begun to sob and yell, a frenzied mixture. 'Edward screaming, obviously, screaming and gagging, coughing on that fucking crook's scalp blood as it filled his mouth and ran down his throat and windpipe. Cascading off the smashed head straight between Edward's lips. I had to drag him off. Can you see this lovely tableau – mother, child and hood? A mother tugging the hulk by one of his ankles off the vomiting child? Then I have to hold the baby up in the air by *his* ankles to let the blood stream back out of his guts. The hulk's dead to the world but not dead.'

'I'm glad,' Jenkins replied.

'Afraid of being an accessory?'

'A police officer accessory.'

'He'll come round. His wife was taking care of him. She didn't seem interested in stopping me after that.'

'Why did they give you house arrest, anyway?' he'd asked.

'Kim owes a lot. Or they *say* he owes a lot, Dominic and Geoffrey.'

'Kim skims?'

'I don't accept it.'

Jenkins was looking ahead through the thick rain at the time but felt her turn to stare at him.

'You knew Kim well,' she said. 'Could you believe he'd do something like that?'

Jenkins did not answer at once.

'Yes, you *do*,' she said. She gave a small whistle. 'This makes it all the more wonderful that you came for us. Thanks.' She reached out from under the child and touched his left thumb on the wheel for a couple of seconds. As a flesh contact it was a bit less than he had with Mair, but it reached him all right. 'So, what was he like at Oxford?' she asked. 'What were *you* like?'

'Oh, like undergraduates.'

'Are you disappointed in him – the way he's gone?'

'Which way *has* he gone?'

'Not your way.'

'There are others.'

She had turned quiet for a while and then said: 'I'm in it with him, you know.'

'Yes, I suppose you are.'

'Yes, I suppose I am.'

'Skimmed how much?'

'Why?'

'So I can judge how serious they'd be about getting it back.'

'They're serious,' she replied.

'Six figures? Seven?'

'I've told him we should leave – to somewhere distant, obscure. Forget the *Terra Nova*.'

'Oh.'

'Doesn't it make sense?'

Did it? As they crossed the bridge, he had found he was not very focused on sense. He was focused on her closeness to him and on the recollection of her finger saying something comradely to his thumb. And on the ruthless, smart, brave way she had saved herself and her child.

And the same today . . .

As Bullfinch continued uselessly questioning Brade, Jenkins stayed stuck with his thoughts of Jane Pillar. Now and then, despite the road and the weather, he had been able to glance at her neat profile alongside him in the dark, occasionally tipping forward over the child as she dozed. It was a long time since he felt obsessed by Mair's profile, though also lovely in its way, distinctive, chinny and forceful.

'To return to the bad with a vicar, Dave,' Bullfinch said. 'How can this be acceptable? How can I defend you to the reporter if you will not talk to me?'

Jenkins said: 'But you yourself, sir, have described these allegations as mere talk.'

'And now I hear this vicar is actually living in with you and Kate, Dave,' Bullfinch replied. 'What kind of ménage is this, for God's sake?'

'Short-term,' Brade said. 'A sort of fostering. He needed looking after. Cliffy's had some shocks. Colleagues are hunting him. Familiar kind of scenario, sir. You know how colleagues can be.'

'Hunting him why?' Bullfinch asked.

'Churchmen are like that,' Jenkins replied.

'They hunt him because he has let them down, just as you, Dave, have let down the –'

Jenkins said: 'Nothing's going to interfere with the *Terra Nova* scheme, sir. You'll be all right.'

'All right?' Bullfinch hissed. 'What the fuck are you saying?'

'You'll be all right,' Jenkins replied.

24

'Perhaps we should get out now, Jane,' Pillar said. He was talking about retreat but he made it sound joyful, a gift, a honeymoon, voice on the up. Surrender sickened him, so act victory. 'France, Italy, Mexico – any of those brilliant places we used to discuss. The kind of welcoming spot you always yearned for. OK, you could have been right.'

'I *don't* think so. Not any more,' she replied and touched his cheek with her fingertips, like consoling a child.

Christ, how come? Suddenly, and somehow, by refusing to move she was moving away from him. 'They'll be here, and bloody soon,' he said.

'Of course they will. We can cope.'

'Dominic at least will come. I think he and his father are quite close. To have him clobbered like that . . . All right, love, you –'

'Darling, how *else* could I get out? We'd failed once. This way it worked.'

'He might be dead,' Pillar replied. 'From what you say.'

'*Who'd have thought the old man had so much blood in him?* Is it *Macbeth*? And most of the filthy stream over and into my child? If Ardnell senior can't take a joke he shouldn't have joined. Yes, an ageing bod, so why accept a job as jailer? He deserves what he gets. He might be all right. I can't care, Kim.'

'I do think Dominic will care.'

'Dominic risked him. Dominic can't hurt us. We're free.'

Pillar nodded, but hesitantly. He wondered about her confidence. Usually confidence was *his* speciality. He could not equal her today, nowhere near. 'You simply walked from Maidrew in the night carrying Edward?'

'*And* the money and jewellery,' she said. 'Walked to a phone box, that's all. It's only a couple of miles.'

'Rough ground, country roads. Terrific, love.'

'There was no pursuit. I could saunter.'

'To find a car at that hour.'

'It took a few calls. The operator helped.'

'I wish you'd called here as well.'

'What do we know about the line to this place? They set up the flat, didn't they? If it's tapped they might have had time to find me, send me back.'

Pillar gazed at her. 'Of course, it's wonderful you're here, Jane, you and the boy, but –'

'The three of us again. We're *strong* now, aren't we?' she said. 'You can tell them get lost if they try heaviness. They've got no hostages. This is what you wanted. Remember when you talked about strength? You've got supremacy back. We can enjoy it, Kim, use it. You have friends in the Bay who'll look after you – the black cop, Jenkins, and perhaps his pal, if the black cop says you're all right. And he will, won't he? I've come to think we're safer here – *we're* safer and Edward's safer – safer than if we did a bunk. They'd trace us wherever, and we've got no protection in France or Italy or Mexico. Those places sound like heaven, but they're exposed. It's *you* who were right. Your project here will be great now. You don't want to run from that, do you? Do you, Kim? It's your *soul*. What a waste to chuck it. All right, perhaps we even pay them the 1.6 once things get going. We can talk about it with them, but talk about it like equals, possibly do a deal, pay them something, something lower, a lot lower, something that lets them feel they've had a win, and gets us out, but no pauperising ourselves and losing Maidrew. This is a *business* situation now. I certainly don't say break the partnership. But make them see there's parity. Make them see it early.'

Of course, he had known there was a shift in strengths again between him and Dominic and Geoffrey, but perhaps she grasped it more clearly, more fully than he could. Those bad minutes at Maidrew had sharpened her perceptions, maybe, and stoked her aggression. 'Jenkins?' he said. 'I don't know how he thinks, how he sees me these days, Jane. He's probably not buyable. I think he could be in love with his job. He's the worthy sort who takes on duties – to law and order, to his colleague.'

'Of course he's not buyable. But he's –'

'He *was* a friend. Things were different then.'

'Kim, I find I feel comfortable here, at ease. None of those horrible open spaces we have at Maidrew. I don't worry about Edward.'

'Well, I admit, that's damned important.'

'We'll be fine.'

'Yes,' Pillar said. He wanted to believe her. Naturally. He would work at it. 'Yes, I think we will be fine,' he replied. They were in the long living-room of the flat and he stood and tried one of those pirouettes he used to perform at Maidrew when fooling to show how happy and assured he was – and to make her happy and assured, too. Today she did not need any boost to her morale. *He* did. The performance should be even more meaningful here because he could do his steps near the *Terra Nova* model. She did not exaggerate – that scheme came from his essence. She deserved everything he could give. She had pulled off a hell of a coup alone.

He thought she looked lovely now. It was five minutes to midday. She had showered when she came in from the taxi just after dawn and washed off some smears of blood picked up from Edward on her forehead and right cheek. Those had scared him at first. She had a key to the flat and let herself in quietly. When he awoke he found her bending over him, Edward asleep in her arms. Despite those blood traces, it was a lovely moment. Then, guzzling coffee, Jane had outlined events at Maidrew, a matter-of-fact voice, no drama or big talk. Afterwards, she slept for a couple of hours. He lay alongside her but was unable to sleep again himself, thrilled, delighted, and ashamed there was no part for him in her escape. He tried to plan how he would handle Dominic and Geoffrey when they heard and came looking for Jane, and for him. She said old Ardnell would recover, but Pillar could not be sure of that. There might be a law angle to all this, as well as the grief and rage of Dominic.

Now, she wanted to cook a meal – 'get back to sweet old domesticity', as she termed it. There were none of her clothes in the flat and she wore a grey jerkin belonging to Pillar and the jeans she arrived in. Although the jerkin drowned her, she looked good in it – irrepressible, lithe. He would have liked to take her back to bed while Edward still slept. But he did not think she would want this. There was a remoteness to her for now. Again he felt that shame at leaving Jane to break out unaided. It was as if she suddenly knew she did not need him.

* * *

Dominic and Geoffrey arrived in the afternoon, both behaving very serene and unshaken. Geoffrey said in that loud, homely voice: 'It won't surprise you, Jane, Kim, but Dominic is being damn reasonable about the injuries to his dad.'

Dominic made a small wave with his right hand to dismiss the compliment. 'We knew she'd try to break out. We'd already witnessed one attempt. I can't object. If you lock up someone of quality like Jane, she's going to fight it. And she'll do what's necessary. My father was in the way. Hard luck, dad.'

'Jane's very concerned about his condition,' Pillar replied.

Dominic used the same gesture again, this time dismissing anxieties. 'He'll lie up for a while. You don't mind if he stays at Maidrew? Best there should be caretakers in, even a fucking dreamy caretaker such as my dad. Fell for it like an idiot, didn't he – the kid's "sickness". Old tales are always the best.' He shook his head a couple of times to signal disbelief that his father should have been so stupid. Then he seemed suddenly to remember something: 'Oh, he has an idea – this is a notion that came to him just before he passed out, apparently, right after the first couple of blows – he's afraid he might have bled over the child and if so he asks me to apologise. The thought horrifies him, I mean it. He can't talk very much, but he did force himself to speak of that. Guilt.'

'No,' Jane replied cheerfully. 'Edward was *fine*. Unaffected. It's kind of your father to fret, but he mustn't.'

'Oh, splendid,' Dominic said. 'He'll be relieved. We'll certainly clear up the bed where it happened and the poker.'

Pillar had made tea. The four of them were seated around the flat's living-room, Jane on the sofa with Edward in her arms, asleep again.

Dominic said: 'My mother thinks dad will be totally all right in a few weeks, without permanent damage to the brain or his balance and so on. She believes some moderation was used in the hammering, no frenzy, and they're both grateful for that, Jane.'

'Obviously, I can't get Garrant into the flat for you to deal with now Jane and the child are here,' Pillar replied. He spoke as though it was only a location matter, a geography matter. It was more. He wanted it understood they could no longer force him to do the fixing for Garrant's death.

'One reason we've come – to discuss alternative sites,' Geoffrey told him.

Jane said – that matter-of-fact voice again: 'I don't know any of the detail of this, but doesn't it sound like something you two had better handle for yourselves? I mean, given the *undoubted* changes.'

'The changes, yes,' Dominic said, his slapdash features all over the place like meat in a stew.

'The fact that you're no longer holding Edward and me,' Jane explained. 'It does have a bearing. This is not to crow, but, yes, a bearing.'

'Certainly,' Geoffrey said.

'I'm not sure how much you know about Garrant, Jane, but he could fuck us all,' Dominic said.

'Which all?' Jane asked.

'The company,' Geoffrey said. 'The *Terra Nova*, everything.'

'How?' Jane asked.

'The police will have him lined up for one death, possibly three,' Geoffrey replied. 'He reeks. He had dealings with us.'

'He might talk?' Jane asked.

'A possibility,' Geoffrey said. 'It depends how desperate he gets. It always depends on how desperate people get.'

'Had dealings with whom?' Jane asked.

'With the company. In the first instance, to prevent an attempt on Kim. You'll remember the crane corpse. He was in the Bay to do damage. We had to have him hit early, and display him. This was magnificent work, but potentially embarrassing now.'

Edward stirred yet seemed still exhausted after the night's troubles and slumped back into full sleep again. Jane glanced down at him affectionately. 'Who in the company did he deal with?' she asked.

'Primarily Dominic and me.'

'This is why I said you'd want to handle it *yourselves*,' Jane replied. 'You'll wish to be really sure the matter's tidied properly. It doesn't seem something that can be delegated.'

For a third time Dominic gave his small wave. Now it might indicate he accepted Jane's argument, perhaps *had* to accept it. 'But who helped you, Jane?' he asked.

'With what?'

'Not the actual assault on daddy. That was a noble solo act, we know. Getting you away though, and back here. This time it couldn't have been Kim. We're certain he was in the flat all night.'

'People watching?' Jane asked.

'We feel a continuing obligation to look after him,' Geoffrey replied. 'Even more lately. Things could get bad here – the other syndicate are still busy, full of envy and evil. A.W. Moss-Cober and so on.'

'She walked with Edward in her arms to a phone box,' Pillar said. 'No aid. It was remarkable. She'd lost her mobile. Confiscated?'

Dominic lowered his cup from his mouth. 'Which fucking phone box?'

'At the edge of the village,' Jane said.

'Vandalised and dead,' Dominic replied.

'Can't be,' Pillar said. 'You've checked that? Why?'

'We might be talking about different boxes,' Jane said.

'Where is it?' Dominic asked.

'And then arriving here in a local taxi,' Geoffrey said. 'As we hear.'

Abruptly the tone of the meeting had altered. Pillar saw and heard the raw suspicion and hostility. He felt some of it himself.

'Wrong,' Jane replied. 'How could it have been local?'

'Exactly,' Geoffrey said.

'And would it matter, even if?' Jane asked. 'I'm here, the child's here, and – pardon the bluntness – you're fucked up. That's what counts, isn't it? We all have to be respectful to one another now.' She stared across Edward first at Geoffrey, then turned and gave Dominic the same.

'What I wondered, Kim, is if you sent the black cop, your chum, for her,' he said.

'Send?' Pillar replied. 'Jenkins isn't someone you *send* anywhere. And I'm not going to bring him into company issues of that sort, am I?'

Jenkins? At Maidrew after all? Could that be?

'We heard of an Omega parked in the village late and starting up at around 4.30 a.m. and belting off. Know anyone with an Omega, Kim?' Geoffrey asked. 'Omegas in the police pool?'

'I'd still be prepared to help you with Garrant, of course,'

Pillar replied. 'If he's a menace to you two he's a menace to the company and the project. We three are partners, equal partners, and I would never deny those bonds, nor the liabilities they bring.'

'The fucking liability's at least 1.6,' Dominic said. 'Don't ever get to think you can do without Geoffrey and me. We've got pull in this city above anything you can realise.'

'Pull with some really top cop?' Jane asked.

'True fucking pull,' Dominic replied. 'Plus we've managed to line up a local replacement for Garrant, probably the best middleman in the Bay, as we now discover.'

'Julian Corbett? Pillar asked.

'He's brilliant,' Dominic replied. 'So, we've got pull all ways. But pull costs big. This is pull that means we need to collect all our debts. This is pull that's vital, but there's no pull that can see us clear if Garrant gets –'

'Pulled,' Jane said.

'If Garrant gets taken in and chatters,' Dominic replied.

'Not taking him *out* in the flat, though, that's all – the child around,' Pillar said. 'Edward's been through enough.'

'Kim's always talking of the loyalties he owes, is *proud* to owe,' Jane said.

25

Cliffy disappeared. For a few mad minutes Brade found himself wondering whether Hale-Garning was right after all and people from the cathedral had watched until he was alone in the flat and then come and taken him to Llandrindod Wells or a defrocking. But everything looked undisturbed. Cliff would have violently resisted any church raiding party and furniture was sure to have been damaged or at least displaced. In any case, his fears of abduction were crazy, paranoid, weren't they? People in orders did not behave like this. It was just after lunchtime and Kate was at work. Brade had taken to looking in at the flat when he could to check that Cliffy was all right and give him a break from loneliness.

Brade called out to Cliff anxiously a couple of times and then before he could search saw a pencilled letter again written in capital letters like an old-fashioned ransom demand or sermon prompts. It had been placed on Brade's copy of *The Great White South*, as if Cliffy knew Brade was sure to find it there, and as if it carried the same weight of tragedy.

> DAVE, NO GOOD, ALAS. I CANNOT REST. THANK YOU FOR CARING. YOU ARE WELL RID OF ME. CLIFFORD H-G. (REV.)

The letter was on the back of a printed advertisement sheet from a firm offering discounts to clergy for winter and summer weight suits, grey, black and navy, winter and summer underwear in a number of styles, and rubber-soled black lace-up shoes. Brade ran upstairs at once to Cliff's own flat and hammered at the door. There was no answer and he used his plastic and broke in. Quickly he went through all the rooms. Hale-Garning's message had a suicide tone and Brade felt very scared. Clifford was not here.

Brade locked up and went back to his own place. He regretted now not having arrived earlier. There had been a few drinks after a pub lunch with Jenkins. Cliff might have felt abandoned. He would never have deserted his telephone duties at the flat unless badly troubled. Although the drinks session with Jenkins had been important, Brade should have kept it shorter. It was Glyndwr who proposed the get-together, and Brade found he wanted to talk about Jane Pillar. And talk. Jenkins seemed half dazed by her. He said he needed advice, and obviously meant to ignore any he did not like. Oh, Jesus, wasn't the Bay situation tricky enough without such complicated sex?

'A terrific woman, Dave.'

'How do you mean?'

'Terrific. Thank God I took that fucking moustache off.'

'Well, yes. But a mother, Glyn.'

'I know.'

'Wife of a one-time close comrade.'

'I know.'

'She's not happy with him?'

'I don't know.'

'Has he let her down?'

'I don't know.'

'So what brought it on? When did you see her?'

'Really terrific, Dave. You'll understand. What you get from Kate. Rapport?'

There had been more like that. No clarity, a lot of appreciation and yearning. 'What about Mair, Glyn?'

'I know. She's terrific, too, and loyal.'

'I don't understand where this came from. Mrs Pillar's only just arrived in the Bay, hasn't she?'

'Depth. Vitality. Resolve. Yet potential tenderness, also, I'm sure. I'm knocked sideways.'

God, women could knock any man sideways. Brade wondered now whether it was still surging grief about Semprina that made Clifford leave. Brade could understand such sadness. In his pain and strung-out state perhaps Hale-Garning was turning vengeful. There had been signs, hadn't there? Suddenly a ferocious thwarted vicar might be on the streets. Clifford knew a bit about Garrant from the journalist. Was Hale-Garning somewhere looking for him? Oh, Cliffy, Cliffy, this is different from a cathedral snatch squad.

Brade waited an hour then went back to work. He spent the evening at home with Kate playing Pontoon for pounds and waiting for a call. At 10.45 the telephone rang. Jenkins spoke. He had not left the bar with Brade and was calling from there now. The amplified voice of a general knowledge quiz master sounded off-and-on behind him with hard geography and sports teasers. 'So what am I going to do, Dave?' Glyndwr asked.

'At the moment, go home.'

'There has to be a chance Kim Pillar will get removed.'

'In a business sense you mean, Glyndwr?'

What is the capital of Kenya?

'Removed, Dave. So she's on her own.'

'This is an open line. You want to take over a child?'

'People who hire a hit man are not going to give up just because he's found hanging from a crane. This Jim Driscoll caff is very much a heartfelt, civic aim of theirs. They'll continue striving to remove competition.'

'Glyn, I –'

Which left-hand batsman is world highest scorer in test cricket?

'This is a marvellous girl, Dave. She can flatten a man one minute and cradle a child the next.'

'What? Which man?'

Jenkins did not answer but Brade could hear him trying to get his breathing right.

'I'm hoping for a call, Glyn. I mustn't talk too long. A priest. Missing.'

Who holds the world men's shot-putting record?

Jenkins was silent again for a while.

'So could you ring off now, Glyndwr?'

'You'll look for him where?'

'Probably the Bay.'

'Shall I come and help? You shouldn't be alone in that state.'

'Get a taxi home. Don't drive.' Brade put the phone down and after a minute lifted it to make sure Jenkins had disconnected. He waited another half-hour and then drove to the Bay. Trying not to be spotted, he parked near the leisure complex and walked to Stuart Street. Perhaps Clifford was hanging about near Garrant's place, hoping to intercept him. Cliffy might not realise that when Garrant went out it would almost always be by car, often in the vintage Daimler coupé, and never without minders. Cliff could be beyond fine points on safety.

Brade did not find him. The gates to Maritime House were closed and he could see a guard in the lodge reading. There appeared to have been no recent crisis, if Cliff stalking would rate as a crisis. All the same Brade was uneasy.

He returned to the car and drove to Semprina's place, in case Cliff had gone there to pay a sentimental visit. Her flat was dark, though, and again he saw nobody outside. In Herbert Street Erica was just back after what she called 'a middling-long trick' in a Dormobile and could not help with sightings of Hale-Garning, though she said she remembered him from the other night. Louise was not around, away somewhere, perhaps on retreat at a convent or working London conferences.

He parked again at the complex and this time walked to the Toledo. Simeon de Courville and a party of friends and so on were a moment ahead of Brade at the door. Briefly, Simeon detached himself from the others and came to speak in private. 'Trouble tonight, Dave?'

'Not from me. How about you?'

'Dave, please. I'm with out-of-town business colleagues and their womenfolk.'

'Do I smell a handgun?'

'I tell them, "You must see the Toledo in its pomp a little before midnight,"' de Courville replied. 'If you are to know anything about the Bay, *really* know about the Bay, this is the where and when.'

If Cliff knew anything about the Bay, *really* knew it, he would have discovered that Garrant came to the club most nights. And he was here now, with his wife, a company executive, Robin Hewlitt, and a guard contingent. To be seen here regularly was how Garrant showed he belonged to the dockland community, was eminent in it and fireproof, yet human and approachable. He had once told Brade he saw it as like Prince Philip handshaking among people lining the route.

Because he was approachable here the London reporter Susan Fiston must have decided to approach. Brade watched her walk across the big room to Garrant and speak. She was in a check shirt, jeans and the suede boots and looked intent and determined. Tonight there was no karaoke but a few people danced. The track sounded to Brade like house music. Some said it was on the way back despite everything. He thought the group might be Deep Dish. The Toledo did try to keep up. Leaning on a stick, Cordial Maximilian watched the dancers. A.W. Moss-Cober was out there with a woman Brade did not recognise, young and very energetic, wearing a red mini-skirt and sleeveless, backless red top. Julian Corbett danced old-style, holding his wild wife Henrietta very close.

Some of Garrant's people shifted nervously when Fiston came so near but Garrant himself listened politely to what the reporter said and then laughed. Perhaps she had asked him to dance. She said something else to him, spoke longer this time. When she finished Garrant glanced across and beckoned Brade.

'Here's a journalist who thinks I did Indiment, Semprina and Pedal, Dave,' Garrant told him as soon as he joined them. 'I don't know if she's going to publish, but I'm glad you're in the club to put her right. Stories like that in the Press – no use at all to the Bay.'

'Did she *say* you did them?' Brade replied.

'Does she have to, Dave? Oblique. Implication. You know how they operate. What did Denis Thatcher call them – reptiles? I believe you've already met her. You heard her, Lorna, Robin, didn't you?'

'Out of order,' Hewlitt said.

'Dave, I certainly don't expect you to tell her about the disgusting tales that link you, personally, and your religious friend, to the deaths of Semprina and Pedal Power. But it would be a kindness if you'd inform her officially I'm not charged with any of the deaths.'

'I know you're not bloody well charged,' Fiston said. 'You wouldn't be out. *Why* aren't you charged, though, that's what I ask?'

Garrant nodded in friendly style. 'If you could inform her officially, Dave, I'm not charged *and* I'm not under suspicion for any of the deaths.'

'Our inquiries continue,' Brade replied.

'My God, what is this, Brade – some kind of truce between you, some kind of arrangement?' Fiston asked.

'Our inquiries continue,' Brade replied. 'No Rico statutes here to make things easier like in the States. We need proper evidence.'

In her booming untroubled voice Lorna Garrant said: 'People from London, places like that, don't really understand the Bay, do they, Dave?'

'I'm beginning to,' Fiston replied.

'But how can you bully Adrian in this way?' Lorna Garrant cried. 'How can you slur Dave Brade – "truce", "arrangement" – is this about something dirty?'

Garrant said: 'Ignorance of the Bay added to a –'

From somewhere on the other side of the dance square Hale-Garning in his church robes but no hat and yelling over the music suddenly began to gallop towards Garrant and the rest. In his right hand he carried an unopened bottle of tonic wine by the neck. He was shouting repeatedly, 'Killer of my love!' His face had the terrible righteous fierceness that would sometimes move in there, and a few good-sized flecks of sweat dropped from his forehead and fell in arcs as he charged towards Garrant. Clifford raised the bottle. Hewlitt and one of the bodyguards moved quickly in front of Garrant. The bodyguard pulled out a small metal cosh and when Cliffy lunged with the bottle hit him once near the temple so that he was spun a little to the side and his bottle came down on Fiston's head and broke. She fell at once, concussed, her shirt and face brilliantly red with wine. Clifford fell also, near her, half the bottle still in his hand, the church robes soaked just above the hem. Brade thought it all like a Middle Ages painting of abuses among clergy. Although Hale-Garning's legs had gone, he was not unconscious and the body-guard bent and would have hit him another blow but Garrant leaned forward quickly and grabbed his arm. 'It's Mr Brade's playmate. He's probably jealous, that's all – perhaps thinks Dave was making up to me or Robin. Harmless.'

Brade helped Susan Fiston to her feet and the barman brought a chair and a cloth for her to wipe her face. 'Is this part of it?' she asked.

'Of what?' Garrant asked.

'The whole thing,' she said.

'There is no whole thing,' Garrant replied. 'This is an incident.'

A small crowd gathered near. The music stopped for a few minutes and then resumed. People in the Toledo were used to incidents. The manager and a bouncer came and the bouncer explained that Clifford had been allowed in despite his garb because he said he wanted to distribute tracts. Cordial Maximilian hobbled over to Brade. 'Is it some kind of love tiff, Dave?' he asked.

Julian Corbett said: 'Can Henrietta and I help in any way?'

Garrant and Hewlitt got Hale-Garning upright. Garrant tried to take the remains of the bottle from him. Cliff fought to keep it. 'I will not be left defenceless,' he screamed at Garrant. 'You are through and through evil.'

It wasn't a bad estimate. Jenkins appeared. 'I'd have been here sooner, Dave, but some fucking jam-sandwich uniform wanted to breathalyse me. It took a lot of argument and so on.' He came close and whispered: 'Did I tell you about Jane Pillar at all? Terrific woman.' He looked around. 'She wasn't here, was she, cracking heads?'

'I want to get the reporter and Hale-Garning away,' Brade replied. 'They're not safe now.'

'I'd say it was Adrian who was not safe,' Hewlitt declared.

'Slanderous suggestions from this reporter, violence from your associate, the vicar.'

'An incident, Robin,' Garrant said.

'You're too tolerant, Adrian,' Hewlitt replied.

'Oh, God, I've struck a woman,' Cliffy said.

Garrant spoke to Hewlitt and the bodyguard. 'I'd like you to help Mr Brade with these two injured folk. Go with him. I don't feel Glyndwr can do much. Take the Daimler, Robin, and drive behind Mr Brade so you can give a hand with the Rev. and the journalist at the other end.'

'You'll be left exposed, Adrian,' Hewlitt said.

'I don't think so. Two men is enough for the time you'll be away. I imagine we've had all the excitement and hazard likely to come our way tonight.'

Hewlitt said: 'But, Adrian –'

'Off you go then,' Garrant said.

'What do you mean you don't feel I can do much?' Jenkins said.

'It's been a party night for you somewhere, has it, Glyndwr?' Garrant replied. 'Celebrating what?'

26

'That was our new man, Julian Corbett,' Dominic said. He put the telephone down. 'Garrant is at the Toledo club now, and with only two security people.'

'Now?' Pillar gasped. 'He thinks we could do it *now*, in the Toledo? Oh, Jesus, Dominic.'

'Now's the crux.' Dominic said. 'Corbett estimates forty minutes.' He brought a Smith and Wesson automatic from its shoulder holster and very carefully checked the magazine, going for coolness, getting nowhere near. Pillar could almost feel sorry for him. Dominic's fingers looked stiff, not quite in his control, and he was making a long, long job of clearing his throat. Even so he spoke through phlegm and the words emerged shakily, half garotted by it. 'I know Geoffrey's carrying something. Well, of course. Didn't we come to the Bay hoping for this kind of chance? What about you, Kim?'

'No, for God's sake,' Pillar replied. 'Guns didn't seem my role here.'

'Role?' Dominic said. 'I forget your *role*.'

'To look like someone nursing a creative business project,' Pillar replied. 'To *be* someone nursing a creative business project.'

'Ah,' Dominic said.

'You think it's fancy talk,' Pillar replied. He didn't have to take shit. His family was back and safe. In any case, he must delay this mad plot until they knew it was too late. His sympathy for Dominic disappeared. 'Would the *Terra Nova* ever get the planning OK if people know I go armed? It wouldn't matter what high-level pull you've bought.'

Dominic stood up, as if the arguments were all a mad luxury. He looked scared and weighed down, but sure. 'You're a partner, aren't you?' He put the gun away. 'Aren't you? We're talking about saving the company, not just about saving the project. We should go at once. Corbett will open a fire-door at the club.'

'Is he reliable?' Pillar asked. A mistake. He knew that instantly. It sounded as if it was his only doubt. In fact, he had *only* doubts. 'Corbett sounded hysterical, almost incoherent, screaming nearly when he asked for you.' Pillar had taken the call first. They were in the Bay flat. Jane had gone to bed an hour ago.

'We told Corbett he could probably reach us here until quite late,' Geoffrey said.

'He knows the scene,' Dominic replied. 'He's recommended. There's been some kind of fracas at the club involving Brade's vicar and a journalist. Corbett's certain there'll never be another chance like it. Come on.'

Pillar stayed in his chair. How long could he stretch the objections? 'Of course, Corbett would like Garrant out of the way. He's the competition.'

'*We'd* like Garrant out of the way,' Dominic said. 'He's a menace.'

'The Toledo is a stronghold,' Pillar replied.

'Listen, you didn't want it in the flat,' Dominic said. 'All right, it's *not* in the flat. Nothing to upset your wife and kiddie. But we buy Corbett's judgement. His judgement is, do it now. Do it there.'

'Will he be around?' Pillar replied.

'He's watching things,' Dominic said.

'Will he be around when it's done? Will he help?' Pillar asked.

'Not his kind of role, as you'd call it, Kim,' Geoffrey replied. 'He's a middleman.' He was on his feet, too, and looking urgent.

'A freelance,' Dominic said. 'He's done what he's hired for – called us with a tip. But you, Kim, and Geoffrey and me, we're boardroom, with interests to look after. Corbett says Brade has been talking to Garrant. So has the journalist, really talking. He's a magnet. It's not good for us. We have to get there. Garrant sent two of his people to help with the injured. Soft soap. He wants to show how gentlemanly and nice he is – Bay old nobility. Brade's not going to wear that. He'll be back to quiz Garrant more, or even take him in. We reach him first, and thanks for the opening.'

'I hope you'll come, Kim,' Geoffrey said. He stepped towards the door. Although he had not produced a gun for checking, like Dominic, now he tapped himself once with a couple of fingers near his left shoulder, as though needing to confirm the weapon hung there. 'Save the company, save the noble *Terra Nova*. And then there's sheer loyalty, team spirit. You were always good at that, Kim, I know.'

'Of course he'll come,' Dominic replied. 'He'll be inside for as long as us if Garrant spills. Indiment was killed because he was stalking Kim. Police love a motive. And then they look at Maidrew and the bank accounts, including what's left of the 1.6, and ask where it all came from. They'll find out.'

Pillar did not know how to answer any of that. 'I'm no help unarmed,' he said, suddenly certain he would go with them. Perhaps it had also been stupid to admit he lacked firepower. There were two guns in this room, and two tense men carrying them, Dominic enraged about rough treatment to his father, though keeping it under so far. Pillar stood. He said: 'Yes, I'm loyal. Yes, I'm a partner. I want the project to succeed.'

'Good, Kim,' Geoffrey said. 'Only as expected.'

'Bring a flashlight,' Dominic replied. 'You identify the target. Plus do the driving. You've been around the Bay a bit. You know the roads.'

'I'll leave a note for Jane,' Pillar said.

'You'll be back, don't worry,' Dominic replied. 'We'll all be back.'

'In case she wakes while I'm out,' Pillar said.

'A note is not sensible,' Geoffrey replied.

In the car, Dominic said: 'Of course, you're right, Kim. This is lunatic. We've allowed something to happen that our mothers warned us of – a situation with no options. But lunatic ploys occasionally work, *because* they're so fucking lunatic and unexpected. Think of the way you took that 1.6.'

'Most of the greatest operations look like rubbish when only ideas,' Geoffrey said.

'Keep the flashlight hidden until it's needed,' Dominic said.

'If his full security is back in place by the time we arrive, do we abort?' Geoffrey asked.

'Move, Kim,' Dominic replied. 'All that talk.'

It was just after midnight, still quite busy on the roads, but Pillar took the Mercedes up to 80 mph.

Dominic in the passenger seat said: 'Corbett will hit the club lights a couple of minutes after you're inside. You put a beam on Garrant for us. We come and go in the dark.'

'But not me. I'll be seen,' Pillar said.

'You're there on a harmless night out, almost a victim when Garrant gets done,' Geoffrey replied in that big comforting voice.

Dominic said: 'Nobody's going to know it's you showing Garrant to us. It's dark, except for him. In any case, Toledo people don't talk to the police, do they?'

'But you're afraid if it wasn't dark they'd talk about *you*,' Pillar said.

'That's not what I'm afraid of. We're two strangers with pistols in our hands,' Dominic replied, 'doing this personally. Forced on us by time. If it's light, his security could knock us down as soon as we're through the door, even if there's only two.'

Pillar parked in Mount Stuart Square and they walked to the rear of the club. The fire-door had been released. It was just after 12.15 a.m. 'Go in first, chat to him, Kim,' Dominic said. 'He did you proud, didn't he – Indiment on the jib? You could thank him.'

'If all his protection is there maybe Kim should come straight back out and tell us,' Geoffrey said.

'We'll have surprise, as long as Kim can charm him,' Dominic replied. 'Kim can. He knows how to gab or we'd have left earlier, with a better chance.'

27

Hewlitt and the bodyguard helped Brade bring Susan Fiston and Cliffy into Brade's flat and left. It had been a crafty gesture by Garrant. Jenkins brought himself. He did not seem as bad now. Kate was sleeping. Good. Brade made some tea and prepared a meal of bread, cheese and onions. They all rested. There was not much talk. He put some brandy in Fiston's, Hale-Garning's and his own tea, but not Jenkins'.

'Did I mess anything up, Dave?' Hale-Garning asked.

'Oh, not much you didn't,' Fiston replied. 'You ought to be in some country parish where the population is sheep.'

'Don't you fucking talk to me about Llandrindod Wells, you smartarse,' Clifford bellowed. Cynthia, next door, rapped the wall.

There was a phone call from headquarters to say some kind of gun battle had begun in the Toledo. 'No detail yet, Dave,' the Control inspector said. 'More than one shot. The club seems to be totally dark. We've got people there and two armed response cars on the way.'

'I have to go out again,' Brade told Hale-Garning and the other two. 'There's booze in the sideboard.'

'Going *where*?' Cliff cried.

'You'll have company,' Brade said.

'But going where?' Hale-Garning asked. 'I'm not stopping with this loud bitch and a piss artist.'

'Steady,' Jenkins replied. Brade thought he articulated it pretty well.

'What you're going out for – is this to do – to do with the whole thing?' Fiston said.

'Which whole thing?' Jenkins replied. 'You people – always looking for big themes.' Again, not too much slurring.

'Well, to do with Garrant?' Fiston said. 'I must come with you.'

'You're injured,' Brade replied. 'You should rest.'

'It's crucial to my story,' Fiston said. 'To see things at first hand.'

'It's not a fucking *story*,' Brade replied.

'My investigation.'

Bullfinch was spot on about their arrogance. '*I* investigate,' Brade said.

'Oh, that right?' she asked.

'I don't want to be left here alone,' Hale-Garning said.

'No, no, that won't happen,' Brade replied.

'If you don't take me I'll call a cab,' Fiston said.

'You don't know where I'm going,' Brade replied.

'I'd try the Toledo again first,' she said. 'It's where everything's at, isn't it?'

'I should be with you, Dave,' Jenkins said. 'If this is something big. We've worked together on it from the start. It would be selfish to exclude me now, drunk or sober.'

Hale-Garning said: 'There's a choice?'

Brade drove them all back to the Toledo. The lights were on again. No music played. A youngish woman in a red mini-skirt and red backless, sleeveless top, and with a stethoscope to her ears, was kneeling by Pillar. He lay face up near where Garrant and his people had been. Brade recognised A.W.'s dance partner. It looked as if she had pulled Pillar's shirt open and now she took a couple of soundings on his bare chest. The shirt and his jacket were blood-soaked. His legs were a little apart, his left arm out straight at his side, the other bent underneath him. Half a dozen uniformed police officers, some with holstered pistols at their waists, had begun questioning club customers.

Brade walked over with Jenkins and stood near the body: 'Just what you wanted, Glyndwr,' he said.

'Did I?'

'"Removed"? Was that your word?' Brade introduced himself to the girl doctor. 'Is he dead?' he asked.

She stood up: 'Oh, yes,' she said. 'There's an ambulance coming but no point. Two, possibly three, shots in the chest. Do you know him?'

'My colleague does,' Brade replied. 'Very well.'

'I'm sorry,' the doctor replied.

'Oxford. He knows his wife, too. Probably he'll break it to her,' Brade said. 'Were you with A.W. when the lights went?'

'Who?'

'The man you seemed to be dancing with earlier,' Brade said.

'Earlier? How do you know? Snooping?'

'Were you with him when the lights went?' Brade replied.

'I danced with a few,' she said. 'What *is* this?'

'The one you were with for the Deep Dish number,' Brade said.

'Oh, Deep Dish. Alec?'

'Yes, Alec Moss-Cober,' Brade replied. 'Were you with him when the shooting began?'

'Why?'

'Were you?'

'I'm here with a party of girls from hospital. A birthday.'

'Jungle slumming? Can you remember if you were with Alec when the lights went, and so on.'

'Nice chap? Sort of . . . tidy?'

'That's A.W.'

'I don't think so. A couple of numbers, that was all. And then when the lights came up again and we saw what had happened I went out to the car for my bag.' She walked back to her friends at a table near the bar, the stethoscope hanging from her neck.

A uniformed sergeant came over to Brade and Jenkins and said: 'This man entered the club through the fire-doors, apparently. He approached Adrian Garrant who was here with his wife and full minder unit. Two of them had been away somewhere but were back when this happened. The lights went. It looks as if someone inside was contracted to do the fire-door and the mains.' The sergeant had an open notebook in his hand and looked at it now. 'At least three shots. When we got the lights on again we found him here. We haven't searched his clothes for identification but I've been given the name Kim Louis Pillar.'

'I know him,' Brade replied.

The sergeant said: 'Garrant and his group withdrew, telling

people they feared he would be targeted next. You know what Garrant's lot are like about security. It's possible there were two unidentified men waiting outside the fire-doors. They seem to have been scared off. Perhaps Kim Louis Pillar was meant to line up Garrant for them. There's a flashlight sticking out of his pocket.'

'It was ghastly, Mr Brade,' Julian Corbett said.

'What's it about, Dave?' Simeon de Courville asked. 'Terrible, terrible.'

'A.W. and Cordial are here as well, aren't they?' Brade replied.

'What's that mean? Don't think you can put this on us, you tireless scheming fucker,' Simeon said.

'What's he getting at, Brade?' Fiston asked. 'Is he a suspect?'

Garrant and his retinue came back into the bar. 'I thought it wisest, safest, not to be here for a while, Mr Brade,' he said. 'There might have been an uncontrolled, destructive gun fight.'

But, of course, he would have to reappear now, to prove he was still alive, still eminent and fireproof, still central to the Bay.

'Why would this man want to attack you?' Fiston asked. 'Perhaps more than one?'

Garrant shrugged: 'People do.'

'Pampered taker of my love,' Hale-Garning howled.

The lights went out again. Immediately, there were two shots.

'Christ, Cliff, have you got a gun? How?' Brade yelled.

A woman screamed nearby. Had Fiston stopped something again?

'I'll find the switch,' Jenkins said.

'You will?' Brade replied.

In three minutes the bar was lit up once more. Garrant lay not far from Pillar, his team around him, two with Walther automatics in their hands. Lorna Garrant crouched, trying for a pulse. Brade thought the scream had probably come from her. She would not find his pulse. The girl doctor hurried back but did not bother to use the stethoscope this time.

Bullfinch arrived in the navy suit soon afterwards. 'What, Dave?'

'It looks like a plan to take out Garrant which went wrong, at first. This man, Pillar, gets hit by the protection, or one of the Jim

Driscoll restaurant syndicate, or by his own associates – maybe accidentally, maybe because he'd offended them.'

'My God, this will kill the *Terra Nova*,' Bullfinch replied.

'Yes, it might,' Jenkins said. 'Sorry, sir.'

'Is he pissed, Dave?'

'Upset, sir,' Brade said. 'Seeing a fine old rugby friend dead.'

'And then someone puts the lights off again and in due course we find Garrant,' Brade said.

'Who did it?' Bullfinch said.

'I wish I could say me,' Hale-Garning replied.

'Who, Dave?'

'Again, one of the Jim Driscoll syndicate? None of them was around when the lights came on the second time. Jule Corbett? They're business competitors. He's gone, too. It would be important to get rid of any weapon.'

'So, where are we, Dave?' Bullfinch asked, eyes glinting with what might be tears. He had suffered some unmentionable loss.

'Yes, where are we?' Fiston said.

'I'd say we're laughing,' Hale-Garning replied, laughing. 'So prayer *does* work.'

'Yes, absolutely,' Jenkins said. 'We'll shake the truth out. Ballistic tests on guns that *are* still here. We can get some of Garrant's people for possession of fire-irons at least . . . I mean firearms.'

'Are you sure he's not pissed, Dave?' Bullfinch replied. 'An appalling double murder. I can do without a lush on the scene. Gravity, for God's sake.'

'That bond with Pillar, sir – bound to cause Glyn disorientating pain.'

28

Floyd Llewellyn was back from his conference in time to conduct the funeral service for Adrian Garrant at Bethel. Jule Corbett thought his father-in-law handled this very well. In his little address from the pulpit about Garrant's life Floyd was able to mix respect for him as a famed dockland figure, although so young, with forceful disapproval of his crookedness. Garrant had attended Bethel two or three times and made a couple of big donations to church funds, and Floyd spoke gratefully of these. But he took as his text Matthew 6, 24: *No man can serve two masters: for either he will hate the one, and love the other; or else he will hold to the one, and despise the other. Ye cannot serve God and Mammon.* He really gave the 'cannot' big power, leaning forward over the congregation, his face sad and angry. He always had his grey hair cut in a prow at the front to imitate Floyd Patterson, and he thrust this at his listeners now for emphasis, with vigorous neck movements.

Corbett was not sure about the impossibility of serving two masters, but he felt that Floyd applied the verse very well to Garrant's career and death, yet without causing more hurt to Lorna Garrant and the children. They occupied the front pew just under the pulpit. It was where Cordial and Simeon de Courville had sat in that meeting when so many of the events which happened since had their beginnings, perhaps even Garrant's and Pillar's death. Corbett found this symmetry touching. Kim Pillar's funeral would take place in London tomorrow.

There was a fine turn-out for Garrant, though no police. People like Brade and Jenkins might attend the funeral of a murder victim, but not when the victim had Garrant's reputation. Many staff and members from the Toledo were present, including de Courville, A.W. Moss-Cober and Cordial. Corbett saw Cordial still had his eye nervously on that other text, the wall text, *Without shedding of blood is no remission.*

After the service, outside in Mount Stuart Square before folk moved on to the burial, Simeon de Courville approached Corbett. Simeon was in a marvellous heavy dark suit with a black silk tie on a white shirt. His shoes were black lace-ups. 'Nice one at the Toledo, Jule,' he remarked.

'Adrian is such a loss,' Corbett replied.

'Cordial, A.W. and myself had a talk up at A.W.'s house – well, when we could – a fucking kid in and out of the room doing bits of some mad play with A.W., and another one upstairs blaring away with music – but, yes, a conversation of sorts, and it was decided in view of how it all eventuated that you was probably entitled to half the fee that would of gone to anyone hired to replace Indiment to do Garrant, Jule.' He put a hand into the pocket of his jacket and brought out a roll of fifties tied with wide blue ribbon knotted in a bow. 'That is, ten grand. There was a bit of argument about the amount. Cordial thought we might of got someone cheaper than Indiment, Indiment being such a star, or supposed to be. But, like A.W. said, nobody was going to take that job for cut rates, not after the crane and mouth tape.' Simeon turned his back, so as to shield the transaction, and handed over the money.

Corbett pushed the roll into his pocket. 'Not to quibble, Simeon, but why only half? Indiment had half in advance, didn't he – so he'd do the job and qualify for the rest. Well, the job's done now.'

'Greed, Jule. Nasty. Nasty. You get other nice pluses out of the slaughter, don't you? A rival gone. Use some of the cash to buy Henrietta a new smock or similar,' de Courville replied. 'Not here today?'

'She didn't approve of Garrant.'

'Some couldn't, it's true. I got to admit, there was off-putting sides to the arrogant shit.'

Floyd came out and joined them while he waited for a car to the cemetery: 'It's no pleasant welcome back, these killings, Simeon.'

'Exactly what I'd just said to Jule,' de Courville replied. 'What, what, I ask is happening to this area?'

That evening at home in the manse, Corbett had a telephone call from Geoffrey Fonnet. His strong Geordie accent sounded really warm: 'Dominic and I are damn pleased, Jule,' he said. 'The club matter.'

'Thanks, Geoffrey.'

'Dominic asks me to say you're due a bonus, and I am with him absolutely on that.'

'Thanks, Geoffrey.'

'Obviously, a bit of a blip for now with our project, in view of the loss of the partner in charge. We think the position may be recoverable.'

'I'm sure.'

'And the main thing is, there'll be no talking from that potentially awkward source. It could have destroyed the firm and injured Dominic and myself personally. We are much indebted, Jule.'

'Who was it?' Henrietta asked when Corbett rejoined her and Floyd in the sitting-room.

'I think one of our London trips would be very nice soon, Hen,' Corbett replied. 'Some distinguished shopping is called for.'

'Mammon been looking after you again, Jule?' Floyd asked. He was about to start a bullworker session in his study and was in shorts and a vest, looking spectral.

'Oh, some professional fees are due,' Corbett replied.

'Mammon been looking after you again?' Floyd said.

29

Brade and Jenkins looked for Susan Fiston's report in *Six Days* on the state of things at the Bay but nothing ever appeared beyond a factual account of the Toledo shootings with no by-line – nothing truly *investigative*.

'It's defeated even her, Dave.'

'Too many libel dangers, from Bullfinch above all, but even Corbett or Simeon or A.W. or Cordial or the Toledo management. The *Six Days'* lawyers must have put the block on. Nothing but very grey grey areas.'

'But we'll sort it,' Jenkins replied.

'Of course. How's Mair?'

'I'll sort it,' Jenkins said.

'Of course.'

'How's Kate?'

'It's going to be good.'

'Of course.'